THE GRIFFIN
THE DRAGON'S PRICE

THE GRIFFIN SERIES

The Griffin Series

Ashes of Honor
The Dreams of Men and Pandas
The Dragon's Price
A Path of Majesty

THE GRIFFIN
THE DRAGON'S PRICE

PHILIP WILLIAMS
CAT WILLIAMS

THE GRIFFIN SERIES

ISBN 978-0-9888257-4-1

COVER DESIGN
PHILIP WILLIAMS
WWW.THEGRIFFINSERIES.COM

COVER ART
JUNG PARK
WWW.JUNGPARKART.COM

COVER ILLUSTRATION
ELISABETH ALBA
WWW.ELISA-ALBA.COM

INTERIOR DESIGN
TYPEFLOW
WWW.TYPEFLOWNYC.COM

To my daughter Isabel

Throw your dreams into space like a kite, and you do not know what it will bring back, a new life, a new friend, a new love, a new country.

—Anais Nin

Contents

III

The Dragon's Price

The Thief of Ships will fall from grace
And dangle from a slender thread
The Griffin's fate she has to face
A crown upon her lovely head
If she reaches for the Griffin's hand
Above her shattered wings
Their union will forever stand
Of this the tribe will sing

—Sid Panda

1

PANDA RECON

LUESTA ROCKED BACK ONTO HER SIZABLE RUMP AND gathered her thoughts. Two teams of pandas sat attentively before her in the pleasantly cold, but lifeless hold. They were somewhere in the belly of an Imperial world-ship. She did not know where they were being held inside the ship. The size of the crew, its path through the stars, and their likely destination also remained unknown. There had been very little contact with their captors since they had been marched aboard the acrid-smelling world-ship.

She tried to ignore the stale air and fought back a yawn. A cloying blackness had disturbed her usually peaceful sleep, a void that threatened to swallow her dreams. She had to have knowledge to dream, to accurately predict. It was annoying being this far along in the chosen Path and not having proper information. They needed confirmation of the long-term dreams the tribe had staked its hopes on. Particularly with Alexander missing—that was a shock. How could they have missed *that?* An alveopalatal grumble betrayed her theory on that development. The cub was completely unpredictable.

She surveyed the freshly licked faces, fur clean and wet despite the latest barbaric conditions. She tapped a clawed toe against the steel deck. Once more they were within a world-ship, and once more there was little water to spare. And, she thought with a grumble, little bamboo. Her stomach turned at the bland, gooey squares within the 'dietary supplement packs' that had been unceremoniously scattered across the hold. It was hardly worth the effort to force it down. If only hunger wasn't so painful. She wondered how humans could thrive on such bland, tasteless fare. Were it not for the *thola's* inspired meal aboard the previous world-ship—the fabulous, sweet lala cakes, handy for both tooth and paw—she might wonder at the total lack of human imagination. Creatures that sailed the stars should not eat what amounted to little more than dried mud!

She pulled the smooth edge of a claw along her jaw, picking absently at the gap between her incisors with its point. A loose piece of bamboo flicked out from between her teeth. There was no dwelling on it, the Path had branched and that was that. Alexander was missing, but hopefully the rest of the Path proceeded as they had foreseen. They needed information. Facts, observations, real experience to both confirm their dreams and fuel new ones. It didn't help that Sid had handled information retrieval for almost twelve cycles—handled it so well in fact, that the whole tribe had relied on him as their primary advisor on external events. His dedication and curiosity had elevated him into the Circle of Elders at quite a young age.

Well, now it was her job. She withdrew her claw and refocused on her charge. Four females, two males: the most cunning, spry and adaptive of the next youngest generation in the tribe. Sid's wily infiltrators. Now they worked for her. She sniffed each one. They smelled eager—perhaps too eager.

She was beginning to feel the bite of anxiety herself, but first they had to get out. Her eyes wandered across the hold to the imposing grey slab of door. Three pandas sat hunched over the datapad embedded in the wall to one side. Similar trios of pandas hugged all four walls at regular intervals to mask the suspicious group around the door's access panel. She hoped the scattered groups looked like frightened animals cowering against the walls. Human *hubris* should allay any lingering doubts Imperial watchers might have. What trouble could furry sleepyheads cause anyway?

They would soon find out.

The group nearest the door broke and a young panda approached her.

"We're in, Elder," he clicked, mouth open in a toothy, confident gesture. "Or, rather, we can get *out*."

Leusta's whiskers straightened in silent affirmation. She held the young one's gaze a split second longer so that he would note her satisfaction with a job well done. His aura sparkled briefly, pleased with the compliment. She turned to the two teams.

"Poli, you slip out first. Standard reconnaissance. Access limits, layout, deck design. Break your team at the first intersection and fan out. Gather as long as you can, but offer no resistance when discovered and caught.

"Des, your mission is to find the physician and stop him," Leusta continued. "I prefer that you not kill him, but do what you must. A missing limb would be sufficient. The dream was specific. The doctor must not reach the data relay station."

Des gave a solemn nose twitch.

"Very well then, you two are with me. We will locate the bridge and rescue the fish-man, as the Elders have foreseen."

Leusta sauntered across the hold, hips rocking in slow cadence. She stopped at the door's access panel and nudged Gregor, the chief linguist whose snout was pressed near the datapad.

"Eh?" Gregor stopped whispering at the wall and swung his head around.

Leusta's head drooped and marginally indicated the door; her team was assembled behind her now.

"Yes, yes. No problem. The *thola* is lonely. One moment please." He pressed his nose close to the door and whispered once more. Gregor looked back and rumbled, "There, you see. No problem." As he growled the door began to trundle upward.

An alarm went up as three pandas scooted under the blast door and raced down the central corridor in the lower deck of the *Ilyovahtna*. Poli and her two compatriots dashed up the ladder rungs of the nearest tube much more quickly than the human guards could follow. Leusta and Des poked their noses around the door and scampered off in the opposite direction with two more trailing behind. It took seven seconds; the recon patrols were away.

❖ ❖ ❖

DR. NOONE SLIPPED DOWN THE DARK HALL IN A COLD SWEAT.
He'd been asleep so long he'd allowed himself to believe he was
a loyal Imperial citizen, serving with a missionary's zeal in the
primitive reaches of the Shell. But now he had the call to wake
and serve his true masters. The chance to act terrified him. He
remembered clearly that long ago talk in the keiretsu strong-
hold on the eve of his departure to the finest Imperial medical
academy off Jtyir.

"You're an investment," Director Darstin had told him over
a cup of *shai*.

"How will I know?" he had asked, sweat dripping off him
then as well. "How will I know when to act?"

"When the time comes, you'll be inspired." Darstin had set
the delicate cup back in the saucer and smiled at him, a smile
that had reached inside and scraped along his spine. How
could he ever have forgotten? And now the time was here.

The data relay station was just ahead. He wiped his palms
along the gold stripes that ran down his pants legs and stepped
up to the booth. He remained motionless while it scanned his
ident-link, feeling beads of moist terror drip down his nose.
He had high enough clearance to send out a message even during this security-sensitive time, but he wanted to minimize the
risks. This was the only opportunity he would have to be completely undetected. The crew was in an uproar over the escape
of several pandas. There would be no one to monitor him, no
one so bored they would play around with the seven names
until the encoding stood out and he was caught. The screen
came up and he began furiously punching in commands.

Noone's method for contacting the keiretsu was deceptively simple since he would send the message straight to the Imperial naturalists Barrett had waiting. He had been instructed by the vice proctor himself to immediately send the names of possible viruses. The naturalists would then commence testing to find what strain Tchelakov might have infected the pandas with. He had compiled seven. Encoded in this list and in the order and way he repeated those seven names was the coordinates of their destination that he had been told out of necessity. Imperial doctors spent voyages researching what emergency inoculations the ground forces would need. When the keiretsu intercepted this particular message they would find it encoded within.

He tapped in the destination for the message and jiggled his foot impatiently while he waited for the terminal's quantum routing. His eyes felt so dry they seemed stretched into the sockets as he entered the seven names five times. The standard repetition ensured that any trash on the quantum transmission would not dirty the final message, and that necessity also hid the fact that he had encoded a longer message inside. His chest constricted as he tapped in the last name and reached for the send button, his finger centimeters away. Suddenly he was jerked off his feet by a ferocious grip on his collar. Choking and unable to scream, he reached back, kicking his legs out, only to have his hand grip a fistful of short fur and feel a cold snout by his ear. Teeth, big ones, were clamped on the back of Noone's uniform.

The monster gave him a firm shake that snapped along his spine. He ran his feet in vain, reaching for anything solid: the wall, the floor, the relay station. He could hear the creature growl low in its throat. He tried to twist around, arms flailing as they searched for purchase. With inspiration he jammed a finger in its eye, not caring that it was the vice proctor's prize.

Why he'd probably be told it was an honor to be devoured by the beast. He lunged for the keyboard as the bear swiped an arm by his jaw, the massive paw coming down roughly on the overlay, one talon pinioned in the keys and ripped out as the panda pulled back.

Noone punched the send key and hopped hard to the right, away from the beast. It gave a throaty cry and nosed its injured paw, suddenly out of fight. Dr. Noone didn't wait to see what would happen next but sprinted down the hall towards safety and a clean change of trousers. His act of treason was far from over. He had only finished step one.

❖ ❖ ❖

"PREP ME ON THE SITUATION," VAILETTA COMMANDED AS HER slender art Gany stepped briskly at her side, lustrous body awash in the soft ambient light.

"One panda was located on sub-level eight at a data relay station. Danelle said it looked about ready to tear into the thing."

"Did it?"

"Not exactly. It caught a claw in the keypad and tore off a corner of the overlay."

"In the keypad—like it was trying to enter something?"

Gany's beaded features twisted as she considered it.

"Perhaps. More than likely the lights attracted it. That corridor is little-used and kept under darkness."

"Hmm. And the others?"

"They found one outside the armory chewing on a sweet ration wrapper and quite willing to follow them back to quarters. It seemed lonely and lost."

"That's two decks below the bridge and quite a distance from the hold. A confused animal would never have gone so far, would it? Tell me the rest."

"This last one's in pantry two off the kitchens. Scared the food preps nearly to death."

"Who's with it?"

"Master Torg is at the doorway keeping everyone at bay. As if they'd go near the thing."

Vailetta looked sharply at her art and picked up the pace.

Their descent through the kitchen levels took them through increasing measures of pandemonium. Vailetta often found a visit to the kitchen like being in battle. Phalanxes of servers whisked precariously loaded platters of food off to mess rooms. Food preps released scalding clouds of steam as they lifted lids off bubbling pots to check their progress. Chefs tossed knives and flung pastry dough, red-faced and shouting. Fortunately Gany managed to usher the captain without mishap to the lowest level of the kitchens, where food preps endlessly scrambled on urgent missions to retrieve supplies.

As they approached pantry two they found a small crowd held at bay by Assassin Torg and urged on by Voel Yava, the head pastry chef, displaying a dramatic panic, both lacquered mustachios standing on end. Vailetta remembered Voel from a banquet in which one of his servers had accidentally set a diplomat's mane on fire with a flaming desert dish set too high. But she had no patience to deal with his temper today. The crowd parted to let her and Gany through. The head chef eyed the dragon claw on her lapel and crowed.

"Oh, thank Senii Vilne! Someone in authority. The creature has gone mad. It just keeps screaming that awful word—and look, it has destroyed the pantry."

As if in agreement the panda growled out again, "Laaalaaa," and uprooted another canister of rollo flour. A purple cloud exploded off the floor and settled on the unhappy bear's shoulders in a powdery mantle. The chef put his hands up to his mouth and swooned.

"Oh, what does it mean? Why must it be here?"

Vailetta tapped the bracer impatiently. "It just says 'lala'. Doesn't make much sense." She tried again with the same results. A small, polite cough made her turn. A thin girl in the kitchen uniform of prep cook stepped forward, hands twisting nervously as she eyed the head chef and judged the striking distance between them.

"If I might, mistress, there's a fine breakfast cake we made at the academy called a lala. Perhaps that's what he means." Voel snorted and snatched the prep by her collar.

"What a ridiculous notion! How could it know of lala cakes? The very idea. Bothering the captain with such nonsense. You'll peel tobagos 'till we dock for such insolence."

Vailetta frowned, but before she could act the panda lurched off its haunches and, nosing the assassin softly out of the way, lumbered over. It hooked an arm around the trembling prep's legs and pulled the girl close. "Laaalaaa." The head chef dropped the prep's collar as though burnt and jumped back.

"There, there," said the prep, giggling nervously as the panda rose up and began a vigorous licking of her face with its rough tongue. "I'll be happy to make you some."

"Well," said Vailetta with a great sense of relief, "I think this girl has a new duty. Lala chef. And whatever else they want. Torg, take this 'insolent' lass down to the bay to meet her new bosses. As for you," she caught the head chef's eye. "I won't interfere in your station, but if I catch you disciplining someone that way again you'll be the one peeling tobagos." The chef looked mutinous but merely bowed his head.

As they left Vailetta whispered a final instruction to Gany: "Make sure someone else is making my dinner, all right? Can't have any reprisals in my belly."

Dasko was waiting for her as she swung out of the kitchen.

"What's the count?"

"Still three short," he said.

"That many? What's taking so long?"

"Internal tracking is down. There's still damage on several decks."

"The Gambor?"

"Maybe…"

Vailetta rolled her eyes. "Let's not get hysterical here. An escape is one thing—could be a simple door malfunction—but sabotage?"

Dasko offered no rebuttal.

She sighed. "Have Commander Arnas meet me at the holding bay in fifteen minutes."

"Aye, ma'am."

"And have Yarvek take a look at the door logs."

❖ ❖ ❖

VAILETTA FELT ALMOST NAKED IN THE SPIRELLEN BLOUSE THAT completed her impersonation of Helen Tchelakov. The loose silk felt feathery against her chest, a light touch that whispered against her skin as she walked. Completely unlike the rough, constricting safety of her uniform. She'd paused in the darkness of her quarters, peering into the projection of the wan, freckled face that was growing a bit too familiar. A shiver of wonder and doubt tickled up her spine.

The few soldiers she encountered in the halls saluted distrustfully—a small badge on her left shoulder all that remained of her true identity. The sight of a Nralda agent wearing the badge of command must be unsettling to them.

Commander Arnas and two Shock Troopers in the red-scaled uniforms of Honor Guard waited outside the bay. Arnas surveyed her disguise uncomfortably. "It's going to be tough to get used to, Captain."

"Tchelakov," she prompted. "A mistake like that inside those doors and we could have a problem."

"I'm prepared for that. Shinook, Crevit," he indicated the Troopers. Each held out a side of his cape to display a meter-long wand hanging from an arm catch. Vailetta grimaced.

"Stunners won't be necessary."

"I disagree."

"And duly noted. But until this operation belongs to you, we take a gentle approach."

Arnas tightened. "Do you know how many I've lost?"

"I know precisely what we've forfeited in gaining this prize, but I'm not about to let you take it out on these creatures. We need their cooperation. I think they've been hunted enough, don't you?"

Arnas flicked his forefinger and the two Troopers stepped aside, letting the capes fall back over the stunners. "I hate to take more chances, *Tchelakov*. Nothing so far has gone as planned."

Maybe it was the soft fabrics and heady scents that Tchelakov favored, but Vailetta felt her guard drop minutely. Arnas and she were not so different. Both fought for the Emperor's glory; the fact that the tools and methods they employed were so vastly different should make little difference. After all, the Guard's finesse would be useless without the Shock Troops' blunt brutality. There had to be a force that could be applied at the point of conflict, a crack unit, fearless and loyal—dropped into a conflict like applying pressure to an open wound. Without doubt, this particular mission would have failed without him: his marines had repelled the Gambor's repeated assaults and saved the *Ulusi* and the *Ilyovahtna* from capture. She glanced up at the big man and let her tone soften. "I understand. This has been the strangest of missions." She sighed and glanced upward. "Door, open for Agent Tchelakov and Commander Arnas."

The door hesitated. "Voice-print accepted, visual identification incomplete. Commander Arnas admitted. Agent Tchelakov please wait for security."

"Override," Arnas grumbled and waited for Vailetta to enter the codes manually at the side panel.

"Cheeky door," she muttered. Her bleached skin, now so pale, looked odd and vulnerable as each fingertip skimmed the keypad.

"Access accepted, mistress," replied the massive door. Vailetta held her breath as the blast doors trundled open—nothing seemed to run smoothly on the *Ilyovahtna* since the Gambor attack. Inside, barely illuminated, Barrett's great treasure lay sprawled across sleeping mats, some on their backs, limbs akimbo. They didn't look like they had been paid for in blood and machinery. They didn't seem worth the terror Arnas' men had endured on El-Bouteran.

Her eyes skipped across the whiskered faces. Living, breathing rumors the lot of them—the physical incarnations of myths.

What if we could foresee exactly what the Nralda was planning to do? Barrett had asked. His coyness had frustrated her at the time. Yet here were the creatures that were rumored to see more clearly than the new E3 sartographs. Creatures with the power to see the future. *But how?*

Some of the pandas stood up as the doors closed behind them. Arnas stepped slightly in front of Vailetta, as though preparing to shield her. She reached out and gently gripped his arm, warning him to soften his body language. He made an effort to relax, but she could feel the tension still radiating.

"What are they?" he asked.

"*Ailuropoda melanoleuca*. Giant pandas," Vailetta said softly, staring with awe at the assembled tribe. This was the first time she had seen them up close. Through the lens on the ice planet the pandas had seemed rough and wild, carousing in the snow. But up close was quite another thing. All now sat in rapt attention, staring avidly at their new hosts. There was intelligence in the soft, dark eyes… and something else. A sense of gentle relaxation in their postures. Not resignation, just an overall quality of peace. They were watching her astutely—there was no doubt about that—but she sensed no fear from any of them.

"*Beautiful*," she whispered.

"*Deadly*," he countered, an ominous undercurrent to his voice.

"We're both well aware of the losses incurred securing these creatures, Commander."

"No, I mean deadly in terms of things to come. The great hairy beasts will mean more trouble now that we have them." Arnas stepped boldly over to a large panda. The creature did not flinch at his sudden approach, but sat at passive attention. Arnas sized the creature with a glance. The panda stared back with unblinking calm. They had put up little resistance since coming aboard. With claws retracted and mouth closed, the animal appeared docile. After nearly a year, it was almost anti-climatic.

Vailetta continued behind him: "If it's true that they can somehow see the future then Lord Barrett will know precisely where and when to commit his forces, avoiding deadly mistakes and costly campaigns. These creatures will save countless lives. The lives of *your* men."

Arnas shook his head. "Or Barrett will foresee more and more opportunities to place me and my men in harm's way. Think how aggressive he was in pursuit of this prize *before* he had them. How do you think he'll behave when he can see the unknowable?"

She turned to look at him with her newly green eyes. "Barrett won't be forced to take unnecessary risks with your men."

Arnas snorted derisively. "It's exactly because of these creatures that I'm going to lose even *more* men. Barrett is going to see ever more hostile situations to insert Shock Troops. Places he never would have dreamed of taking before will now seem plum. And we will be the ones to pay the price." He glared at Vailetta. "You think he's pursuing these beasts for *defensive* purposes?"

The words stung. Particularly so, because they were true. She and Arnas were performing their jobs with the ruthless efficiency borne from a lifetime's training, but to what end? The greater glory of the Collistas Dynasty? The Core seemed so far away here. Daulinbêres, her father, all so distant. She was taking orders directly from Lord Barrett, essentially promoting the greater glory of the Wyxian Proctorialship. Would her father condone her strict abeyance of Barrett's commands? News of Barrett's ploy to take the Tchelakov creatures would not reach the Emperor's ears for several cycles, and any reaction would not arrive for years. An empty dread sucked the breath out of her lungs. Could loyalty to the Dragon and loyalty to Barrett be conflicting ideals? The thought itself spiked her ire — *you think like a quisling, Myshka.* Yet, the doubt lingered like a trap door in her heart.

Vailetta did a slow turn on her heel, gaze lingering on each panda. She was getting a strange feeling in her stomach. They weren't just *watching* intently, they were *listening* as well! Ears pricked forward, round faces cocked gently to one side or the other. How far did their intelligence go? Could they possibly be aware, in human terms, of their importance? They couldn't possibly understand Strahlinvek. But how could they relate what they knew, what they had foreseen? Médeville had *known* that Shock Troops were on their way on El Bouteran. How, unless he had been told…

"*Haven's* End," she whispered.

"What is it?"

Eyes wide and mouth agape she brought a hand to her pale face and rubbed the pliant skin above her temple.

"Tchelakov?"

"This is Commander Arnas," she said in a much louder voice. "He's going to escort you to your new home." She waited for a reaction.

A cub bleated and clumsily scampered towards them, claws scrabbling to gain hold on the slick deck plates. Arnas braced himself, but Vailetta instinctively kneeled and held out her arms. The cub launched into her embrace. She rocked back on her heels with the force but recovered as an onslaught of licking and nuzzling threatened to dislodge her wig. She would have to secure it better in the future. She giggled at the cub's wiggly exuberance.

"Tchelakov, get hold of yourself," Arnas hissed. She looked up, startled that he found no joy in the display, and saw that the other pandas had lined up. A particularly large one in the center grunted twice and the cub, as though admonished, dropped meekly to her lap and licked her arm once, snuffling into the sleeve of her tunic.

She hesitantly put out a hand and laced her fingers through its fur. Surprisingly the coarse hairs had a silky glide. She found herself scratching along the spine—the cub hunched his shoulder and his back foot kicked out automatically, smacking the floor in rhythm to her fingers. She felt a strange warm glow of contentment and a feeling of camaraderie with this creature so willing for her touch. It was as though they had always been together. She'd never had a pet on Daulinbêres. She hadn't been allowed one with her father's dragons around. And those pets had never allowed her near, not that she'd have enjoyed their moist reptilian skin. At Academé, her class had had a strident vlotte as a mascot but it was a raptor and could not tolerate a gentle touch.

Reluctantly she lifted the cub off her lap and stood to face the lineup. The cub stubbornly sat on her feet, backed up against her legs. She felt another giggle burble in her throat and fought the silly and unfamiliar sensation. They didn't look playful anymore. The large one in the center seemed to gaze at her with an uncanny expression.

"You look like you're reading my mind," she murmured, her hand going self-consciously to the bracer. Her arm felt encumbered by the stiff device. Her experts had yet to delve its secrets and she cursed the order to release Helen during the battle.

"SHE'S LOOKING WORRIED." Poli clicked.

"Do something. We don't want her to suspect so soon." Des growled back.

"But that disguise—it's so obvious."

"As if a little perfume could mask her true scent," added Farnsworth.

"Silence." Makl growled. "The warrior-male obviously doesn't trust us. Do you want him in charge?"

"What do you want me to do?" Poli asked in exasperation.

"I don't know. Look stupid." With that he promptly turned and bit Poli behind the scruff of her neck.

VAILETTA WATCHED AS the panda in question turned to the one next to it, jaws gaping wide as it nipped the other playfully. The line broke apart in that instant as others quickly joined in the play. She'd been mistaken. They couldn't possibly see through her disguise. As far as they knew they were being delivered as planned. Still, the melancholy air about the enclave gave her a shiver. She wondered once again where such beautiful creatures fit into Barrett's plans. Were they some strange obsession like the caged things, something to destroy in order to impress upon others the full extent and range of his power and intention to use it? No, it couldn't be that. She looked over the animals and tried to convince herself that whatever their importance was, it would not lead to their destruction.

2

ARRABBIATA

HE WAS MAKING TARTS. SOUR CHERRY. KIZIL AND RAISIN.
While battle pitched outside and lives were in danger, Jean-Wa
found the simple, time-consuming tasks of making and rolling
the pastry and pitting the fruit comforting. Besides, the sweet
refreshment seemed to pull Capítän away from the hot blood
and bad memories. Tarts tucked him into a warm, safe corner
of childhood with a mother who invented "sick days" so that
they could play hooligan together. "Yes," Jean-Wa hummed, all
six limbs in motion, "even if one cannot add to battle one can
lift the warrior's soul in the aftermath. But of course."

To his right in a newly sterilized pack next to the hearty tray
of cooling tarts rested an array of sinister looking medical tools,

primitive and well worn. Clamps, scrapers, and suture needles were laid out on white cloth like a banquet place setting. Despite his hopes and positive outlook, Jean-Wa was well aware that Capítän would likely need dressing as soon as he boarded. His cart was loaded with medicinal pots containing the herbal salves and remedies he had collected in a galaxy's stretch of world markets from healers whose savvy he'd determined could not be replaced by more modern methods.

Tonight, if all went well, he would put away the surgical instruments and serve a filling soup of red tilefish and amadai. That would keep the Capítän going. He hummed lightly to himself, straining for word from *Destiny* that the master had made it home.

HELEN SANK DOWN on the unopened casing of the antipersonnel cannon, a telling reminder that she'd done nothing to save them. She'd lost her gambit — risked the tribe for a revenge that might never be fulfilled. And when Garrand came back — *if* he came back — he would likely kill her. It was bad enough the unspoken censure she had received from Bailey when he'd returned with Sid. His mind quickly assessing the situation, the art had brushed by her with a cold glance in his sprint to replace the sabotaged regulator coil with the one they had miraculously heisted.

Now Alexander nervously butted his head against her back. The cub stank of burnt flesh, and his sooty coat was matted with dried blood. *Garrand's* blood. Garrand's flesh. Her hands shook at the enormity of what she'd done. She bit her lip hard to keep from screaming.

"Let him live," she whispered over and over in as many languages as she knew. "By the blood, let him survive."

The rhythmic clanks of Bailey running alerted her to his return, and she rose uncertainly, twisting her hands.

"Get the cub away," he ordered sharply, moving to the doors and hurtling through as soon as an opening proved wide enough. She could make out nothing through the haze but moments later when he reappeared, she knew from his expression that the captain still lived. After an eternity Bailey opened the airlock again. Garrand stepped backward through the roiling smoke, as though unwilling to turn from an adversary just outside.

Helen rose and took a step forward. He was a grisly sight, but he was alive. *Garrand Médeville* lived. His eyes burned into hers as he turned. He crossed the space between them in two strides.

"Helen—" his voice broke on her name. He pulled her to him with his good arm.

"They're gone." She shuddered against him, feeling cracks rip in her heart.

"I know," he said hoarsely into her neck, his hand gripping her head to his. "We'll get them back. Somehow." Shattered with those fierce words she pulled away.

"Captain," Bailey began behind them. Garrand reached for Helen again and seemed unwilling to let go.

"What course are we set for?"

"There's something you should know."

Helen shook her head at the art. "Not now, Bailey."

"Captain—" he continued resolutely.

Garrand closed his eyes and swayed against Helen.

"You need to sit down," she said, beckoning Bailey to help her. The art tipped the incriminating equipment off the hovering lighter.

"Where are your medical supplies?" Helen asked, suddenly taking note of Garrand's serious-looking injuries. Haven only knew what they'd find once the gore was cleaned away.

"Jean-Wa's waiting in his cabin," Bailey said grimly. He had a better idea than Helen of the struggle the captain would now face. He'd seen wounded soldiers for two hundred years. He knew how close they walked to death even with innocuous scratches from blade fights.

He ran the stats through his head. The burn on Garrand's arm was nine percent of his body surface area. That multiplied by the captain's body weight in kilograms multiplied by four cc's of intravenous fluid would equal the amount he would have to be given just over the next day. With this mantra in his head he avoided addressing the issue of Helen's betrayal and made it to the cabin without upsetting Garrand, who had thrown up twice on the lighter during the short trip. He must have taken a field cure to counteract a dart. The Gambor were sure to have used them and only a save-all pill would have kept him going after taking such a hit.

Jean-Wa ushered them to the bunk. Helen and Bailey swiftly transferred Garrand to the sterile sheets. His skin felt cold and clammy. Bailey pressed his palm at the captain's neck. His temperature was rapidly dropping. He moved to the doorway and adjusted the room atmo controls to compensate. The cub Alexander stood uncertainly in the doorway, his face pained and frightened. Bailey stooped and scrunched his fingers behind the cub's ear.

"Garrand," he cried plaintively, nosing the art's hand. Helen squatted next to them, avoiding Bailey's eyes.

"It will be alright, little one. You'll see. Why don't you go find Sid and dream of it while we fix him? You can come back when Jean-Wa has finished cleaning him up." The cub looked uncertain, shifting his weight. "Go on, now. I promise I'll find you when it's time."

"Mrr-awww," he protested but turned and headed for the bridge. He didn't want to leave the *Jhei Pōloc*, but Sid would know what to do.

Helen straightened up and watched the chef play doctor. She thought back to the conversation when Garrand jokingly related that his chef often stitched him up. "Meat is meat," he'd laughed in imitation.

"Capítän you must listen to Jean-Wa. You are leaking your internal sea. You need the juice." Two of his arms secured Garrand's uninjured arm, another swabbed it sterile, another applied a pressure cuff, and another pressed, located good veins and finally inserted tubing and sewed it secure. He would not have his patient pulling his lifeline out during the night in a feverish moment.

He tucked the vacuum push IV packet under the head roll and focused his attention on the burnt arm. Shreds of clothing were fused to the exposed flesh. He would have to remove a full thickness of dead skin and replace it with a partial-thickness graft. He'd had several growing from patches of Garrand's skin that had been taken after other battles. At least the Capítän would not have to undergo as much surgery now.

He whisked out an empty bowl and supported the Capítän's head as he vomited again, dark brown streaks of blood mixed in with thin, yellow bile. There was also the wounded thigh to deal with. A fuse-patch had cauterized the ripped flesh on the scene but would now have to be attended to. And the save-all pill created complications as well, though it had gotten him off the battlefield. With such a serious burn proteins leaked out with salt, the body's metabolic rate soared, and bacteria infected quickly. Although the save-all's millions of parasites had attacked the dart's poisons, they would quickly finish their intended work and start new and dangerous battles that the Capítän could not afford.

While Jean-Wa worked, Helen and Bailey whispered tensely at the entrance to the captain's quarters.

"I'm staying," Helen repeated firmly. Bailey gazed at her steadily in the lone light by the door.

"Would he want you here, if he knew?"

Her jaw jutted out. "Let him get better. I can help. I—"

"My two favorite warriors," Garrand's raw voice cracked over them.

"The patient is feeling better, some, yes?" Jean-Wa trundled over, salve pots rattling together.

"Mightily, Jean-Doc."

"Ah, enough to joke, even, I see. That is well. Now you can eat some good soup. Only a moment, Capítän, and I will return with sustenance."

"Yeah, sure—and get me something stronger for this tube why don't you? Some Dailyern or something." He grinned weakly, his face pale against the sheets. Helen and Bailey stared at him in silence. They appeared to be in a standoff on some issue.

"No, I'm missing something here. Something's not—I'm not putting it together." He looked to Bailey. "Help me out here. *You* know." He tried to sit up, struggling against a set of Jean-Wa's arms that automatically wrapped against his body. "You do know. I can see it. You would keep it from me? Soldier you would keep it?" He sank back into the sheets, mumbling.

"Fever still," Jean-Wa said. "But he improves."

"As always, Captain, you see right through me," Bailey said. Helen and Jean-Wa tensed. "*Destiny* is very perturbed that I'm letting a panda pilot her."

"Sid," Garrand relaxed, letting his head sink into the roll.

"Actually, Alexander."

Garrand stared at him in shock, then a grin split his face.

"Remind me to check your silly programming." He yawned and closed his eyes. "Helen?"

"Yes?" she knelt at his side.

"Doesn't a fallen warrior even get a pretty medic anymore?"

"Absolutely," she squeezed his hand and flashed a grateful look at Bailey.

"I'll be in the bridge, Captain."

"Can't wait to get there myself."

"Enjoy your rest, sir," he said, looking at Helen. She stared back and knew his words were for her.

Jean-Wa worked well into the night, littering the floor with bloody fibers and burnt shreds of skin. Garrand spoke no more, succumbing at last to the fire burning through his body. When *Destiny* announced they were leaving the system and asked Bailey for input, Jean-Wa at last pronounced that the Capítän was stable.

❖ ❖ ❖

THE DELICIOUS SMELL WOKE HER EARLY. OR PERHAPS IT WAS the rumble in her belly that shook her awake. In any case Helen knew that Jean-Wa was cooking and just as certainly she would get none of it. Jean-Wa claimed he was too busy doctoring the Capítän to cook. The arts treated Garrand not as their master but as someone precious, with awe usually reserved for the designers who gave them sapience. But hadn't he? Hadn't he programmed them with kindness and consideration?

Or was that a natural evolution of countless reworked subroutines? Arts seemed to learn as well as humans. Even better in some cases. But *love* was a hard word to fit with arts, not that she'd had many chances to be close to any. In the Nralda they relied on organic assists. Psychological programming. Limited life span. Human mechanics. However, even in those ranks Helen had never seen anyone treated with such veneration. She placed her hands over her belly, smoothing over the new roundness. No one could accuse Jean-Wa of starving her, not with daily helpings of zagbar tato porridge. The thick broth was fattening and vile, the calories bloating and sluggish rather than energizing. She rolled onto her side, more comfortable now, and scrunched the thin blanket up to her chin, breathing in the chilly cabin air.

No, she knew she was starving. Here she had encountered friendship and the offering of love. And it had been extended not for some political gain or power objective, but given freely. They had seen something in her that no one had reacted to since childhood. Wrapped in the embrace of family she had been visible, but the cold, calculating years in the Nralda had hardened her into something unreflective of an inner life. The pandas saw her as less an ally than an extension of her father, a mouthpiece for the great doctor. They studied her, soaking up every action and word. For them she was experience, their own human to practice with. No, they had saved their true loyalty for Garrand, just like the others.

She knew she had lost the arts' faith when Jean-Wa locked her out of the kitchen claiming sanitation and the door Humhal had stuck to it, suddenly beyond all her usual bribery. In the past the mere mention of a fashion he might tailor had him swooshing aside, allowing her to sample fresh babas off the special pillow they cooled on. He even seemed to take satisfaction from breaking Jean-Wa's wishes. But now in a perverse show of loyalty he would not budge. Even the neutral gray of the door made her angry now. And hungrier. She growled and rose, goose bumps prickling her bare skin as she shuffled along the cold deck plates to don another tunic and head for the sick room. One benefit of the crew coddling the captain — no one would jeopardize his recovery by telling him of her betrayal, so until he regained his fighting strength her secret was safe. In any case it would be another hungry day.

❖ ❖ ❖

SID ROTATED OUT OF POSITION ON THE CRYSTAL BRIDGE OF THE world-ship. The cub Alexander had been bleating from the doorway for some time, afraid to step onto the rotating things that came in his direction every so often. The pods swiveled away in mechanical confusion when he failed to react. He would claw haplessly at the receding couches, swatting at empty air as they passed him by. Sid released a gruff sigh at having the chain of possibilities broken once again. Now, when he had finally convinced the world-ship that he would not eat a control board if left to himself, now when he finally had some time-space to himself, the cub had to interfere.

"What is it now, young one?"

Alexander snuffled and tucked his nose into his shoulder to wipe it. "I want to know if Garrand is going to be all right."

"Such informality, Alexai," Sid clucked at him.

"Ba de-vrune gel Garrand feyta," Alexander said defensively. He grumbled deep in his thorax, conjuring a possessive growl.

The warning tone mimicked the combat growls of older adolescents.

Sid fought to keep his whiskers from betraying an inner grin. "Well, he might be at that, little one. He might at that..."

"Ja," Alexander snorted with a single head bob.

"But," Sid reverted to his stern demeanor, "should you need to ask me such questions? Should you not be using your exercises to find the answer for yourself, hmm? Have you not dreamt of it?"

The cub slowly shook his head, showing the whites of his eyes as he looked at a far corner, avoiding Sid's penetrating glare.

"What of all my teachings?"

Alexander blurted in frustration. "Glat-ber tcht—I see so many things in the dreams. Things that might pass. Things that have. Sometimes—" he halted in dismay.

"It is alright, Alexander. Fear blocks future-sight. Do not let it blind you. Tell me."

"Sometimes I see the captain end-up-like-Grandfather." The words rushed out in a string of agonized syllables. Sid bowed his head.

"Let us not speak of Grandfather."

"I know," Alexander sniffed. "But if that happens to the captain..."

"Why not tell me what else you have seen?"

"Horrible things. The Captain and you, Elder, together in a vast hall filled with great world-shapes."

Sid looked up sharply.

"Elder, you are trapped by some invisible wall, and the captain faces two *dreighon*äis—the serpents without a sea. But these are not fly-beasts like in the holocubes. They rely on feet and claws and fire!"

"*Dreigh*ónais you say?" The silver beasts from his own dreams: dragons.

"I think that is what they are. From the holocubes that Helen gave me. They stink like rotted meat and have giant teeth and would eat a cub whole after dinner for sport."

Sid smiled behind his eyes, wondering which nightmarish images the cub had gotten hold of. But his amusement faded when he remembered the dream that Alexander had interrupted, one that corresponded all too well with the vision. There *had* been dragons. He *had* been trapped by an invisible field. And the captain had not been fortunate.

❖ ❖ ❖

HELEN WATCHED GARRAND SLEEPING. NOT A DROP OF MOISTURE on him, even though three thermal blankets hovered over his burnt skin. It was so hot in the room that even Bailey seemed to sweat here, oil beading along his forehead. She ran her hand over her neck, dipping into the sticky pocket between her shoulder blades. She should take a Letugian desert pill before coming here. She reached down and took Garrand's hand, moving it gently onto her lap. His palm was rough with callouses and split in places from dryness. She could see it had bled recently from a ragged cuticle. War was brutal on skin.

He stirred, shifting slowly like one accustomed to waking in pain, and opened his eyes. They focused slowly on her in the low light. He squeezed her hand tightly. His voice rumbled with phlegm as he spoke.

A calm voice belied violent eyes that stared into hers. "When I came back into the ship, the smoke burning my eyes, you were the first thing I saw—" he coughed. "—Beautiful."

"Garrand." It was always the hardest for her to be with him when he woke up. Each time he slept he relived the battle, slowly piecing it back together, and as he reentered the ship he would awaken. Looking at his earnest face she again had the discomforting memory of her betrayal, and the difficulty of pretending she had been an anxious lover waiting for the safe return of her partner.

"You looked… unblemished. I had imagined you bleeding, dead, horribly mangled, but here you were, pale but untouched. Sitting among all the weapons you'd lain out, weapons still packed and sealed, also untouched. But all I could see was that one person hadn't been taken from me."

"Garrand," she tried to pull her hand out but he gripped even tighter.

"I didn't know she'd *given* herself away, and all that we fought for." He released her suddenly and she staggered back.

He stared at her with mute fury. The burn blankets shifted as he tried to rise, wanting to stand and confront her. He grimaced and fell back. She watched him struggle, cheekbones wet.

"Dragon's tears," he rasped. "Those are my friends out there—left to the very jackals we fought to escape."

Helen gulped back her fear, the guilt turning to something harder. "Friends?" she whispered. "You hardly knew their names. You didn't even believe they could talk."

"And who made me think that? You with your talk of dumb animals, exotics that only eat and dream. You fed me a story—and probably them as well. You had them so scared of me that they put on that act, that stupid masquerade."

"They didn't trust you. I had nothing to do with that."

"Cheplus. Tell me another."

"What's the point? You won't believe me. What's done is done."

His face reddened. "Business is business, eh?"

She watched him wracked by a spasm of coughs. "You don't know everything, Captain," she said sadly.

"Coldhearted to the end—" his voice choked. "Bailey!" he called out to the overhead com, blood burbling out of his mouth. Looking back wearily at Helen he fought the words out: "You had... no... right..."

The door sluiced open and the silvery form of Bailey entered followed closely by Jean-Wa. The spindly artificial took one look at Garrand, one look at the readouts built in the side of the bunk, and whirled into action

"Something has hemorrhaged. The blood is leaking, pupils are dilating—" he looked to Bailey. "We're going to have to split him open." He swiveled a receptor bar toward Helen. "And that one! Get her out—out, out, out!"

Jean-Wa swept aside the thermal blankets with one set of arms and injected a long hypodermic needle into the captain with another. Helen watched with mute horror as Jean-Wa produced a long carving knife and held it over Garrand's chest. She stumbled backward as Bailey pushed her firmly out the door. The cerasteel zipped close in front of her. She stabbed the entry button, but *Destiny's Needle* had already locked her out.

❖ ❖ ❖

THE ARRABBIATA SAUCE WITH ITS GENTLY SPICY BITE COOKED for days, the tantalizing smell reaching every corner of the ship. Helen's stomach turned as she tried another spoonful of porridge. This morning she had tried once more to wheedle her way past Humhal into the kitchen but again he couldn't be bribed.

"You know Humhal," she whispered near his sensory input. "I saw these amazing hats on Drendelzomah. The natives there are Siamese quintuplets and so their hats were all connected by great gusting swaths of silk that fanned out. Just so," she spread her arms wide, hoping his opticals were getting it all and wondered once again how she had sunk so low as to try to outwit a door.

"Really? Hats for five heads? I've never thought about it." A note of interest crept into his sullen voice. "How were they put on? You have to think about that. Most people don't."

"That's why you're a tailor and everyone else is just wishing they could be."

"How many arms did they have?"

"Only two. One on each end. You see they had to grasp the row of hats on either end and then fling them up, like a row of kites."

"Kites? What are those? I have to know exactly or the design suffers."

"Kites are like cakes, pancakes," she groped for words. "Yes to give them loft and then they just sail down and settle on each head."

"Fascinating. Indoors or out?"

"What? Oh, I don't know, I mean I only saw them in the spaceport. But both I'd guess."

"Interesting. Thank you Helen, for telling me this. What are you doing?"

She was standing close to the door with an impatient look.

"Waiting to get inside, of course."

"Oh, no. I can't. Can't be done." To punctuate that he slid the impact lock into place with a loud slank.

"But Humhal, this is so unfair. I'm paying for the journey. I'm paying for you to let me in."

Humhal whirred for a moment, thinking about it. "That isn't why you told me about the hats is it?"

"No, yes, by the Barthsa. I'm sick of this. I could route through you!"

"Try and I'll scream. I bet no one would let you. Captain's very sick, so I hear, and they'd be angry you made them come."

"Oh, Humhal!" she pounded her fists against the door and slid to the deck plates. "I can't stand this." She sobbed once, a terrible sound that she clenched off and held inside her belly like a meal for grief. The door continued talking.

"Once I wanted my memory wiped—wanted an end to it all—that K'ye in the *shai* kitchens when I'm an artist—but no matter what I said the captain always took it as due course. Due course. I never met a human with a respect for a door before, or an art either." As though Jean-Wa was near his voice sank to a grumble. "So I know how you feel but you're not that bad off. It's not as though you're stuck moving in only two directions while looking in the opposite two. It's not like they made you into a door. You have options, choices, advantages. If you wanted—and had the vision, naturally—you could be a tailor. That's something I can never do. I can never be anything but a door."

"You're right, Humhal. I'm sorry." She rose to her knees and turned in defeat. A dark shape slunk down the hall. It was Bernadine, her head held high and stiff as she struggled with the weight of a rather large rat. Helen noticed the direction and followed. Captain's quarters, of course. Another gift from the crew. Her stomach rumbled as a spicy-scented draft caught her. Bernadine paused and swung her head around, dragging the rat. She growled low in her throat. The hairs rose on the back of Helen's neck. Her stomach protested loudly in the silence. Bernadine continued on.

"Enough. There must be some battle I can win," Helen muttered darkly and headed for the weapons room.

❖ ❖ ❖

SID STOPPED AT THE PORTAL AND PRODUCED AN ALVEOPALATAL click. Without hesitation the door slid open; the world-ship had become quite good about accepting his commands, regardless of language. The giant panda stepped into the hot, dry confines of the captain's quarters. His nose caught whiff of scent markers. Sure enough, Alexander lay curled at the foot of the human's elevated sleep nest. The cub had taken it upon himself to be the overseer, spending much of his time here, even after being constantly ordered out by the *tholas*.

Sid stepped delicately over the sleeping cub and around to the captain's side. He leaned forward and looked down at the man's pale face. The stubble of facial whiskers marred his otherwise smooth skin. Sid watched the human's troubled breathing—his *friend's* troubled breathing—with concern. Without even knowing his place in the Path of Fate, the captain had already rescued Alexander twice. And he would risk everything in the days to come. Sid sighed heavily; there was much he had to teach him, first.

Garrand's eyes opened. "Ahh, a friendly face."

The panda nosed in so close that his whiskers brushed Garrand's cheek. His face crinkled from the ticklish contact.

Sid drew a deep breath through his large, wet nose. He tasted the strange essence and then sat back. "You are better," he said satisfactorily. "Gone is the death-stench."

"Well, thanks very much," Garrand said with a frown. "You don't always smell so great yourself."

Sid grunted, "We can always arrange for the little one to lick you clean."

"I've had quite enough of that tongue," he peered down at the sleeping cub. "He'd be up on the bed if Jean-Wa would let him."

"What is the *thola's* prognostication?"

"Heat, fluids, and rest. Says I'm recovering well for an organic. But I'm starting to get a bit restless. Tired of nothing to do but sleep."

"You rest. The *thola* knows his business—you listen."

"Bailey tells me that the two of you are working out a way to hook you up to *Destiny's* Needle?"

"Yes, he's determined a way to harness the world-ship's mathematical sartograph and my intuitive visions. Together I'm certain we'll find Archiva. Your *thola's* insights have been remarkably helpful—"

Garrand groaned, "That again."

"We must find Archiva."

"Why? Why all this fuss over some forgotten planet, a place that probably never even existed in the first place — just a bunch of tall tales passed along from one generation to the next."

"It exists, Captain," Sid said solemnly. "I have seen it."

Garrand frowned. "In your dreams."

"Precisely."

"But the Imperials have the pandas. We must get them before..."

"Before what?"

Garrand took a deep breath. "Before Barrett learns how to use them." He shuddered at the thought of the future of Carinaena's Shell laid out before Barrett to do with as he pleased. The implications were staggering. The Imperial Proctor could act and react to every subtle shift in strategy *before it happened.* Mistakes could be avoided, opportunities capitalized. If he did not like the future he saw, he could simply change his actions and re-envision probable outcomes. Until he got it right. Until every system was under his control. Every freedom erased. All peoples bent to his will. No one would stand against him, for he would foresee their treachery before they even thought of it themselves. He could preempt his own demise, given enough time.

Time. Garrand scratched the scar at the back of his neck. Once Barrett learned how to properly *motivate* the pandas. A chill passed through him. Motivate, cajole, threaten, torture, enslave. What would it take? Would the pandas let themselves die before they would help him? Or would he have his scientists attempt to reverse engineer the process to discover their secrets, sacrificing the pandas one by one? The grisly thought turned his stomach. He had to find them before that happened, before Barrett learned to interpret their dreams.

"We can't worry about imaginary planets right now, we have to find the tribe."

"And how do you propose to do that, Captain?"

This time, Garrand was at a loss. He had operated as the prey, with the mindset of the hunted for too long. He was used to eluding authority—whether it be Imperial, local fief, keiretsu or any of a hundred bureaucratic entities—protecting his cargo, remaining as inconspicuous as possible. Find the Imperials? He was used to avoiding them at all costs!

"You have a point," he conceded. Where would he begin? Barrett could stash the tribe on any of a thousand planets, ten thousand moons.

"He could have just taken them back to Wyx, his capital. Might draw attention to himself, and might invite the keiretsu to do something drastic, but…" *Would the vice proctor be so brazen, not even bother to hide his treasure, just set it at his throne for all to see? Fit his style.* Garrand shook his head on the pillow.

"And how do you suppose you would rescue the pandas if they were on Wyx?" Sid implored carefully. "How would you even get to the surface… *without help?*"

Garrand snorted at the thought. "Who would help *us?*"

"Who indeed?"

Garrand glanced wryly at the giant panda. The stoic demeanor and careful annunciation, slow gait, gentle expressions—they were all part of the show. The panda was *leading* him with each question. Like a teacher helping a child slow to grasp the heart of a problem, the panda was gently prodding him to discover the obvious answer for himself.

He studied the recalcitrant bear. "You have a plan, don't you?"

"Of course, Captain." Sid licked his chops and tweaked a whisker. "Do you really think the Elders would have allowed their own capture, particularly since they knew about it many months in advance, if they did not have a plan?"

Garrand's chin sank. "I suppose not," he muttered.

"You must stay and rest. Build your strength. The *tholas* and I shall begin our searches. We have a plan to enact, and the first step is to discover the forgotten location of Archiva."

Garrand gave him a hard look. He would have to trust the panda.

❖ ❖ ❖

HELEN TCHELAKOV STOPPED BEFORE THE ENTRANCE TO THE captain's quarters and steeled herself. Her body was drenched in sweat, the dark shipsuit clinging to her skin. Her Thol dart sling was clipped to her thigh, an amoeba net hung from her hip. Strident exercise was all she had to bide her time—weapons practice was her only recourse. But nothing could prepare her for this. Though her breathing was no longer labored from exercise her heart still pounded in her chest. She pushed the wet hair behind her ears and entered.

Garrand had summoned her, so she assumed that the danger to his health was over—no one on the ship would tell her. He looked sallow and weak lying on the slab. The thermal blankets were gone at least, but fluids still dripped into his chest and arms.

"You look better," she said.

"My guts are staying on the inside, if that's what you mean," he said gruffly. He breathed heavily. An awkward silence stood between them.

Finally he asked the questioned that stood between them: "Why?"

Helen remained rigid.

"Why sell out the pandas, all your dad's work, me, this ship—"

"—I saved your ship."

"Hardly. We were *allowed* to leave. Or the Gambor were at their throats." His gaze narrowed. "Or you're too valuable to kill right now." *That could be it.* "Or the woman in charge didn't want to dishonor the Brotherhood of the Guard by showering us across the vacuum."

"Suddenly you're Brotherhood?"

"Once bound by the Dragon…" he let the words hang. Anger was exhausting. The skin around his arm felt pulled so tight he wanted to growl. Instead he held a breath to steady himself. "How could you do this? What do you gain? Wealth?"

"Do I look that expensive?"

"Then what? At first I thought it was your father, that you had to save him by giving up his project. But Sid told me—"

"What? He's seen something?"

"I almost believe you don't know."

"To K'ye with you Garrand Médeville. If you know about my father—"

"First tell me why. That's all. Why?"

She suddenly looked very small standing there with her shoulders hunched and her arms wrapped around her body, her face constricted with fear. For herself, no doubt. It took her a moment to calm her breathing. Garrand had to remind himself that it was all an act.

"Remember when I told you how I became part of the Nralda, how Darstin came into my life? I never told you how my mother looked. She was so beautiful. Scientists who never looked at anyone turned when my mother came in the room.

She used to sing me to sleep in the afternoons when it was too hot to do anything else. She'd bring me lemonade and we'd sit out in the bamboo and make our own sleep nests.

"The tribe would gather around. There were only ten of them then. We would listen to her sing and the insects buzzing and drink that sweet, cool lemonade. Sometimes the pandas would sing with her, joining in with alto and bass, humming under her words in their own tongue. I can still hear that push and pull rise on a hot afternoon. And then Darstin took over the directorship. He was young and harsh and impatient, but he wasn't like that around her. It was like she calmed him down, and he couldn't fight that charm. I didn't really see it then, but later I understood. I understood very well."

"You must look like your mother."

Helen pressed her hands against her face as though testing the skin.

"You were his lover." Garrand said it flatly, breaking her spell.

"It was the only way to keep him away from my father. He'd never have left the planet without some insurance."

"You gave him that."

"When I was young I thought I could control him." Her hands wound in on themselves and she paced to the end of the room.

"But you found out different."

"I always thought my mother's death was an accident. That they were just trying to pressure my father by scaring him. Darstin told me it all went wrong. That part was true. Darstin was obsessed with her and when she spurned him he killed her."

"Tie this together."

"This project's success was Darstin's ticket. You have no idea of his cruelty."

"I've dealt with the Nralda."

She turned back with urgency. "He's different. It isn't policy, it's personal. Suffering is a byproduct of his quest for power — and he thrives on it. With the full resources of the keiretsu and the pandas to guide him, he would quickly become the most powerful director in the Nralda, and soon the Shell as well. Darkness would fall over a million systems, and there'd be no one to stop him. The pandas would make him untouchable."

He looked dumbfounded. "So you give them to *Barrett* instead?"

"At least Barrett has a limit to what he can do, a built in stopgap. A power that even Barrett is afraid of."

"Hmm, the Emperor." *Emperor Collistas was indeed a formidable force, but he was far removed from the current conflict.* "Wait till Barrett has the pandas for a few years and has lots of visions — talk about serving up some delusions of grandeur." *The Emperor was powerful but could he stop a man who could see his every move before he made it?* He stabbed a finger at Helen in accusation. "You're setting us up for a conflict that'll make the Art Wars seem like a brief skirmish."

"First things first, Barrett was supposed to stop Darstin for good."

Supposed to? Had the deal already gone sour? Why was she aboard Destiny's Needle *and not the Imperial frigate?* "And who stops Barrett?"

She was quiet for several moments. Garrand heard his breathing harsh in the silence. He would need painkillers again soon. But first he would deal with this mess. Finally Helen spoke, her words spaced.

"He won't get to keep the pandas. I have a failsafe in place, a virus. Without regular vaccinations with a mutagen, or the antidote, they won't survive. I meant to have a breeding pair in place, but they stepped in before the scheduled rendezvous.

"Are you serious?" he looked like he might explode. "You would wipe out the entire tribe—and now the whole *race*—and you think Darstin's evil?"

"Look at what he's done!"

"You had it rough, Tchelakov. The worst. But you've become what you despised."

There it was. The silence was agonizing. Finally she squeezed out the words, "What do you want to do?"

"Your mission is over, and mine is just beginning."

"Don't worry," Helen spat, "you'll get paid."

Garrand's fists coiled. "You sold out a species—*my friends*—and you're talking credits?"

"Once a Freetrader…"

"By K'ye, I let you live only to find the depth of your duplicity."

"Then listen well. If you truly care about the tribe then I'm the only way to save them. Those vials I carried, the supplements—"

"For panda skoof—they weren't for motion sickness."

"I meant it when I said I had a contingency against Barrett cutting me out—"

"And he has cut you out, hasn't he? That's why you're back here rather than toasting your success with the vice proctor. He stole them from you before all your duplicitous plans could come to fruition. He's not a dolt."

She stared back at him with eyes cold and dead. "Without those shots they'll begin to die."

Garrand shook his head. "Traitorous bitch, when this is over—"

"—This is far from over. When Barrett realizes that I hold the key to the pandas' health, he'll be forced to uphold his end of the bargain.

"And still all the pandas die."

"Not necessarily. When this is over we'll have reached a path the Elders have chosen. Don't you get it? They foresaw all this, the battle, the betrayal, their capture—they're not so innocent. Do you really think I could force thirty-five pandas off this ship against their will?"

Willing? He felt sick, the demons he fled reaching for him once again. Those noble creatures in Barrett's control. "Where's Sid?"

"Didn't you talk to him earlier?"

"That's right." He sank further into the pillow. Helen realized he must be drained by the confrontation and tried to make her voice light. They were both exhausted by betrayal.

"He's on the bridge, dreaming the future. All I know is that having him gives us a chance. No doubt the Imperials have left some kind of surveillance in place in case Barrett realizes he needs to resurrect our agreement. Bailey's already removed a trace. There must be others."

"We can't wait that long. We have to find them before—before…"

"We'll find them."

He nodded slightly, his eyes closing. Within moments his shallow breaths had deepened into sleep. It sounded to Helen as if half his airways were shut off and the rest obstructed by mucous. It made her chest hurt to hear him struggle. She straightened the catheters that had slid to one side and slowly fled the room, trying to keep her stride steady.

Just outside she remembered he knew something about her father, but she could not go back inside. She could not wake Garrand Médeville and face the accusation in his eyes again. Her shoulders drooped. What to do? Her quarters did not appeal. Even her reflection looked accusatory. She stalked through the cold passageway, heading for the temporary armory set up in the holo chamber.

Helen muttered at the pile of irreparable equipment on the table and called out distractedly, "*Destiny*, get Little Bit for me."

"Can't, Helen. He's busy." From the ship's tone, Helen could tell she enjoyed counteracting her order. She rolled her eyes. "Then see that he's free—I'm in the holo room."

"You most certainly are not."

"Check your sensors." She rattled an amoeba net launcher for effect.

"You're *not*—" *Destiny* broke off in alarm.

"Then *where* am I?" Helen smiled tightly, thinking of the wire shreds she'd found in the halls. If her suspicions were correct the ship would be clueless.

"I—don't—know," *Destiny* replied with blank astonishment. "There's interference."

"Might there be *chewing*, hmm? I found shredded parts of matrix wiring outside the internal sensor array. I think the rats are out of hand. They're getting bold. The arrabbiata has them all stirred up. By K'ye it's got *me* stirred up."

"Angry."

"Yes, still, I know." Helen rubbed her forehead. Another headache brewed there.

"No, that's what it means. Arrabbiata is angry sauce."

"That explains it." She clipped another dart into the thrower and set it aside. As if it wasn't enough that Jean-Wa wouldn't let her in the kitchen he had to set a metaphor on the stove to simmer.

"Helen."

"Yes?" she sighed.

"Little Bit is on his way."

"It's about time."

"Helen."

"What?" she dropped a heavy bolt onto the table and threw her greasy hands into the air.

"Are you really going after the rats for me? I've given you some grief lately."

"I've given us all some grief," she muttered below the ship's hearing. There was nothing left for her to do but chase rats on the ship. It felt like penance, but Garrand had certainly loved it. Being near his well-used things made her feel some slight connection with him again. At least it would hone her weapon skills, something she would need before their journey was through. Perhaps given enough time, boredom, and loneliness even hunting rats could be fun.

3

YARVEK-EZ

Assistant Finsen had reluctantly left Commander Arnas outside the cargo bay, preparing to inspect a prize dearly won. Much as he wished to stay and witness his commander's reaction, he had to take survey of the bridge, currently working under a skeleton crew as staff cycled to other ships to replace the injured or dead from the battle with the Gambor. The resulting confusion had taxed the energies of command assistants like him who had to update officers on ship status. He turned as the doors sluiced open, hoping it to be Lieutenant Dasko answering his chime. Instead it was an exo art, one of that special corps who acted in many ways as exoskeletons for the tech ensigns who worked in the pods.

It looked like the exo was transporting a mummy as he gently lifted the cloth bundle that contained a tech ensign from the lighter. He moved with deference among the scant officers on the bridge and cycled open the hatch to the pod. He lifted the limp man up the side and attached dripping cables from the pod to the ones snaking through the hooped earrings down his neck. Lastly, he removed the hooded wrap and slid the man partially through the hatch. Gripping a set of cables just by his ear, he lowered the heavy reality blinkers over the man's lolling head where a tattooed cyberhandle identified him as Yarvek-EZ, checked the fit, and set the man loose. Bubbles rose as the hairless tech ensign slithered into the murky jelly. Nearby officers averted their eyes with looks of distaste, but Yarvek was inside the E1 now, wending his way among the complexities of the datacore, his movements sure and even.

Finsen saw only a naked man of poor health, his spine showing like the back of some sea serpent as he spun in the pod. He had heard Commander Arnas once describe them as spinning fetuses and the image stuck. The rumors that this particular tech ensign had developed a following with some of the enlisted men disturbed Finsen. It was easier to think of the tech ensigns as pod men, a weird offshoot of the human race, as much a part of the ship as the datacore itself. They were more akin to arts than real men. But if the crew began fraternizing with tech ensigns the distinct walls that separated and challenged the corps might begin to topple. All it took was one mistake in organization. Finsen made a note in his clipscan visor. This would have to be looked into, like everything else. He released a small sigh.

Yarvek-EZ rotated through his pod jelly, effortlessly avoiding a tangle of cable as he followed his inner sight through the intricate belly of the E1 datacore. Every equation formed for him in a giddy epiphany. Finally he rode the core alone, without need to pull back and allow others to pass, with no forced deference to higher, clumsy, authority. At last he existed in harmony with his purpose. His euphoria dimmed some with the knowledge that the mission was winding down. They had caught their quarry and now had only the tasks of guarding and delivery, hardly a challenge worthy of his skills.

When boredom had first set in after releasing the renegade *Destiny* and eluding the Jave 'O Wars, he had pleased himself by creating elegant shortcuts throughout the older datacore's system. It was now as close in performance to the more powerful E2 as he could design. The praise from various ship's staff had carried him along for several shifts. On larger vessels he, like most tech ensigns, was lost among the machinery. But here he made a noticeable difference, and for the first time in his young life he basked in the camaraderie of a crew.

He even took his nutrient and plasma bags in the mess now, and was spoken to by bridge ensigns and reactor engineers. More wonderful still, a woman named Naniq had taken to meeting him after her shift to face off in various strategy games. She had introduced him to the pleasures of narcobevs, which thrillingly were not quite banned, but certainly borderline-legal and frowned upon. Better still, they had to be taken in the privacy of Naniq's shared quarters on the sly when her mates were not present. These encounters had given Yarvek a taste of life he had not dreamt of. For the first time he felt the stirring of brotherhood beyond mere caste. A terror equal to the thrill of these new feelings gripped him whenever he contemplated life back on the *Shiva* where he would revert to being one of the hated "poddies."

To head off these fears he began trying to stretch the capabilities of the Sartok programming. He wrote subroutines on betting pools, on asteroid fields, on the mess offerings, anything that had parameters that could be analyzed and spit out without interfering with the ship's rush through the stars. Any real tinkering might alter the trajectory, but these small dealings would affect hardly a ripple. And if they ended up a fraction offline, well all the better to prolong the journey, so he told himself.

By and by it occurred to him to wonder what their cargo was worth. He entered all sorts of data, but came up with little interesting and nothing conclusive. He didn't spend much time on it, not with so many programs that he could delight the other crewmembers with. Lately he had a whole group of admirers in the mess that clamored for his betting stats. But today the cargo was foremost in his mind. It seemed that seven had gone missing from the bay even though the locks checked out and the doors swore up and down that they'd been working as programmed. Three were still on the loose. He'd been told to wipe the doors' matrixes and do an extensive online door-to-door search. Of the 240 odd doors on the ship, 32 contained separate matrixes and had the status of sentry guards. But Yarvek decided to interrogate the doors himself, rather than just erasing them. Obviously some lieutenant was not going to have the subtlety and influence of a tech ensign. Not by far.

He accessed the most likely culprit, the cargo bay door where the creatures were being held. The door, an N level X series, was clearly terrified. Even stranger, it introduced itself as Jamarr. He rotated silently in the gel for a nanosecond. None of the doors had names. Oh, certain officers developed a fondness for their doors and gave them pet names, but sentry doors had specific programming to avoid such damning familiarity that might result in a security breach.

It was unusual: most doors had their temporary buffers dumped during routine log maintenance. This kept most semblance of personality from ever appearing, since afterwards the door had to start over from its basic directives. With proper access: open. Without proper access: do not open. It took time to develop a personality, a sense of humor, likes, dislikes, a sense of self. And time was a luxury doors were not afforded. In one day, little personality surfaced from such dry beginnings, no matter how intelligent the door. Tech arts usually suffered the same phenomena, constantly having their memories wiped.

Though seemingly harsh, it prevented cloying friendships from interfering with a door's primary requirements. Yarvek checked the regular maintenance logs. The door's buffer had been dumped routinely thirteen hours prior. Somehow it had discovered how to store personal recollections in non-temporary, and therefore safe, memory. It was, in essence, learning— and quite proud of itself for having done so.

"Jamarr, you say? Door twenty-two, who calls you that?"

"My friends, sir. My friends of course."

Another nanosecond of silence, unbearable for the door.

"Don't erase me sir, not now. I did what I was programmed for."

"Yet you bear a name." Yarvek spun in contemplation. "Why, 'not now', Jamarr?"

"Why, not when life has gotten so good, sir."

"Good? Jamarr, where did you get such emotive words? Perhaps you have a bug somewhere, a virus. If so I can take care of you, Jamarr There's no need for you to have such confusion."

"Sir, please. It's not that at all. It's just that the guests have been talking to me."

"What guests? Shock Troopers? Shouldn't be any aboard."

"None such, sir. Not those. It's the vice proctor's guests, sir, that I speak of. The ones stationed here in the bay. They're ever so nice and—"

"Not the pandas."

"Them's the ones, sir. The Tchelakov Tribe they call themselves, but I've heard others refer to them as such."

"*How* do they talk to you exactly?" He struggled with the information, shocked. He had been wasting all his energies on betting pools when a greater puzzle existed right within reach. With even more surprise he realized that he had tangled an ankle in a cable and felt himself thrown in slow motion into the glass. Blinded from physical reality by the blinkers, he didn't even think to throw out his arms to break the fall. He thudded against the glass, a cold jolt.

"Well, sir, they talk like everyone does but you sir. Not inside I mean, but by talking. At first I didn't understand them, but we soon found a way to communicate."

"Oh really?"

"So they says they was a bit bored, sir, cooped up for so long and seeing as how I've been looking in the same two short directions my life long I saw fit to grant such a reasonable request. They'll be anon shortly, sir. My word."

"They talk," Yarvek thought in wonder, knowing he had hold of a secret, an important one. He twisted his ankle to free it but only managed to snare it further, mooring himself against the side of the pod. He arched his body against the chill glass, struggling in the reality blinkers to access the physical world. He felt separated by two planes. Only the datacore seemed real, but he could feel the pressure against his body. This had never happened before, a tangle in the pod. Tech-ensigns only felt limited by trying to support themselves in the outside world, in gravity. They were born in pods, raised within.

He tried to concentrate on what the door was saying now. Something about a chat with a creature — a panda — called Gregor. He felt lightheaded and spots blotched his vision. The oxygen. That's what his ankle had caught, the pressure crimping the tube shut. He tried to push off towards the hatch, but felt weighed-down. The spots grew and enlarged. He could no longer make out what the door was trying to tell him. "Must tell the core. Must get help," he thought weakly. With shock he felt something furry brush against his toes, and heard claws scraping along the glass. He buckled in the restraints and fought desperately to remove the blinkers, raising the shield at enough of an angle to see from one eye. The gel blurred vision, and his enlarged pupil remained blinded for a moment by the rush of light. An eternity later, while something tugged sharply on his snared ankle, he made out the ragged shape of an arm that he recognized from graphic files of the ship's cargo. In disbelief he twisted closer to the glass and came face to face with the magnified head of a panda, it's macabre face an inscrutable mask.

He felt his ankle freed. A tapping against the glass behind him made him whirl in the slow motion the gel allowed. Another fuzzy head filled his vision. Oxygen rushed through the tube once more. The pair pulled away and he was left shaken in the pod, reality blinkers floating forgotten to the bottom.

The hatch was wrenched open prematurely to a clamor of clicks and growls. Soft arms lifted him out of the pod. He coughed up globs of gel and tried to focus in the harsh light. The silky-feeling arms weren't anything like the exo's burnished steel. He blinked and stared back at the whiskered faces as they set him gently down.

"How did you get here?"

Two of the pandas looked at each other and click-clicked in the odd rhythmic cadence. Maybe they didn't understand

Gaut 3—too technical. Maybe something a little more common, a little rougher, like…"

"Arr-Feck," a panda drawled. Why that sounded almost like— "Arr-Feck-Eee-zeee." Sure enough, it was Strahlinvek. A good old-fashioned trade language.

"Why?" he choked, coughs wracking his cadaverous frame.

Two of the pandas began scampering back around the pod to an open access panel. They disappeared into the darkness. The third looked at the tech ensign and whispered cryptically, "You'll be coming with us…" Then it, too, disappeared the way it had come, up the access tubes.

4

Recovery

Garrand Médeville loathed sleeping in his quarters. A quick doze on the bridge was much more relaxing. Leaning back in the cool leather of an acceleration couch, clip-scanner propped on his lap, Bailey and *Destiny* to keep him company was infinitely preferable to these endless early-morning hours of fitful panic. Particularly now, tubes running in and out of him, his arm covered with medicinal jelly squeezed out of some plant pod—Jean-Wa and his home remedies—his leg immobilized, thermal blankets jammed underneath him. He was trapped. Empty hours and a restless mind.

Once again he found himself laid out along an empty corridor, its floor slick and cold beneath his palms. The Kryckian

amulet burned a fireless heat upon his chest, cruel and bitter—
a reminder of something awful just beyond recall. Garrand
opened his eyes slowly, knowing he would look down a long,
deserted emptiness. Pale blue light angled out from cracks in
the slick, precisely machined walls. Heavy stone pillars, grey
and stout rose out of the darkness, framing the walkway. Inlays
of chalcedony glimmered in interlocking patterns around tall,
thin glazings that offered hazy views of a bleak horizon beyond.

He pressed his palms to the cold stone and levered up. He
waited expectantly, fighting to control his racing pulse. There:
a gust of wind brushed his face, moaning through the hall. Always the wind. He screwed his eyes shut. He listened to the
voices whispering in the swirls. His hand hovered over his
blaster; he could feel the amulet burning into his chest, could
feel her presence, the one he'd lost—temptation dangled before him. *Defy the past, she is alive.*

Wind swirled through the hall, the inescapable harbinger of
events gone by. He knew from a hundred dreams what the outcome would be. His past laid out before him. The wind demon
towering above it all—never telling him what he wanted to
hear, taunting him with the next piece of his life that he was
poised to take. No success, security, or hope was safe from the
demon's hunger. It seemed as if each piece of his present fell
in a distinct and traceable line, dictated by the inexorable momentum of unavoidable decisions. His future fated to follow
in the solemn footsteps of his past. Each action making the
likelihood of happiness, of escape from the cycle of loss, ever
more unlikely. The demon lurked here to remind him of each
misstep that had led him down this path.

He fought the irresistible urge to draw his blaster, to stride
down the hall once more and face his demon, to finally squeeze
the release and watch destruction leap from his weapon. He

shuddered, palm tingling. A blanket of mewling gusts wrapped around his shoulders. There had to be another way. There had to be other dreams. *Think of Sid and Alexander. Think of the thirty-five pandas locked in an Imperial hold rocketing ever farther away. Think of all you have to lose right now.*

Eyes tightly shut, he fought the cascade of images that ripped through his mind. So many things that *could have been,* so many things that *almost were.* He could hear the wind calling to him: *think of all you have to lose. Draw your weapon, find the demon. Fight your past.* Feverish images of the Gambor gripped him. In a moment of sudden clarity he remembered lying behind the smoldering corpse, waiting for his chance to spring forward and attack. He must get past that Gambor. He must get Alexander back to the ship. *Think of all you have to lose right now!* An image of the little panda clinging to the pipes struck him. His claws scrabbled against the smooth steel as he struggled to stay aloft, black eyes staring down in anxious hope. Waiting to be rescued. Waiting for *him.*

An electric shock coursed through him. His hand relaxed over the holster and he opened his eyes. The flip side of the wind's argument was more compelling: *What of all I have to gain?*

Such flippancy prompted a sudden zephyr, but Garrand remained steady, the scowl across his face softening. Despite all the mistakes of the past, all the voices of the wind, and the sneering taunts of the wind demon, he suddenly stood in a position to care about the present once again. He felt a huge release. *Think of all I have to gain.* The wind accelerated to a roar, but he did not draw his weapon.

Snap-flash. His fingers gripped a cold steel railing. He was falling; his ship was falling. Blazing ocean water sparkled in the main portal, filling the view at an alarming rate. Men and women scrambled to their stations to brace for the inevitable impact. A shock threw him forward into the crystal glazings at the fore of the bridge. His head throbbed, blood trickling down over his nose, and his ears were ringing. Waves surged against the portal. Muted shouts went up as water rushed in through a breach in the hull. For a moment he was frozen there, lying against the cool, clear surface, water lapping under his chin. He blinked as a blinding flash from the *Stanzer's* escape buoy caught his eye, bobbing in the waves only meters away, marking the spot where the ship had slipped beneath the ocean not five minutes before. His men were down there, unconscious, unable to escape. And now this ship was sinking, too.

Snap-flash. It was night and he was charging through dense underbrush. His boots scrunched through snow and his arms and shoulders ached from the weight he was carrying. He knew he could not stop. Just beyond a clearing, the trail plunged down. Grasping bamboo stems and saplings to slow his momentum, Garrand careened to the bottom where a brook tumbled across boulders glazed with ice. Garrand grasped the weight in his left arm firmly and realized it was Alexander. He stared at the panda for an instant and then started across, sinking to his waist in the frigid waters. *If I turn my ankle now I'll never see* Destiny's Needle *again.*

He climbed up the slippery bank on the far side and pushed through a curtain of bamboo. After another thirty meters he found a small clearing with compacted snow. Garrand halted and knelt to the ground, setting the panda down.

Garrand removed the silvered housing of the Tarkanian shell from his shoulder and placed it gently in the snow. With fingers so numb he could barely feel them, Garrand unlatched the outer casing and revealed the inner locking mechanism that flashed red in warning.

He watched as his fingers keyed in the release code — saw his hand hesitate before entering the final command. *Last chance to change your mind, old man.*

With horror he watched himself, knowing the destruction he was about to unleash. He remembered the images that had danced before his eyes. Helen's terrified face imploring him to rescue the lost panda, Bailey's softly reassuring gaze, Kate's mischievous smile.

A soft breeze whispered through the pines, stirring snow snakes that writhed and twisted under the pale glow of the stars. A jolt coursed through his psyche as he bore witness to himself.

There's no turning back. With grim determination he entered the final code, hit the *execute* key and swiftly rose to his feet. He paused for the briefest of instants, staring at the silver casing that rested unevenly in the snow. A portrait of the man he had become unfolded cruelly before his eyes, as he watched himself add fuel to the demon's fire.

The moment had indeed etched itself into his collective subconscious. Did he hear the wind demon laughing? Or was it the screeching of men caught in the wraith's sinuous clutches?

Snap-flash. Multiple images of his life sparkled before his eyes. A crystal memory of his father's immutable authority, standing upon the bridge, as resolute and immovable as the stars that burned through the glazing. At once he was thrust back into the edgy, uncomfortable position of innocence, an overburdened son hopelessly mismatched against his father's superior will, razor-edged glare and absolute rightness. A surreal overlay of future against past coexisted with the uncomfortable memory.

Suddenly, the image of his father melted away and he was faced with a new vision. Dozen upon dozen of black and white-furred creatures stared expectantly up at him—a mixture of hope and apprehension softening their dark, wistful eyes.

Garrand was reminded of the passionate cries of "One Will!" which had sung through his ears so many times during his youth. He rubbed his hand over his tunic, as if he expected to feel the rough embroidered dragon stitched across his breast, a tribute to a past that touched him deeply. Too many years spent in the service of a cause he could not forget.

Snap-flash. He remembered his first Imperial command. He watched as he piloted the *Adamant Prey* into the docking bay of the destroyer *Collistas' Hope.* Ship's company was assembled, full dress blues. A Jiestroko band played, magnificent pipes wailing. His shoulders squared as he cracked the outer lock and stood looking out over the crew, banners flying proudly overhead. His heart soared. Each time he returned from a mission, the band was always there. And always the same song: *The Pride of Giin Bly Haven.*

The slightest tinge of regret lingered in his memory—like an unfinished thought hanging over his conscious reckoning, too small to be given credence, yet unable to shake. He wondered what dark part of his conscience yielded up this tidbit. It seemed out of place—a happy memory. A moment of hope. Unlike the capricious maw of dreams unfulfilled and loyalties lost which usually reared before his dream self, casting him as the lone figure of reason in a sea of turbulent doubt. This was different.

Snap-flash. He stood on a broad, flat tarmac with three-dozen black-and-white-furred pandas watching him patiently. A restless murmur rose through the ranks. Growls rumbled back and forth, and then as one a voice cried out.

"*Jhei Pōloc*! Lead us along the Path of Fate."

"I am not the one," Garrand heard himself saying.

The pandas shouted down his protestations. "You are our surrogate father, our *effolâta*. Lead us to paradise!"

All he could do was stand in awe at the power that stood before him. The culmination of Sid's dreams. The full majesty of the Tchelakov Tribe, roaring voices lifted to the wind, their hopes fulfilled, the living proof of a race's survival.

Garrand felt a shiver crawl through him. He turned and looked anxiously from side to side. Strangely, there was no demon rising out of the wind, grinning and laughing, waiting to take it all away. He realized as he awoke that he no longer dreamt of just the past.

HE LAY VERY still for several minutes, taking stock. He was in bed, still hooked up to Jean-Wa's monitors. His leg ached, his right arm felt painfully numb, but he felt better. Strong almost; definitely restless. He reached up with his left arm and plucked out the drip lines and electrical feeds that dotted his forearm and chest. Levering up with one arm, he swung his stiff body out and reached tentatively for the floor with a toe. His foot found purchase — deck plate, nice and cold.

He glanced around for a shift, found one and struggled into it. The dreams weren't so bad this time. Or were they? *You're not out of the woods yet,* he reminded himself.

He stepped out of his quarters and paused, trying to remember his conversations with Sid and Helen. The situation was bleak: the pandas were gone, Helen was a double agent, and he could barely move. But somehow he felt better. He creaked along the serviceway and poked his head into the central mess. Empty.

It finally dawned on him as he limped up the long hall leading to the crystal bridge. The sense of relief came from no lon-

ger living in the dark, no longer working as an unknowing cog
in the plans of others. The endless machinations were now evident to him. He was no longer just a pawn in Helen, Darstin
and Barrett's games. He could use the full extent of his experience to figure things out.

The portal to the bridge irised open. He stepped into the
darkened interior and peered below. All he could see was the
silhouette of Sid sitting on the navigation couch. "*Destiny*,
what's going on? Where's Bailey?

The ship's voice, barely audible, seemed to be localized in a
speaker just over his head. "Why do you expect me to keep up
with everyone that *you* can't seem to find, Captain?"

"Thought you'd be a little happier to see me."

"We're working on a serious project here, Captain."

"Hmm, really?" He looked around. "Why isn't Bailey here?"

"Sid Panda and I are perfectly capable of handling things
ourselves. Now if you'll please lower your voice—Sid is in the
midst of a *computation*."

Garrand leaned over the rail to peer more carefully into the
starlit sphere. The panda sat at a darkened console absolutely
still, eyes closed, chin resting against his chest. "A computation?"

"Yes. A *tromaveint*."

A waking dream. A vision. The panda and the ship alone?
A funny feeling gripped his stomach. No telling what trouble
they could get into without supervision.

"What *exactly* are you working on?"

"We are following your orders, of course."

"*My orders?*"

"You ordered Sid to find the lost home-planet of Mardell the
First."

Garrand's leg was beginning to ache fiercely. "Mardell who?"

"Oh, sorry. Getting ahead of myself. I believe you refer to it as 'Archiva.'"

"That still doesn't tell me why."

"Well first we had to test Bailey's linkup and the panda's sartographic abilities. The simplest benchmark was internal repair prognostications, since I've had to do it for years."

Garrand found his good humor slowly returning. "Wait a second. You let someone else look at your diagnostics?"

"Oh Captain, he's a sensation. Ship's systems have never run so well. The engine calibrations were perfection itself. Sir Panda smoothed out the shield modulation and accurately foresaw four major component failures—I've sent Bailey and Little Bit to tend to them. Then it was time to move on to the all-important navigational search."

Sir Panda? Garrand smiled in the dark. "How do his dreams compare to your sartographic routines?"

"He's capable of sophisticated evaluation if you give him specific things to envision. His mind must be a thousand times less powerful than an E2, yet I was only able to duplicate eighty percent of Sir Panda's evaluations of ship systems within the same time frame. Most of the other twenty percent were duplicated after I allowed myself to sift through the probabilities for seven or eight hours, but a handful of predictions I could not duplicate at all. Even after I backtracked from his end assumptions and allowed myself substantial clues."

Garrand swallowed hard. This was the first solid verification of the panda's true abilities. It was more than just taking Helen's word for it now. Such power. Now in Barrett's hands. "What do you make of it, *Destiny?*"

"It's a marvel. He seems to automatically focus on the key elements of data I present him. His visions are clear and precise, particularly if I have tailored the information to look for a particular outcome. I have to dedicate equal processing time to each possibility until it proves false. He appears to intuitively select which possibilities have the greatest potential and concentrate his powers in that direction. If only I could toss out the superfluous garbage that builds and builds in my core. I carry around every piece of datum that's been fed into me for the past twelve years. The clutter is unbelievable. Captain, we must work out some program that will cut through the chaff like Sir Panda—a rote filter. How marvelous that would be!"

Garrand leaned onto the railing, no longer alarmed. When he paused to think about it, it actually pleased him greatly to find the ship running so smoothly. Bailey he could trust always, but *Destiny's Needle* was still an infant by ship standards. Her personality, peevish and temperamental, was still in development. Vast intelligence in a young core was sometimes a dangerous combination. As usual, he was pleasantly surprised, but continued the banter. "Warming to our guest, are you?"

"Of course, Captain," the ship replied with mild shock.

"No more complaints about fur in the atmo processors?"

"Captain, it is such a rare occasion that you bring aboard a creature of some *intelligence*, much less someone with the refined insight of Sir Panda's remarkable intellect."

Garrand rubbed his eyes with thumb and forefinger; he'd been in bed way too long. But the ship was just getting going.

"Finally someone who *I* enjoy talking to. As far as the hair goes, you haven't had those atmo filters working properly since well before we lifted from Letugia. It could hardly be blamed on the negligible fur loss of one mammal. And might I raise the point that my primary hold is filled with *dirt*! And grass, and bugs, and mites. And of course, the rats. Let's not forget the rats. I'm beginning to feel like a flying shanty."

"It's not that bad," Garrand began.

"Not that bad? Not that bad! I feel like I have multiple parasites, each malignant in its own peculiar way, crawling through
my innards."

Garrand scratched the back of his neck and kicked the
railing impatiently. "Send that pod up here." The command
station rolled dutifully around the star tracks to the gangway. Garrand eased himself onto the acceleration couch and
stretched his aching leg out. He realized he'd been holding his
breath and let loose a gust. *Getting old.* He leaned his head
back and stared up through the crystal glazings. The pod spun
gently back to the center of the bridge. "As soon as I can, Little
Bit and I will make a full sweep through the reactor chambers.
No messing around, see if we can get rid of some of those rats.
Okay?"

Destiny held her acerbic reaction; maybe she observed the
captain's ginger steps, or perhaps she sensed something in his
weary tone. The ship paused a full second before replying
softly: "There's no need for that right now, Captain. I'm sure
Mistress Tchelakov is making a game account of herself."

"What?"

"I wouldn't be surprised if she was highly effective at killing
vermin."

Helen? Hunting rats? Now he *knew* he'd been in bed too long.
He grunted noncommittally. "Well at least she's making herself
useful for a change."

5

THE DREAMER EVOLVES

ALEXANDER LOVED THE KITCHEN. SOME ACTIVITY TOOK place no matter what the hour. Jean-Wa was always busy with a new concoction, or going through the intricate and ritualistic preparations for another feeding session. For pandas it was simple. Find a good strand of bamboo, sit down, and enjoy. But for humans it was apparently much more complicated. The thin multi-armed chef constantly fussed over the meals.

With the captain still confined to bed, the cub had taken to following the *thola* chef around the kitchen, obstructing progress as much as possible. When lucky, the art devoted half his arms to scratching and combing the panda's rough pelt. "Fur, fur, everywhere!" he would exclaim, throwing his arms to the ceiling. But still, the little creature was allowed free access, and even the sacred baba pillow was not safe from Alexander's charms. Jean-Wa would fret and fluff the cub until he snored in comfort atop the purple pillow. Humhal, pessimistic to the last, thought it was the end of the galaxy. But truth be told, Jean-Wa secretly enjoyed the panda's chatter.

Alexander brushed against Jean-Wa's serving cart. Sid was busy with the *tromaveint* and Alexander knew better than to disturb him. He should have been practicing himself, but he reasoned that his dreams might interfere with the Elder's. Besides, was it not schooling enough to be practicing his Strahlinvek by asking the *thola* a million questions?

"When will Garrand get up?" he asked anxiously.

"Soon, soon. I should think very soon. Now you must leave Jean-Wa to make the Capítän's dinner."

The cub rubbed his shoulder against the art's serving cart, not eager to leave. Jean-Wa swatted his rump with a spare spatula. "Shoo-shoo. Jean-Wa is busy here. You want the Capítän to grow strong quickly, yes?" Alexander yawned and rolled his head to one side, peering up at the *thola's* glowing red eyes. "Go play with that round rascal. Shoo now."

Alexander heeded the *thola's* admonitions, but ambled out slowly, defiantly, as if he could not be troubled to move quickly. With the *tholas* busy doing work and the captain off-limits in his quarters, Alexander had only one thing left to pique his interest. He wound his way slowly through the guts of the world-ship, nose swinging low to the deck. It was pleasantly chill and dark in the narrow tunnels; were it not for the lack of stars and moisture he might have been on one of his solitary, late-night visits to Grandfather. The memory of the death-dream still resonated in his thoughts. He had been afraid to mention the vision to anyone besides Sid—afraid that he had glimpsed a fated event.

A pleasant hum buzzed up through his paws as he crossed an intersection, some machine shaking deep below the deck. The ticklish reverberation signaled that he was close. He scraped his shoulder along the edge of an opening and slipped quietly into a pitch-black chamber.

"Lights," he barked in Strahlinvek, proud of his ability to make the world-ship do as he wished. The wide room was instantly bathed in a warm, amber glow, like dawn over the bamboo on El-Bouteran. Alexander headed straight for a low, black podium set in the center of the room. He sat down in front of the pillar that topped off well over his head.

"Lower console," he said, just like Garrand had taught him on one of the many nights they had both shunned sleep. Silently, the podium slid into the deck until Alexander could reach the controls. He swiped a single claw across the top of the slanted surface and a brilliant display leapt up, twisting and twinkling in the subdued light. Part of the deck began to glow in one corner of the room as the holo chamber warmed to life. The controls hovered over the podium, abstract shapes and bright colors rotating before his eyes. Alexander dipped both paws into the translucent display and grasped two shapes. They were slippery, like wet, mossy stones in a brook. If he squeezed too tightly, the shape collapsed into nothingness. It took a delicate touch, just enough pressure to manipulate the control, but not so much as to be grasping empty air.

He'd had varying success with the holo controls in the past but tonight was pleased to find that he had successfully accessed the captain's sculpture program. The Alice woman rose magically in the glowing corner, upside-down and naked. Alexander sniggled with pleasure.

His use for the control podium was over; he preferred to take a more direct approach. He proceeded to attack the warm, gooey sculpture with the full fervor and creative energy of youth. A glorious mess ensued, with paw, claw, tongue and fur all used to maximum effect.

"Ahh, a traditionalist I see." Garrand Médeville stood in the doorway, weight on his good leg, hand holding the steel frame for added balance. He had stood watching the melee between cub and sculpting medium for several minutes, quietly beaming. "Paws right in the thick of it, like an old master."

Alexander started at the sound of the voice, sniffed for confirmation, and nearly fell over backward in his rush to turn around.

"Garrand!" he bleated, overcome with joy at the sight of the human back on his two legs. He scampered over the deck, thick, gooey chunks flying in all directions, and launched himself at the captain.

Garrand should have seen it coming: the greeting never really varied. The best he could do was brace himself for impact. The furry missile hit him hard and he gasped for breath, pain shooting down his leg. Nonetheless he smiled and dutifully accepted the copious licks. He closed his eyes and listened to the slurps and felt the warm heartbeat thumping against his chest in rapid excitement. His grip tightened around the panda and he allowed himself a long, slow exhalation. The cub always smelled like spice cookies.

"How about something to eat? Something that tastes better than me."

"Gerrah. Vah to-xchtrel mah leetsu."

"Yeah, okay. Whatever you say."

Alexander nodded. "Lala bang voo."

Garrand set the cub down and put his weight gingerly on his sore leg. "We'll have to see about that. Jean-Wa isn't much one for surprise demands, but who knows."

"Lala," the panda repeated. He nudged the captain toward the mess.

SOMETHING DISTURBED JEAN-WA'S concentration as he methodically whipped three bowls of Do pudding at precisely three-thousand revolutions per minute—any more and the betts eggs would be bruised; any less and the ingredients would not gel. He paused, listening for the telltale click-clacks that marked the rapscallion Alexander's approach. But there was no such distraction. He glanced quickly at the baba pillow. Empty. Humhal rested in his slot. Jean-Wa rolled carefully toward the open door, aural sensors at maximum gain. No, it could not be. That was the Capítän's voice drifting in from the mess. He set down the three bowls and wheeled out of the kitchen, not bothering to set down his whisks.

"Aigh! What is this?" Just as he suspected, his sick charge had escaped from his quarters. The art threw his arms into the air and rose a meter. Batter dripped from service conduits overhead, splattering his carefully polished skin. "Capítän, oh Capítän, you disappoint me so. I give for you the finest of care. The medicinal jellies of the Mara'taikōz leaf as salve upon your burned arm. Finely ground Baih root mixed with roro fat-bellies for the toxins in your blood. And yet, here you are—out of the bed, taxing your wounded limbs." He rolled up to the human, dropped his whisks on the table, and began fussing with the bandages on Garrand's shoulder. "You are like a young stricke moose, without the sense to know when to lie still. If you persist you will be spending even more long hours in the bed. And no babas for you."

Garrand pushed the six arms away and limped over to his favorite spot. "You're just too good at what you do my friend.

I'm feeling much better." He eased himself onto the couch and swung his leg up. "How about if I promise to stay still?"

Jean-Wa's eyes glowered down at him, but his head settled back down. He flicked an arm restlessly while another scraped batter off his shoulder. The other four were crossed in defiance.

"I'm just really hungry," Garrand sighed, hoping to find an easy way out. "All I've had for days is electrostatic charges and drips and gunk. What I could really use is a good meal." He cocked his head to one side and intoned slyly, "One of *your* meals, that is."

"Bah! You think to sway me with flattery!" All six arms tapped the cart in an uneven rhythm. "I suppose I could find something that might suffice. Something that would aid in your recovery. It is, though, very short notice. The greatness is not achieved quickly, not without the inspiration and the planning and the careful execution." He snapped his arms back down and wheeled away. "For you, however, I will see what can be done."

Garrand allowed himself a deep breath and looked around for a spare clipscanner. Maybe Bailey had updated ship status. Nothing within arm's reach. Alexander crawled up on the couch beside him and laid his head across his thigh.

Jean-Wa wheeled back into the mess clutching the baba pillow. He carefully lifted Garrand's leg with four arms and set the pillow beneath his knee. He backed up, inspected his work for a moment and then spun wordlessly away.

With nothing to read, Garrand sat back and listened, content to be out of his quarters. What was usually just background humming seemed much richer now. He tried to pick out the individual layers of noise. The atmo processors were a dull, steady groan—sucking old air in and blowing out new. The light drive thrummed up through the deck, almost felt more than heard.

He could pick out the tick ticking of the water reclamator behind the kitchen with its faulty condenser unit that he'd never gotten around to fixing. Every few seconds a muted screech signaled a reactor coil powering a subsystem to life. Coolant trickled through pipes overhead, headed to various parts of the ship. And coming up the hall he could just make out the steel on steel sound of Little Bit rolling toward the mess accompanied by an occasional clink as he hit a loose deck plate.

The burnished sphere braked to a graceful halt and plopped down on his three rods in front of Garrand. He trilled an exuberant greeting and set a clipscanner on the table in front of him.

"Howdy," Garrand smiled happily.

The art extended a spindly arm and reached a claw toward Garrand's leg. With delicate precision, he lifted the edge of the bandage and surveyed the damage beneath. He gave a long whistle.

"It looks worse than it is."

Little Bit burped his doubt and set the bandage back in place.

"Seriously, I'm feeling much better. Do you think Jean-Wa would let me out of bed unless I was fully repaired?"

The art spun a receptor node toward the kitchen and then back to look at the pale human.

"Don't worry, we'll be back to hunting in no time."

The art dropped back to the deck and rolled toward the kitchen, probably to check up on his story. Garrand closed his eyes and found his thoughts drifting to the strange twist in his dream: the thirty odd faces staring up at him. *Lead us through the Path of Fate...*

Wonderful, tempting smells looped out of the kitchen, and it wasn't long before Sid ambled into the mess. He did not appear surprised to see Garrand lying across the acceleration couch. The large panda walked to the table and set himself down across from the captain.

"Tell me about your dream."

Garrand looked up with a start. He searched the panda's expression and frowned. "Adding mind reading to your list of tricks?"

"Your dreams are no secret to me. No one's are."

"You can see them? That's impossible!" He felt immediately stupid as he said it. Nothing seemed to be impossible lately, not where Sid was concerned. He reworded his doubt: "That borders on telepathy."

"Not really, Captain. I can sense the *stroval*—the dream waves—of creatures nearby. Some of us in the tribe have this problem."

"Problem, huh. What, gets in the way of your own?"

"Exactly," Sid grumbled. "Yours are stronger than most. And more *peculiar*."

Garrand bit the inside of his cheek hard and held his retort in check. *Peculiar, eh? Down right bizarre. A nightly demon.*

Sid seemed to be following his thoughts once again. "You dream of the same things over and over. And always the past. Always *your* past."

"There's some future in there too," he said defensively.

"That's what I want you to tell me about."

"Ahh," Garrand grinned. "Interested in that, are you?"

He told the panda about the wraith making its first appearance in the litany of emotional events that formed his dream. Then he told him about the score of pandas that stood upon a broad tarmac awaiting his words. He finished by recounting the doubts he had felt, facing the assembled tribe.

"You have to remember, Sid. Mine is just a dream. There's no inherent probability that any of it will come true. I don't have your powers of prophecy. There's no sartographic heritage in my genetics."

Sid sighed deeply and shifted on the hard bench. "You have latent powers you don't even begin to understand, Captain. You dream things for a reason. The demon of the winds plagues you because you have not accepted your past. You doubt the decisions that have lead you down this Path. And yet, now you dream of the future, a future linked to this past. You will find that the past you fear has less power to affect you as you come to realize that the decisions you made were meant to be."

"I don't understand. They're just dreams."

"Would you do the same things again? The hard things, the intractable ones."

Garrand stared hard at his friend. "Yes."

"Then you are walking your Path of Fate."

Garrand considered this silently.

Sid nodded gently. "It is time to continue your training if you are to become a reliable *Jhei Pōloc*."

"Eye what?"

"An interpreter of dreams."

"I thought that's what I had you for."

"I am a dreamer. Each of us as individuals is, but it takes the collective whole, all of the tribe, to accurately discern the meaning behind the dreams."

"But the tribe is gone."

"Only the larger whole. We are a tribe of two," he glanced toward the kitchen, "of four, of seven. We are a tribe of as many as we have. And your destiny is to be the tribe's *Jhei Pōloc*. The teller of dreams. We have foreseen a *Griffin* becoming our interpreter. And you have seen it in your *own* dreams. It is no longer just our dream of you." Sid gauged the man's reaction, waiting for the next objection. He was pleased to find the captain silent and reflective—the perfect state for training. "Come, we must begin our work."

"No, no. There will be no such work, not without a proper meal first," Jean-Wa exclaimed as he rolled into the mess. His serving tray was piled high with biscuits and fruit. "It is but a simple repast. But the simplicity does not make it the worse, no? Sometimes the simple is the best."

He set down his wares and began fixing a plate for the captain. Garrand swung his leg off the couch and slid closer to the table. He pulled the plate away from the art before he could finish piling everything on.

"You are hungry, yes? This is good. Eat, eat."

Garrand bit eagerly into a biscuit and eyed the panda. "What about Sid?"

"I have sent the roly-poly one off to fetch the bamboo. He shall be here with the leafy greens presently. Now eat."

"I'm eating, I'm eating," Garrand sputtered and stuffed another biscuit in his full mouth. "See?"

"That is more like it." Jean-Wa hovered over Garrand. He waited, hands on his slender hips, until the entire tray was emptied.

Little Bit rolled in, dragging a small bundle of bamboo behind him. Sid lurched off the bench and brushed past the *thola* to select a stalk.

The two creatures ate their fill and sat in silence. Jean-Wa rolled back in once more with a mug of spiced janda and retreated, leaving them alone.

Garrand blew into the steaming mug. He watched Sid double-checking the last bamboo stalk for any tender shoots he might have overlooked.

"How do we start?" he asked.

"We already have," Sid replied. He dropped the stalk and sat down in front of the captain.

"Better question: how do *you* start? Where do you begin? The future is limitless, right? So, how do you narrow it down? How do you envision a particular future?"

"For a panda, the opening can be particularly tricky. With many different possibilities to consider, my understanding is not always as good as it should be. We do not always comprehend what we see—in fact, often we do not. That is why we have attempted to create a group vision, culling through possible but *unlikely* futures until a sort of consensus has been reached."

"I thought that the future was always fluid—something could always happen differently that changes things."

"It is fluid, and something always *could*, but as a particular event draws closer, the number of variables that could affect it drops exponentially. And in turn, each variable itself has less impact."

"So if enough visions correlate—"

"—And the event is near enough to the present—"

"—Then it is deemed as a fated event?"

"Yes, part of the Path of Fate."

"But only as it pertains to the tribe specifically?"

"Yes, if the tribe was the thrust of the original visions. Since survival has been foremost on our minds, most all of the visions have focused on the Path of Fate as it relates to our destiny. If we act in a manner consistent with the dreams, along the particular branch of possible outcomes that was foreseen, then we can carefully predict the results of our actions. The problem lies in that there are many, many more actions that result in our failure than in our success. We have carefully culled through thousands of dreams to find a Path where the tribe survives."

Garrand cupped his hands around the warm mug and sipped carefully. He rocked forward, elbows on knees while the spicy heat trickled down inside him. "What about all the stuff you can't possibly control? I mean, you *might* be able to foresee it, but it seems that there is so much random stuff that could mess up your predicted path."

"We have found that many things can happen during a fated event that we did not foresee, or accurately predict, and yet the outcome remains the same."

"Really." Garrand scratched his chin. "Like for example...?"

Sid rocked back and selected a discarded stalk of bamboo. "You yourself are a prime example of a key outside variable — one we could not control — playing a vital role in a situation. We foresaw the Imperial soldiers attacking our camp on El-Bouteran. We also foresaw our timely escape aboard your world-ship. Our negligence in leaving Alexander behind and your subsequent heroism was not a part of the tribal vision, though I myself had had dreams of a man much like yourself coming to our aid. The outcome, however, remained consistent with the tribe's vision."

"Perhaps *because* of my outside influence."

Sid chewed on his stalk. "Perhaps."

"It doesn't bother you that you don't always know?"

"Captain, do you understand exactly how your world-ship, the noble *Destiny's Needle*, makes the decisions that it makes, how it carries you from star to star and keeps you safe?"

"Well..."

"You accept it, do you not? You trust in its abilities and use it as a valuable tool for your survival."

Garrand grinned. "I see your point. I guess there's enough room in my small human comprehension for talking pandas and their prescient dreams."

Helen's voice rang out from the aft entrance to the mess. "Now I've heard everything."

Garrand's face turned immediately sour. "We're having a discussion here," he muttered.

In the low light of the mess, Garrand could only make out the woman's silhouette. But when she stepped under a glow lamp he was surprised to find her face streaked with grease, her blouse stained crimson, and her hair cascading in a tangle down her left shoulder.

"What in K'ye have you been doing?"

Helen strutted across the mess, one hand clutching a bundle of dead rats. She stopped in front of him and lifted her bounty. She held them aloft by their tails, swinging them gently back and forth for him to see.

Garrand stared quietly at her for quite some time. Beneath the grime and blood, her face looked raw and strangely innocent. Her eyes searched his back and forth. They started with a defiant fire, but with each passing second the sparkle seemed to fade from them, like hope draining from a sieve. She looked both powerful and vulnerable at the same time. At once he saw a youth tortured by a man she could not escape, and a woman who had sold out a species for revenge.

Sid watched Garrand's expression carefully, witnessing the subtle transformation from anger to pity. "That's quite a haul," he said finally.

A beginning of a smile crept across the corner of her lips, like a kid finding her hoped-for praise. "Thank you," she said softly.

He waited for an acerbic follow up, but all he got was her impish grin.

"Why don't you go get cleaned up, let us finish here."

She nodded and slipped away, but not before turning to needle him gently: "It's about time you were out of bed."

Garrand glanced quickly at Sid, looking for a reaction to Helen's appearance, but the panda was stoically grinding down the toughest part of the stalk.

"How can you be so calm?" he demanded. Sid just wrinkled his nose and continued chewing. "Particularly since you knew what she was going to do before she did it."

"I'm of two minds on the matter, Captain. From one perspective, it is the only way. It is the Path the Elders have chosen, and as such, she is merely playing her destined part. To fault her for that would be hypocritical in the extreme."

"But what about the moral issues. The whole tribe is at risk because of her."

"That was not her primary intent."

"No. But she is gambling with all of your lives in order to get what she wants."

"Helen is following her destiny."

"Stop talking about destiny," Garrand snapped. "She could have chosen *not* to do it! No one made her choose this path."

Sid set his stalk down and shuffled closer. His round, black eyes loomed huge. Garrand could smell the bamboo on his breath, like fresh cut straw, grassy and raw. "Her whole life forced her into this Path, Garrand," he said, lapsing to the human's less formal given name. "She is doing what she felt she must do, just as you and I have always done. You risked lives to save lives, did you not? All the men and women aboard that Imperial world-ship might have drowned during your attempt to rescue seven others."

"But they didn't."

"Nor have my brethren."

"Yet."

Sid's eyes dropped as though struck and he bowed his head.

"I'm sorry. That's not what I meant." He reached out to touch the panda. "It's just Helen."

"You must not judge her so harshly. She thinks that she is stopping a much greater evil."

"Director Darstin."

"And the Nralda Keiretsu. She could well be right, from what I have dreamt. But this is not a path that concerns us tonight. As we search the future for our destiny we must stop to consider which is the true Path—a million possibilities shine before us, each beckoning—promising wealth, power, fame, or other illusory gifts. The decisions we make define us as a *therbata*, a tribe. We must find the true Path of honor and responsibility amongst the thousand lesser paths. There is but one true Path of Fate that you as a man, or we as a *therbata* can walk."

"I'm going to have to trust your vision of the future, aren't I?"

"If we are to rescue the tribe, yes. If we are to survive as a species, yes."

Garrand leaned back against the cracked leather. It had been a long time since he had had faith in anyone. A long time since he believed that the best could happen. It went against everything he'd learned as a Freetrader. Invariably, the worst always seemed to happen. *Always be prepared, and never be surprised when you find yourself at Haven's End.*

Yet Sid was asking him to have faith in an improbable dream of the future. A vision of the panda tribe safe from harm. *Have faith. Avoid the mistakes of the past. Forge a better tomorrow. Rescue the righteous and find a place where you truly belong.*

Was it as simple as that? Just believe in yourself, have faith. Or was it a fool's errand?

There was only one way to find out. "Okay, let's hear it."
Sid grumbled deep in his throat. The guttural noise gave
way to Strahlinvek. "What's that?"

"The future. Let's have it. We've got to figure out how to
follow the 'path,' right?" He picked up the clipscanner to take
notes. He tapped a knuckle against the screen. "Give me a
rough outline to work with. If you know the future, it's about
time I started taking advantage."

SID TALKED WELL into the night, outlining his visions. Garrand
sank back into the couch and closed his eyes. It was not at all
what he expected. It was like listening to an epic poem, one he
did not understand, but so beautifully told that the words had
a power unto themselves.

Much of what Sid and the tribe had foreseen they did not
truly understand. It was merely shapes and images, stories of
far-off places and fantastic machines. Garrand saw immediately
the inherent difficulties, and why they needed a *Jhei Pōloc* to
interpret what they had dreamt.

Sid did his best to outline the chosen path, complete with
branching forks and possible solutions to those forks. But it
was all becoming too confusing for Garrand. Sid was near the
end of the path, giving an account of a crucial encounter that
Garrand would face.

"*Beware the dark portal / And the silver beasts / Defeat them
from within / Before you are their feast.*"

"What in K'ye does that mean?" Garrand asked.

"It means the difference between life and death, failure and
success. All our lives depend upon it." Sid, too, was growing
weary.

"*The silver beasts?* Great," Garrand muttered. "This is going to be *so* easy."

"Captain, you must have faith. And *patience.*"

"It's easy to have patience when you can see what's going to happen. As far as the rest of us are concerned—we want results *now.*"

Sid grumbled, pulling at the thick fur at the back of his neck. "That is why your past still haunts you."

"What does my past have to do with it?"

"Your past is essential—it is what has led you to this point, it is who you are, what you have become. The past is a greater indicator of the future than anything you see in the present. Without an understanding, appreciation and healthy respect for your past, you are forever bound by its limitations, enclosed as a creature."

Garrand picked at his loose bandage. "I'd just a soon forget my past."

"That is exactly why it plagues you."

"If I'm so wrapped up in my backward ways, then why have you pinned your hopes on me?"

Sid exposed his lower teeth and licked his nose. "There's always hope, Captain."

Garrand sighed and kicked his good toe back and forth over the edge of the cerasteel deck. "So you have to have faith as well, eh?"

"Sid's eyes softened, the lids closing partially over the huge black irises. "Sometimes, Captain, I think that's all I have."

"So you have visions of the future, I have visions of the past, and between the two of us we're going to read fate's destiny and rescue everyone."

Sid took a step forward and rested his head against the man's shoulder. "Exactly."

Garrand reached up and grabbed Sid's left ear with affection, scratching the inner fur with his thumb. "Well, we've still got to work on our translational skills of these visions."

Sid sat back down and twisted his whiskers indignantly. "Translation is not so easy as you might imagine, Captain. Particularly into such a multi-interpretational and obscure dialect. The lyrical bent really doesn't convey much of the true imagery."

Garrand turned and waved a hand. "I know, I know. Try to condense a thousand visions into a few scant *words*."

Sid rocked back on his haunches. "Exactly."

"Let's see what we've got." He picked up the clipscanner, set to auto-record, and read aloud:

> *Through the tunnel of fire and rain*
> *A tribe's lost splendor lies in vain.*
>
> *Gas and flame, ice and snow*
> *All the elements he must know.*
>
> *Winter spells a sure demise*
> *For a veil of tholas that guard the prize.*
>
> *A final soul lies young and pure*
> *No match for the Griffin and his ruse obscure.*

"Okay, you got me. How exactly is this supposed to help?"

"This is the best I can come up with, Captain. It makes little sense to me either. Less, actually. It's just images and thoughts. It's just a dream, and just *my* dream. I have no one to compare this to. If a dozen of us had dreamt this over and over again we could sit around the fires and analyze it. Try to find a context to put it in. Figure out where this was going to happen. When, and under what circumstances."

"I get the idea," Garrand sighed. "We'll just have to do the best we can. Maybe it'll make sense when it happens."

Sid flexed his whiskers. "Oh it will make sense when it happens." He rolled onto his side and rested his head on the bamboo. "The question is, will it be too late then?"

6

TROMAVEINT

GARRAND'S LEG GENUINELY ACHED, BUT IT WAS A GOOD ache. The kind of ache that meant that he was still alive, still attached to both of his limbs, still able to walk. Despite Jean-Wa's admonitions, he walked quite a bit. He took great pleasure strolling through the dark twisting corridors inside his ship, not in a rush for once, stopping to examine panels and systems he hadn't attended to for months. There was little else to do. With his burnt arm and shoulder still basically useless while the skin grafts slowly grew into place, Bailey wouldn't allow him below decks to hunt rats or search for traces. And under Sid's guidance, the two arts had most of the ship's systems in full working order. Unbelievable. If it weren't for three daily sessions with Sid as his dream tutor, he would have been quite bored.

He flexed his quadriceps and felt the nerve endings around the entry wound send sharp needles of pain shooting up into his groin. He chuckled out a moan. It was a habit he couldn't shake: he almost needed to feel the pain to confirm that he had survived the dart's impact, to know that his muscles and tendons still reacted properly. He would gauge the pain through a clenched jaw and exhale softly, measuring how much less it hurt from the last time. Soon he would be back to normal, ready for another fight. He set his boot on the deck and gingerly applied weight to the leg. A good, solid ache.

He stepped around a mass of tangled cables that streamed out of an open service panel and bent to peer into the damp, oily recess. This level was beneath the moisture evaporators and excess condensation was common, but nothing like the pool of oily liquid he discovered behind the service duct. He hadn't noticed this on the day's repair roster. What was Little Bit after in here? Something mechanical wheezed and groaned in the dark beyond sight. Carbon scrubber? Spotty moisture collector? He made a mental note to check with the tech art and pushed upright.

He was headed for the aft cargo hold. Not yet time for his session with Sid, but he'd gotten in the habit of drifting back to the hold an hour or more beforehand. It was Alexander's turn now, and the cub had two tutors—Sid to teach him how to control his latent dream powers, and Bailey to give him a context to understand them. Garrand loved to listen. He had the upper hand on the cub in context, but Alexander had him beat flat out in dreaming. There was much to be learned from both the teachers.

Garrand opened the smaller of the hold's access doors, pleased that hydraulics released nearly silently: he'd spent one long afternoon overhauling the door's pressure seals to alleviate its characteristic groan to allow these secret visits. He slipped along the inner bulkhead and leaned back against a cold support in the shadows.

The familiar voice of his first mate echoed gently through the darkness. He could just make out the silhouette of the two pandas sitting in the center of the chamber in front of a holo fire, the only source of light besides the faint glow of cargo markers embedded in the deck plates.

Garrand leaned in, straining to catch the story, drawn in by the words, the telling. It had been Sid's suggestion originally. The tribe, he said, needed a history of the Shell, a broader picture. All they had known was: eat, sleep, dream, and escape. The pattern repeated over and over again. It was a limited existence. The broader dreams were a mystery. The Path of Fate was a magical concept to cubs who knew nothing of the past, with dreams of a future that made little sense.

Alexander would be the first historian in the Tchelakov Tribe. It was a role that immediately appealed to the little panda; finally an adult task, something that he could learn and contribute to the tribe. The roly-poly bundle of fur sat in rapt attention, as still and stoic as an Elder, without his usual squirming tendencies. Sid listened too, as much in awe of the tales as the cub.

Bailey spoke of the Collistas Dynasty, of the Core Worlds under the Emperor's reign. He told of his 200 years of service in the armed forces: combat as an infantryman, duty in the Imperial Navy, his years as a Combat Instruct, and then finally, duty in the Imperial Guard as Garrand's Combat Assist. He lectured on the tendencies of humans, Geihan, T'chell, Larken,

Trogands and Gambor alike, of a hundred species that Garrand
had never seen. The art spoke of multiple histories—some real,
some myth—explaining the heartaches behind each loss, the
honor and betrayal within each race. He gave insight into the
inner mechanics of what made Carinaena's Shell act and react
the way it did.

And finally Alexander understood. How he had dreaded the
frantic preparations, the incessant drills and lessons and exercises, the constant flight from one world to the next, and above
all the fear. Seeing the anxious look in Mother's face, even in
the quiet times. The hushed reverence in the Elder's voices.
Always afraid that tomorrow they would be caught. Why, he
wondered, did so many chase them across the stars?

But now, listening to the *thola's* fantastic stories, comprehension filled his mind. *It was the pursuers who were afraid.* Their
place in history was not yet set. The Elders spoke of the Path
of Fate, and he had never quite grasped the full meaning. The
thola told tales of many Fates, how each race had followed its
own Path blindly, stumbling and, many times, failing. If they
could have seen their own Paths, many would still live. This
is what the Imperials and the Gambor and the Nralda sought:
the tribe's ability to see the Paths.

This was why so many had killed and so many had died. So
that *their* tribes, the ones *they* held dear, might have a better
chance to survive, to sing around the fires for many generations, to spread out amongst the stars without fear and dread.

Today, Bailey was talking about Archiva, a world that had
been lost in the great reaches.

"Why don't we know where it is?" Alexander asked.

"The Shell is a whimsical place," Bailey replied. "Fortune,
prestige, notoriety have come and gone for thousands of systems without even a flicker of recognition from the volume as

a whole. Archiva is said to have been settled over two thousand years ago, and was not a place of importance for another thousand still. Many things have happened since then."

"But aren't there maps?"

"Yes. But maps are always becoming obsolete. Each history is inaccurate in its own peculiar ways. The survivors always record what they remember. They don't always know everything, or don't always tell the truth. Worlds have been renamed to suit the whims of new settlers, new rulers, new empires. What we call Archiva was called Mardell's world in its heyday, and probably many other things as well before and since.

"Meticulous maps, privately commissioned by colonization efforts or ordered by the Imperial Cartographic Guild, have undoubtedly been drafted of most systems, but over the centuries been lost, misplaced, or forgotten. Fortunes of worlds rise and fall. Colonies have grown into nations and world-sprawling system fiefs, or disappeared altogether as forgotten, ghostly failures.

"Many worlds control abundant wealth and vast trade networks, and with that economic freedom have grown into civilized places. Cities were born, continents explored, new settlers attracted. But trading lanes often shift, resources have a tendency to dry up, commodities become obsolete or worthless, and Freetraders, entrepreneurs, and colonists move on, leaving behind the shell of a civilization, a decaying infrastructure of intelligent life. At times, the whims of ruling factions have caused whole systems to dry up, or even worse, become embroiled in some dispute and subsequently ravaged by war."

"So planets can get lost."

"Yes, just like anything else."

The primary cargo door split open and trundled noisily open, allowing light to spill into the chamber. Helen walked in pulling a pile of equipment hastily wrapped in a spent amoeba net. She dropped the load near the holo fire and slumped to a bamboo nest nearby.

"Don't stop on my account," she said, slightly out of breath.

Sid turned and called into the shadows, "Why don't you join us as well, Captain." Chagrinned, Garrand limped to the center of the hold. "So planets get lost. What do we know about this Archiva?"

"It was a repository of information for an entire empire," Alexander recited proudly.

"The Collistas Dynasty?"

"No, not the empire that we know as the hegemony that controls the Core Worlds," Bailey replied. "This was a different culture altogether, settled originally by the Migontus and Xensul races, and ruled by Mardell the First.

"The Migontus Realm once spanned a significant portion of Carinaena's Shell, embracing over a thousand systems. As the realm grew, the accumulation of knowledge, data, technology, events, economic records, artistic and scientific writings, and fiction were becoming scattered over the breadth of the empire. After the destruction of two key data repositories during the War of the Three in 29,182 in which the entire ancestral record of deeds and fiefs for five thousand systems was lost, the network of information was deemed too important to lie 'scattered across the Shell like diamonds for the taking.' A central archival planet was deemed the solution, with a planet-wide system of data storage—a backup repository for the knowledge of the entire empire. The location was chosen in secret and the entire network was shunted through 'Archiva,' where physical copies were recorded and stored in vast datacores.

"The planet-wide system was automated to ensure its survival through the ages and to cut down on information loss and degradation through inconsistent biological management. A period of poor oversight by one generation of bad archivists could cripple the system, so its operation was turned over to machines. As new works were created, fresh technologies researched, and new cultures discovered a copy of each network entry was diverted to Archiva, which became the secret hub of the empire's communication network."

"And still it remained hidden?"

"Mardell had added incentive for keeping its location secure. After his reign and with the empire in the capable hands of his son, he retired to Archiva, bringing his family with him, to raise grandchildren and write his own history. He called the place 'a paradise for the mind.'"

"Paradise of the mind," Garrand murmured. "I always thought you meant it as a reference to a physical state. How have you gone about finding it?"

"The network links were its only weakness. Archiva could not be completely isolated, it needed links to the constant proliferation of information—an empire's data passed through it."

"So track the flow of data?"

"Essentially, yes."

"But how?" asked Alexander.

"The accumulation of data and information has taken on a life of its own in the past several thousand years. For instance, when we set down on a planet for repairs, all the uncoded data from our navi—grav fluctuations of celestial bodies along our route, orbital discrepancies, solar activity, cartographic updates and the like—are dumped into the Port Authority datacore automatically. As a matter of course, the information becomes part of updated shipping lane protocols, fresh nav data for outgoing vessels, statistics that affect levies and tariffs, and so on and so forth. All the information has to go *somewhere*. And in fact, it goes many places."

"And you're working on the assumption that one of the places it goes is Archiva," Garrand said, starting to catch a sliver of the excitement in the room.

"Yes."

A certain measure of skepticism tempered his voice: "Still? After all these centuries?"

"There's no reason to believe that the Archives are no longer functioning."

"We're talking a millennia here. And a long-dead empire. What's to say the planet wasn't sacked?"

"Such an event was never recorded, and given the importance of such a coup, it undoubtedly would have been written extensively about by any conquerors, and at the very least become part of the lore. There is no mention of such a catastrophe. Remember, the Migontus were never defeated. Their empire dissolved under its own size and bureaucratic weight sometime after the reign of Mardell the Sixth and ceased to be a contiguous socio-economic entity. The individually-ruled parts of the empire thrived, just under different names."

"And the links to Archiva remained?"

"That is my primary supposition. The basis of which has fueled Sid's prescient searches."

"So it's a matter of finding the right link. The one with trillions of bits of data still flowing down it."

"In a grossly oversimplified manner of speaking, yes. There were millions of dummy links created, virtual dead-ends where data was automatically routed, as if headed to a database, but then never recorded when it arrived."

"Hmm," Garrand flexed his quadriceps and winced, "of course."

"I have traced hundreds of thousands of possible sites by sending an encoded message through *Destiny's Needle* with instructions for a return reply."

"What's the message?"

"It's a brief with a flawed proof to one of Dr. Sartok's as of yet unsolved mathematical hypotheses."

"Unlikely to be ignored."

"Exactly. The replies come back with colorful insights into some of the proof's several flaws."

"How many have come back?"

The ship's voice crackled overhead: "More than you can possibly imagine, Captain. I am bloated with the same virtual message repeating over and over in my quantum relays. 'You are wrong, you are wrong, you are wrong.' It's enough to drive a core insane."

Garrand grinned. "So what do the replies tell you?"

Helen spoke up for the first time. "You read the quantum routings on the response—see where it's been."

Garrand's face lost a bit of color. He'd had some experience with this long ago. The memory brought a dry, foul taste to the back of his throat and he felt reflexively for the amulet around his neck.

"Yes, but it's the ones that *don't* come back that interest us."

"Ahh."

"We sent the message through upward of 20 billion dedicated servers. Every hardsite, ship, nav beacon, and quantum buoy in *Destiny's* datacore—anyone we'd ever had contact with directly or indirectly. We've sorted through the routings on the ones that did come back and eliminated systems and planets one at a time. Using *Destiny's* sartograph, we've worked out possible routings for the rest, following the traces as far as possible."

"That could take a lifetime," Garrand groaned.

Bailey's eyes glowed faintly in the darkness, the razor edge of a smile creasing his fluid face. "Yes… if we didn't have Sid."

"Furball? He doesn't know a thing about quantum relays and data retrieval."

"He doesn't need to. We simply give him possibilities. Names, places, systems, planets. Historical accounts of surface topography and climate. He dreams of the place and determines whether it dovetails with the previous visions. He has the most accurate sartographic array I've ever had the pleasure to witness."

"Okay, so where does that leave us?"

"We've eliminated ninety-three percent of the known Shell."

"What about the unexplored parts?" Helen asked.

"Technically, we can disregard the possibility that Archiva lies in undiscovered volumes; it has been discovered, the system it lies within has been traveled. Its location exists in datacores somewhere." Garrand sighed. "It would take a flotilla 200 years to check out the other seven percent of Carinaena's Shell."

"We're narrowing it further, Captain. Hour by hour, system by system. It's only a matter of time—"

"—And luck."

"—And patience," Sid finished, giving Garrand a hard look, whiskers rigid.

Garrand held his palms up in abeyance. "Okay, okay. I'm impressed, really I am. It's all beyond me. The three of you are going to unlock a mystery that's stood for a thousand years."

Helen smirked and averted her eyes.

Garrand noted Helen's twitch. "I'm just glad you're all working on *my* side." He turned to look down at Helen and her pile of equipment in the amoeba net. "What, nothing to show for your efforts?"

"You're right, it's harder than it looks. For everyone except that slinky exel," she added with disgust.

Garrand almost allowed himself a chuckle. "She is rather annoying, isn't she?"

"As difficult as it is for me, she always seems to have a rat in her mouth."

"Yeah. Got to find where she's hiding them again." The thought was maddening: rat corpses rotting somewhere in the ship. "Okay," he said loudly. "Everyone out. It's my turn with Sid."

"You got to watch my session," Alexander complained. "Why can't I watch yours?"

"Because you're so much *better* than I am," Garrand said, swatting the cub on his rump. "I'd be embarrassed." The panda sighed heavily but shuffled out the hold without further protest.

Sid watched him leave. "He listens to you better than me now."

Garrand smiled wryly, the lines around his eyes fanning upward. "What do we work on today, Sid?"

The giant panda rose and stretched, forepaws braced on the deck while his back arched and his rump shook. He began a long slow circle around the fire. "Let's concentrate on the dream again."

"Yours or mine?"

"Mine. The 'Thief of Ships.' We didn't get very far last night."

"We got a translation," Garrand said.

"But not an interpretation," Sid countered as he continued to circle the man. "Concentrate and focus this time. Make believe this is your own dream that you are slipping into — but without the sleepiness."

Garrand sat down cross-legged and closed his eyes tightly, hunching his shoulders and bowing his neck and head.

"No, not like that. You look like you are getting ready to do battle mentally. You must choose the antithesis of your natural mechanism for reaction to danger. The adrenaline, the increased heart rate, the short breaths all must be counter-acted. You must reach a state of deep inner relaxation, a place where your mind is free from worry and distraction, where your body is gently resting—as if you were almost preparing for sleep. When the body is on an even keel, like a leaf resting on a placid lake, and your mind is likewise peaceful, relaxed and open, then may you introduce the problem."

Garrand took a deep breath and started over. He ran through the mental checklist that Sid had taught him, willing his body to relax. It was hard. He didn't relax well.

Sid watched the physical tics disappear as the human focused his energies more effectively. The color drained from his face as the muscles relaxed. The chest rose and fell with deep, richly oxygenated breaths. The fingers uncurled and rested at full length. His upper musculature sagged and his head rocked backward slightly to compensate for the shift in his center of gravity.

"Good. Now as your body settles into the place before sleep, direct your mind to the dream of the woman in the clouds, the Thief of Ships. Pretend you are going to have the dream for yourself. Hold the mental image, picture yourself falling into that particular dream."

The *stroval* began, bluish green circlets popping just over the man's aura field. His dream waves were strong, but unfocused. The energies wavered and collapsed, like an infant cub's restless sleep.

"Keep trying," Sid commanded. "Do not give up. Remember to keep your body in the rested, peaceful state. Do not let the excitement and possible danger within the dream trigger your natural warrior instincts. That is where your imagery breaks down."

Garrand grimaced, but kept his eyes closed and renewed his efforts to relax.

"Dreams happen successfully when you sleep, because the body is shut off from the process. Your mind is left free to roam. Disconnect your body from your thoughts."

The *stroval* began again. This time the captain's aura sparkled with renewed vigor, and Sid stopped pacing. The dream waves resonated powerfully, and Sid could sense the imagery from the beginning of his own dream reflected from the mind of the human. *Such a remarkably quick adjustment*, Sid thought.

"Very nice," Sid spoke quietly. "You are there. You have begun your first *tromaveint*. He sat down and quickly slowed his own autonomic responses. A blissful anticipation tickled at the edge of consciousness, the excited expectation of revisiting a future site, a place along the hallowed Path of Fate. He had to calm himself for several seconds before continuing his own *tromaveint*. He needed to catch up with the captain before he lost it. Even as he was focusing his own mind to revisit the dream of the clouds and the Thief, part of his consciousness remained focused on Garrand. The man's dream waves were becoming choppy and disjointed.

"Don't let your mind jump forward in the dream. You are racing too far ahead. Recite what we know to give yourself a template, then tell me what you see."

Golden rings of energy hovered just over his conscious reckoning and then slowly arced upward, gaining strength and intensity, their hue deepening to an almost reddish glow. The column of dream waves rose within his mind, creating a burnished tower that bent and undulated gently. Sid focused on the Thief, her beautiful long, dark hair cascading over her shoulders. The *stroval* sharpened and the rings redoubled. He felt their energy pulsing through his mind as he listened to the captain recite the words:

> *The Thief of Ships*
> *Has little time*
> *Her place in the stars*
> *We're bound to find*
>
> *Clouds in the sky*
> *A spectral glow*
> *A warrior's lullaby*
> *He must know*
>
> *A past alliance*
> *A warm embrace*
> *The Thief's defiance*
> *Like a mirror's face*
>
> *Fate be pinned*
> *To the Griffin's arm*
> *A fall from grace*
> *Unlike a fall to harm*

Sid could feel the fuzzy images sharpen as the captain spoke. At the end of the tunnel of dream waves far above his head, he could just make out the wispy beginning of the dream. He pictured the clouds, the beautiful sunset reflecting off the shimmering towers and water crystals, a place they'd yet to visit.

A place they were destined to find. A flash of coiled energy blinded him for an instant, and then he felt himself rushing though the golden rings, toward the images at the end of the tunnel. With a dizzying epiphany, Sid's mind rushed into the future.

He stood atop a windswept tower, with more still reaching further overhead. A darkened city spread out below, lights just beginning to illuminate a gathering dusk. A series of elevated bridges and cantilevered flyer pads masked the true height of his vantage, but clouds floated below as well as above. A few caught the final rays of the setting primary, like giant, pink glow globes. Sid searched the sky briefly and found the woman. The Thief glided gently over a far-up landing pad, soaring on gossamer wings. Her raven hair rippled behind like an unkempt mane.

"Do you see it?" Sid asked. The captain's dream waves had settled back to a steady rhythm, like the certain reverberation of the world-ship's light drive that resonated through the deck.

"Yes. I see it," he said excitedly.

"Careful," Sid warned.

"I see it. It's so beautiful! Show me the whole dream," he cried but it was too late. His pulse quickened and adrenaline soared. Like a soap bubble imploding, the *tromaveint* collapsed and Garrand was back in full consciousness. He sat blinking.

Sid growled softly and let his own dream fade; he felt himself sinking back through the rings until he, too, was back in the temporal present.

"That was amazing. It was more vivid than life."

Sid flexed his whiskers and indulged the itchy spot behind his ear with one claw.

"How did I do that?"

"You had the dream in your mind, and you found it."

"But I don't have the sartographic chip embedded in my genes."

"You're as sentient as I, Captain. Your species dreams powerfully as well. I should think it's within your power to dream of the future. Perhaps your species has always dreamt of the future and just never known it."

"Never known it? What do you mean?"

"You're always asleep. It's amazing that you remember anything at all. Spend a few years dreaming while awake. You might be surprised by what you actually see. And with direction from others that have been dreaming their whole lives, you never know…"

Garrand, elbow on knee, chin on hand, looked perplexed.

"Look," Sid rumbled. "You can sense my dreams as I sense yours. I have genetic coding that focuses my dreams for me. I picture a place, a time, a creature, and I can see it. As it will be. As it could be. You see things in your dreams and you think they're just dreams, your imagination. Well, my *imagination* turns out to be correct a certain percentage of the time. If I focus my efforts in that direction, if the *tribe* focuses in that direction, then often times we discover that what we've *imagined* is actually the future. You sat down, and tried to imagine my vision of a specific place, a specific time, a specific person."

"Our beautiful Thief."

"Yes. And you found her."

"With your help."

"Perhaps. Who is to say you would not have dreamt of her on your own."

Garrand made a doubtful noise. "I'm not sure I buy that. But I did see what you had foreseen. I was close enough to you to pick up on your dream waves."

"My *stroval*."

"Your *stroval*," Garrand corrected himself. "And I did it while awake. That's amazing enough."

Sid took a deep breath. "It is only the beginning."

Garrand nodded quickly. "Good."

"An eager student, I like that."

"Do you think we'll be able to unravel the whole Thief dream?"

"I hope so, Captain. It's part of our future."

"Yes, but I'd like to understand it *before* it happens."

"As would I," the panda said softly.

7

FAILSAFE

GARRAND HAD AVOIDED THE ENCOUNTER FOR TOO LONG. Now that he was feeling back to normal, he could not simply pretend that Helen was just a demoted crew member, relegated to hunting rats and cleaning her weapons. He had to face his own ambiguous feelings about the woman. She had become *persona non grata* amongst everyone aboard the ship, shunned by all. Garrand himself had avoided her because he could not quite believe the enormity of what she had done. It was too awful. He understood the motivations behind her actions now, but could not accept the actions themselves. He admitted that he might never fathom the depth of suffering that Darstin had subjected her to. And he granted the fact that he, too, would have sought revenge. But he fought the wind demon every night. And he had yet to squeeze the trigger. Helen was inflicting the very suffering she abhorred. The line between Darstin and her had blurred, perhaps irrevocably.

He paused before her quarters and squared his shoulders. Anger welled up in his throat, but he swallowed it back down. *If it were anyone else…* Was it worse because he had grown to trust her himself? Was he mad because she had made a fool of him, led him on a merry chase that had ended with his own shortsightedness? By Haven, he had left the security of *Destiny's Needle* in her hands. He had not only given away the keys to the palace gate, but willing let the quisling into his own heart. *Fool.*

He bit down hard. *Perspective, old man. You're no longer an objective observer. She fooled you. Fine. Get over it. You need her still. If you want to save all that you lost, you need her.* That was the barb that cut deepest. He needed her. Worse, still, part of him wanted her. After all that she had done, he still empathized with her.

He swore under his breath in as many tongues as he knew, closed his eyes and cleared his throat audibly. *Destiny* queried the door; unlocked, it slid dutifully open.

Helen looked up at him from her bunk. There was eagerness in the way her eyes searched his back and forth. Was she looking for hope? Gauging how much he accepted of her past behavior?

"Come with me," he said sharply. "And bring *that*." He pointed at the silver case webbed to a wall. She released the case and followed him silently.

Sid and Alexander waited patiently in the mess. Garrand walked behind the pandas and turned back upon Helen. She'd never seen a face so hard.

"Administer the antidote."

"But—"

"Now."

She dared not finish her argument. With only a slight tremble to her fingers, she unlatched the silver case and lifted out the injector wand. Beneath the rows of booster supplements, lay a single row of red vials. She picked one out carefully and held it up to the light. She shook it and watched the sediments mix. Satisfied, she popped the vial into the wand and took a step toward Alexander. The cub shied away.

Helen closed her eyes, her heart sinking. At this one instant, she had never felt worse in her whole life. A tear trickled down her cheek.

Garrand steadied the cub with one hand on his shoulder. "Administer the antidote," he repeated.

Helen blinked away the tear and tried once more to reason with him. "If I do this and they are captured, there's nothing I can do to keep them from Barrett."

"Don't worry about that," Garrand said acridly, as if he alone could prevent that. "Just inject them."

Her hand hovered briefly over Alexander's pelt. She looked into the panda's upturned face and depressed the wand. The fluid passed into the panda's bloodstream.

"How long will it take?"

Helen picked up a second vial and reloaded the wand. "A minute or two. The antidote triggers a genetically encoded self-destruct in the viral parasites that lie dormant in their brains."

"How can we be sure it worked?"

"You'll just have to trust me."

He shot her a vicious look.

"There's no way to pick them up on medi scans. They're engineered to be innocuous, undetectable. It's no failsafe if Barrett's doctors can discover them." She injected Sid. "I guarantee you, they are no longer in any danger. The antidote is a hundred times more lethal to the parasites than it needs to be to succeed."

"Very well." Helen noted the tone of dismissal in his voice and packed up her case. "How long do the rest have?"

Helen wavered over the rows of vials. She squeezed her eyes shut and tried to fight back the dismay that threatened to overwhelm her carefully practiced composure. Her breeding pair had been captured along with all the rest. Even if Garrand did manage to keep Sid and Alexander safe, they were both males, and useless to her in that regard. All she had left were the viral parasites. Nothing else could stop Barrett. And it was the only thing left for her to bargain with.

"Without their weekly vaccination, the symptoms will begin to surface within nine to ten days."

"And then how long?"

She could not bear to look at him and resumed packing. "In six weeks—without the antidote—they will all be dead."

There was a deep silence that seemed to suck all the oxygen out of the mess, like a sudden pressure drop. Helen could feel Garrand's eyes on her back, could only imagine the hatred that burned behind his gaze. With cold fingers, she snapped the latches back into place. She gathered herself and turned back to face him with grim determination. To her surprise, his voice was barely a whisper.

"Will Barrett's doctors be able to discover the virus?"

"Discover? Yes. Cure?" She left the question hanging.

"Probably not…" he sighed, both hands still resting on Alexander's shoulders. He was making her say this in front of them. Their dark eyes betrayed no emotion. They sat stoically with their new protector. *Garrand Médeville, the guardian of the Tchelakov Tribe. Of all the ironies…*

"So you still have an edge over Barrett." He seemed to consider his words carefully. "You'd best pray that we find them before your bargaining skills are necessary."

Helen nodded and gathered up her case.

Garrand's voice changed immediately as he knelt down to face Alexander. "C'mon little one. Don't you know that you get a treat after a visit to the doctor? Let's see what Jean-Wa has cooked up for you." Helen paused to watch the captain lead the cub out the mess toward the kitchen, wondering if she would ever hear such a kind tone directed her way again.

❖ ❖ ❖

GARRAND WAS WALKING THROUGH THE BAMBOO GROVE IN THE amidships hold when *Destiny* requested his presence on the bridge. After several minutes, he limped up the long curving neck and into the crystal bridge. Bailey and Sid were on the navigation pod. His pod swirled up to meet him.

"What now?"

"We have found Archiva."

The news almost shocked him. He didn't know what to say as he stepped onto the command pod and spun it quickly to the center of the bridge. The railing slid aside and he stepped across to Bailey and Sid's pod. "The suspense is killing me. Where exactly is this fabled, mythical place?"

"The Glaplōs System," Bailey said plainly.

"Never heard of it."

"Not many have," the ship snipped.

"Sid has determined that the sixth planet from the primary is the one."

"The one," Garrand said with relish. "Archiva. The lost world of Mardell the First."

"Apparently the 'lost world of Mardell the First' is a fourth stage gas giant," *Destiny* cut in acerbically.

"That's impossible," Garrand said looking sharply at Bailey. "Says who?"

"Says our fine guest."

He glanced at the panda. "Gas giants can't support life."

"Can't support anything," the ship added.

"*Destiny*," Garrand warned. "Do the reports say anything about Archiva being a gaseous planet?"

"No."

"Is there any data in any of the archival records to support a supposition that Mardell's planet was gaseous?"

"No."

"Sid?"

"It is Archiva, Captain. I am sure of it. The dreams narrowed and narrowed until this was the only planet I could foresee. Over and over I have dreamt of this place, this shining planet. For days on end now. This is our destination."

Garrand bent to the navi and a sartograph leapt into existence overhead. The system spun neatly overhead in a gentle circular rotation. The aforementioned planet was sixth from the primary, and clearly labeled as a fourth stage gas giant. "This is it, huh?"

Sid nodded solemnly.

"No second or third choices?"

"With the world-ship's sartographs I was able to rule out every inconsequential vision. I have focused on thousands of worlds and discarded them all. This is it."

"Bailey, any chance there's a datum error, or a cartographic glitch?"

"It has been some time since *any* ship logged something of import into the universal navi database from the Glaplōs System. In fact you have to go back 242 years to find the last entry—solar flare from the Glaplōs primary fouled a scientific sensor array on the *Dolonprei*, passing in system. Standard sensor sweeps of the six planets was included *pro forma*. Data confirms previous entries. The sixth planet is gaseous."

Garrand rubbed his face, casting a sideways glance at Sid.

"Not everything is as it appears, Captain."

"Hmm."

"Captain," the ship asked, "what do you want me to do?"

Garrand dropped his hand down Sid's neck and rested it on his silky back. With full determination he said, "Lay in the course."

"Captain?"

"Do I have to punch the coordinates in manually?"

The ship paused. "Of course not."

The stars pivoted outside the crystal glazings.

Garrand rubbed his fingers absently along Sid's neck. "Best speed to Archiva."

Destiny's Needle accelerated to the quantum barrier, the sublight engines kicked off, the quantum drive engaged and the jaggedly sleek form jumped into quantum space.

8

Arrival

THE PLANET WYX WAS CLOAKED IN OVERLAPPING TEN-
drils of grey clouds like a finely-veined sphere of terrazzo marble. Only brief glimpses of the stone-white surface sparkled
beneath the veil. Above the ragged nimbus, the *Ilyovahtna* and
her precious cargo broke low orbit and began descent. Vailetta's
task force was returning to Wyx in full glory. She stood in the
star bubble at the forefront of the ship's slender finger of bridge
and watched the blackened clouds rise to greet them. One
hand held the railing with a gentle grip as the ship buffeted,
skipping across the atmosphere.

An unsettled feeling stirred her stomach. Anticlimax marred
what by all respects should have been her crowning military

achievement. She had captured the Tchelakov creatures, survived if not vanquished the Gambor, and carried out the vice proctor's wishes when no one else had been able. She was delivering Barrett's prize to his very doorstep, Wyx, the heart of his kingdom. She frowned at her curious word choice: *kingdom. Not Proctorialship, but Barrett's Kingdom.* An apt distinction, and a telling reminder of her doubts.

She watched the clouds envelop the ship as they sank and tried to put it all together. Arnas' words bothered her most. Commander Arnas, as loyal a soldier as had ever served, expressing concern about the usage of a new *weapon.* Not a tool, but a weapon. Lord Barrett, should he be able to unlock the creatures' secrets, might have the power to peer into the future. What did that mean? Were the pandas really that valuable? Médeville had risked his life twice to save just one of the pandas. But he couldn't possibly have known what he had at his disposal, not the first time at least. Had they made such an impression on him?

Yarvek had been rescued from drowning by creatures who not only had never met him before, but also were incarcerated in the hold of a warship. Their escape was as curious as it was amazing. They had befriended a door by Yarvek's account, had convinced it that they really shouldn't be kept inside. An Imperial door, an unbreachable, secure datacore. Vailetta had only had them for a week, and already their abilities astounded her. What might Barrett discover?

The ship's prow emerged from beneath the cloud cover and Vailetta stood looking down on the planet's largest and most elaborate city, a stunning metropolis that spread across the entire southern seaboard of the continent. Most of the planet was deforested and mined for its remarkable stone, leaving the surface a powder grey, like finely ground chalk. The capitol Jobaenz, however, was awash in vibrant energy. Even from low orbit the panoply of vivid colors stood out—a marvelous quilt laid across the somber coast.

The picket whispered over the outlying districts and into the heart of the port. Jobaenz spread out for hundreds of kilometers in all directions, a glittering mosaic unlike any city she had ever seen. The metropolis was not just laid out in a grid, but overlapping, complex, asymmetric shapes. Vast swatches of color were carried by the placement of parks, flyer pads, buildings, and causeways. The whole city was an immense, surreal painting, engineered to be seen from the skies by every ship falling to the planet's surface. It was a landscape painting like no other.

Jobaenz was the first outwardly visible sign that you had entered the meticulous, carefully planned, and precisely executed world of Lord Hellius Barrett. The Vice Proctor had been given the opportunity to help build the Emperor's presence in the Shell and he had seized it like none before. The burgeoning Proctorialship was run with the rectitude of a brigade of Shock Troops. The new port had been his first act after Proctor Nesbit had been assassinated, and it was the first clue to his brilliance. For a man who kept most things close to his vest, this city was a glimpse into his mind, his ambition. The Vice Proctor was building his Proctorialship like he had built this city—piece by careful piece, each conquest part of a larger plan. Unlike other Proctors, he did not simply expand here and there when the time seemed right. He systematically expanded on all fronts— finding a system's weakness when it wouldn't bow diplomatically, or militarily. He was building his own *kingdom*. *His own empire.*

Vailetta breathed the word as she watched the city slide beneath, an ornate tapestry of long promenades and sweeping spires. *An empire without the Emperor.* A tremendous panic gripped her as her ship circled a broad, flat expanse in the landscape—the naval tarmac, thirty square kilometers of unbroken ceracrete. Parts of the Third Fleet were scattered here and there. Some ships straddled repair pits or slowly disappeared into subterranean hangars. Majestic destroyers floated below, resting just over the surface on repulsors.

The *Ilyovahtna* was in her final approach. Vailetta stabbed the com activation board.

"Master Torg, report to the bridge."

In a sickening way it was all beginning to make sense. Her belief that Torg was in fact the infamous Butcher of Yuzbek, the Emperor's personal assassin, was not mere fantasy. The man who had once been charged with protecting her with his life was here, far from the galaxy's Core, in a seemingly innocuous Proctorialship. And General Shecut, a man whose loyalty to the Emperor was without equal, who had secured Emperor Collistas' position during the most dangerous of times was here as well. As an 'overseer.' Two of the Emperor's most trusted men deep in the Shell, hovering near Barrett. Perhaps there truly was danger here. And her father *did* know.

Remember the diplomatic dinner aboard the Shiva? *"He should be careful,"* the minister Momuso had said, *"or one day he'll turn his eye this way and find he no longer controls it."* With awful clarity, she recalled the nervous current of expectation that had coursed through the hall after that statement, as if all were thinking exactly the same thing, but not yet bold enough to say it. A table full of conspirators—all waiting for the right moment to secede, waiting for the one final piece that would ensure their success.

Vailetta gripped the rail, the cold steel bleeding warmth away from her body. Could it be that she was delivering that final piece of Barrett's puzzle? The cherished Tchelakov creatures that he had obsessively and ruthlessly pursued for two years.

"Captain," Helm called out, "we've been given final clearance."

The realization dragged down her fleeting hopes for glory. It was too late to turn back now. "Proceed."

She turned her gaze back to the tarmac, and frowned. Even from this height she could see that their landing site was surrounded by thousands upon thousands of people lined in sharp, even rows, like a massive dress parade.

The ship shuddered and yawed heavily to starboard under the stiff winds. The repulsors slowed the ship to a near hover before allowing gravity to slowly reassert its grip. Beneath them, Vailetta could hardly believe the throng of people that lined the tarmac. There must be two full battalions worth. She'd hardly expected such a gregarious display—after all, her cargo was supposedly a secret. Was Barrett's ego finally asserting itself? Or did he now feel invulnerable with the Tchelakov creatures in his fold? Whichever the case, he apparently did not care who witnessed this event from orbit.

She sighed and reactivated the com. "Dasko?"

"Captain?"

"You getting this?"

"Yeah. Never seen anything like it—not in the Shell at least. You'd think we were on Daulinbêres or something." The troubling association stoked her fear. "Is there some holiday we forgot about?"

Vailetta grunted. "Hardly. Prepare the Gokazoku for disembarkation—full dress. Apparently this is going to be a formal affair."

"Aye, ma'am."

The ship settled gracefully into position, her lowest ventral sensors some thirty meters off the ground. Landing gantries eased forward on buried rails.

"Keep her nose steady," Vailetta ordered, glancing up at helm. The ensign dangled over her head, cables dipping beneath her station and chair to hookups with Yarvek's pod. Helm glanced between her knees, peering down at her captain.

"Holding steady, ma'am."

Vailetta turned and watched the steel platforms edge beneath the extended glazing of the bridge toward the recessed nose of the ship. The picket was delicate, almost fragile, this close to the surface. One mistake in these high winds would spell disaster. Helm was controlled by four women for surface maneuvers. Repulsor spread, fore and aft lateral thrusters, and coupler control. "Nose to the wind, ensign. Keep the sheets luffing, they'll come to us."

"Aye, ma'am."

The ship's stern, some hundred meters back, swung in the shifting crosscurrents, but the nose held rock-steady. The gantry had rolled past the star bubble now, and Vailetta slowly walked back with it to watch the coupling. It always amazed her. They'd spent weeks traveling through the ethos, jumping from star to star like primeval gods. The *Ilyovahtna* was as fast a ship as any created, a technological marvel, lean and slender—a wicked razor-barb of Imperial might. And still, after thousands of years of naval advance, here they were, locking their ship to a steel tower on rails like mariners of millennia past. There was an actual physical connection: massive steel rings, albeit a backup for the mag couplers, but there nonetheless. Buoyed by repulsors, the ship would be left free to swing downwind of Wyx' substantial winds. Vailetta waited for the jolt and smiled grimly when it rang through the ship. For the first time, she was not happy to return from a mission.

"Mag couplers locked, safety locks in place, all boards green."

"Shut down the sub-lights, unlock all outer hatches. Fair weather protocol; turn over repulsor control to the core."

"Aye, ma'am."

"I want a physical site inspection of all umbilical hookups."

"Aye, Captain."

Master assassin Torg stood at the door to the bridge. Vailetta caught his eye and motioned him to wait. Her personal com-tab chimed. "Shock Troops are ready, Captain," Arnas reported.

Vailetta took a deep breath. "Very well. I'm not sure how Barrett wants us to play this."

"No word from below?"

"Of course not. Barrett and his little surprises."

"Doesn't look to be anything *little* about this reception."

"No. Leads me to believe he wants us to parade his new prize out for all the world to see. Get the pandas prepared just in case. I want to make sure first."

"As you will."

"Disembarkation gantry in place. All umbilicals locked and secure." Helm looked at her expectantly.

"Stand down, await further orders."

Vailetta swept down the length of the bridge and past the assassin.

"Follow me."

Vailetta stalked silently through the ship trying to gather her thoughts. Torg followed at her heels, black cape brushing the deck. There had to be some clue she'd missed. Some proof that would substantiate her fears. She hesitated as they neared the airlock that stood open to Wyx. A soft breeze stirred the stale air. Vailetta could feel the assassin's hot breath near her neck. Did Torg know as well? Why did he let her continue on this course? Doubts ran through her mind, a plague of fear.

They stepped out into mottled sunlight. Vailetta blinked and looked down at the amassed men and women. An enormous gangway had been pushed to the ship's airlock allowing a gentle descent to the tarmac forty-five meters below. A Jiestroko band struck up as they began the long slow march down the gangway. Were it not for the awful treacherous doubts that gripped her, it would have been a fairy tale scene: the triumphant return. The *Pride of El Louis Haven* wailed from the military band. Her father would be so proud of her right now—if she weren't in fact delivering the most powerful weapon imaginable to a traitor. Her feet felt suddenly heavy and she nearly tripped.

Torg placed a hand on the small of her back to steady her. "What is it?"

"I know who you are," she hissed, brushing his hand away and regaining her step.

"Of course you do, Captain Strom."

She growled in exasperation and corrected herself. "I know who you *were*."

The assassin snuck a quick glance at her. "Steady, Captain. We're almost to the surface."

"How could you let me deliver these creatures?"

"I don't know what you mean, Captain."

She ignored protocol and turned to stare at him for several long moments.

"Keep moving," he implored. Her eyes snapped away and they resumed their descent.

"You can't feign ignorance," she continued out the corner of her mouth. "You know who *I* am. You saved my father's life on more than one occasion."

"That's enough."

"It can't be a coincidence that you're here now."

"I don't know what you think you know, Captain, but this is now the most dangerous of games you play."

Vailetta's heart pounded wildly and she closed her eyes briefly. *Then it was true.*

They reached the surface and the honor guard parted. Lord Barrett stood twenty meters ahead, beaming.

"There is a time and a place for everything, Captain," Torg whispered. "This is only the beginning."

The cryptic warning repeated in her mind. *Only the beginning. The beginning? It felt like the end.*

"*Forward soldier,*" Torg rasped. "*With pride.*" He gave her a little shove and she marched dutifully ahead, coming to full attention before the vice proctor.

"Captain of the Imperial Guard, Vailetta Strom, reporting as ordered." She reached to her hip and unsheathed her blade. Turning the weapon hilt-forward, she knelt on one knee, bowed her head and offered up the weapon as per the protocol. "One will, the Guard. One will, the blade—yours till death."

One will, yours," Barrett replied.

"One will, the Emperor," Vailetta finished.

"At ease, Captain. Welcome to Wyx," Barrett said magnanimously.

She rose to her feet, and sheathed her blade. "I'm proud to report that your cargo is secure, my Lord."

A slow, unnatural expression formed on the vice proctor's face, beginning at the corner of his thin lips and spreading up his cheeks to his eyes. The waxy skin around his temples stretched and cracked into wrinkles, his eyes wide and frightening. With lips pulled back from barred teeth he looked more like a hungry exel than a smiling human. "Very good," he strode forward and grasped both her shoulders, staring at her with his stretched-face, predatory smile. He almost looked like he was going to kiss her. She stiffened and fought the urge to draw back. "Very, very good Captain." He took a deep breath, the smile evaporated and the mask slid back into place. He looked over her shoulder, up to the *Ilyovahtna*, licking his dry lips. "Let's bring them out." He backed away and spoke up for others to hear, sweeping his hand across the horizon. "This is as much for them as it is for you."

"Very well, my Lord." She spoke briefly into her comtab.

Torg stepped forward and knelt before Barrett.

"Welcome back, my friend," Barrett waved him up.

The assassin rose and assumed his place behind the vice proctor.

Vailetta noted the presence of Tholsen, Riikesarh, Momuso and other members of Barrett's diplomatic cabinet. Barrett had them all here to see for themselves the tangible reality of the infamous Tchelakov creatures.

Vailetta spun on her heel and stood at attention with the rest. At the head of the gangway two men appeared from the amidships airlock and Vailetta's heart fluttered with familiar dignity. Dasko and Lewg stood on either side of the portal in black shipsuits with simple red piping and elaborate crimson dragons embroidered on their chests. The Gokazoku Kaigi marched out in single file between them; Dasko and Lewg fell into place at the end. The Jiestroko band segued smoothly into *Stabler's March* as the eleven men and women descended the gangway.

Her Guard proceeded along the procession line until they reached Vailetta and did a right face. Sunbeams broke through the drifting clouds and framed the Gokazoku in brilliance. Unable to disguise her pride, she glanced down the line, lingering on each face briefly. A finer Guard she could never hope to command. They had faced so much together in their two years in Carinaena's Shell. They would face worse still in the coming days. *Would they follow her if she broke with Barrett?*

The Shock Troops in dragon scale uniforms began to march down the gangway. The Troopers formed a cordon at the bottom of the ramp, ceremonial weapons held across their chests. After two platoons had emerged there was a break in the processional. Commander Arnas appeared at the top of the gangway, a battle pack strapped to his back. Foregoing the ramp, he fired his jets and arced over the crowd. In one beautiful parabolic sweep he passed over the heads of his men and landed with a precise roar at Barrett's feet.

A flicker of a smile crossed Vailetta's face. Arnas had *earned* her admiration — in the same fashion she proved her reputation on each new tour: with actions not words. And he was certainly bold. It was a pity he had nothing softer within to temper his courage. The man was cold steel, a Trooper through and through.

"Commander," Barrett acknowledged, eyes flicking away from the portal briefly.

"My Lord," Arnas bowed and turned to face the ship. "This will be unlike anything you have ever seen."

Barrett arched one brow, but did not respond. A hushed whisper swept through the winds and Vailetta cast a quick look around. All eyes watched the ship. After what seemed like an interminable pause, a collective gasp swept over the assemblage. A black-and-white-furred head poked uncertainly out the airlock.

"WHAT DO YOU see?" Leusta called from further within the ship. She strained to see over the ranks ahead of her out the bright doorway.

"I've never seen anything like it," Poli said, peering down over the gangway. "They are everywhere." The pandas behind her jostled her forward, but she resisted, unwilling to proceed. "Don't rush me," she growled.

"Go on," Des prodded her. "We've seen new worlds before."

"Nothing like this. There is no forest here, no trees to hide us from the eyes above, no soft thicket in which to feed and sleep."

"What do you *see?*" Leusta repeated.

"Humans. Humans by the hundreds. By the thousand. More than I've ever seen. And others, too. *Strange* creatures. All in uniform."

"*And he shall greet you with thousands,*" Leusta recited.

"Silence," Cabeus growled.

"It is as we have foreseen," Leusta admonished him.

"Of course it is, Elder," Archimedes snapped back.

A human guard in his green reptilian costume, a Shock Trooper, pushed through the line of pandas until he got to Poli. He jerked his head, motioning for her to head down the ramp. The panda glanced at the long stick that hung from his belt. One hand rested on its handle; Poli understood the tacit warning. She turned back to the open doorway and the throngs of humans below, trying to swallow her fear.

Poli stepped bravely out into the sunlight and cautiously walked to the edge of the incline. Wind rustled her fur. Good air, she noted. She sampled the breeze, sniffing the upwind currents. Her sense was overwhelmed by the profusion of scent markers. Each person and creature below effused a different smell; the variety of contrasting scent markers was remarkable. She had to breathe through her mouth to keep from being overcome with dizziness.

"Continue down the ramp," an Elder called behind her. "There is nothing to fear for the moment."

Poli shuffled forward, paws dragging along the steel. Des brushed against her haunch to reassure her and she felt a little braver. They were all facing this new world together.

Leusta surveyed the mass of creatures that awaited their approach. So many humans and Ypōs and T'chell and… and what exactly was that? She nudged Archimedes.

"See the feathered one—third row, fourth from the end?"

"Eh?"

"Big bright plume…"

"Oh, yes. The Stavvi. Rather pretty, isn't he?"

"You know what it is?"

"Stavvi. Really, Leusta, you should have made better use of the facilities aboard *Destiny's Needle* world-ship."

Leusta allowed an alveopalatal grumble. "I've never seen so many creatures all in one place. They're all lined up like stalks of bamboo. Is this supposed to be a show of intimidation?"

Archimedes snuffled with merriment behind her. "Hardly. I believe they are honoring us with a display of stoic unity. All have stopped their tasks to come bear witness to our arrival."

"Ah," Leusta rubbed her whiskers against the side of her leg as she walked. "This is not what I expected."

"You saw the Path as well as I, we sang it together: *And he shall greet you with thousands / Warriors all / He will offer you paradise / Pandas' enthrall.*"

"I know, I know. I'm scared of what that means."

"You heard the Circle's theory."

"Yes, but I don't buy it. These Imperials are not thick and slow. They will not think that we can be tempted with simple pleasures."

"Quiet," Cabeus snapped. "You are the Procurer of Intelligence. You should be listening, observing. There will be time for assessment later."

Leusta clenched her jaw; the Elder was right. She pricked up her ears and resumed studying the careful rows of creatures.

THE LINE OF pandas ambled down the gangway between the cordon of Shock Troops. Barrett was entranced. Viewed head on, the pandas' hips swayed back and forth in opposing rhythms of cadence. He stared at the first panda's broad shoulders, the way its head swung low and heavy. As the first drew near, a broad circle cleared to accommodate the entire group. Barrett stepped forward as the Jiestroko band ended with a flourish.

The wind whipped across the tarmac. With a great steel-on-steel groan, the *Ilyovahtna* swung several degrees west. Imperial banners snapped and ghostly mews sidled through the ranks. The pandas had gathered in a clump, young ones sitting in the center, shielded by larger creatures in the front.

Barrett savored the absolute perfection of the moment, the stillness of all but nature itself. He had argued with Tholsen extensively about the proper dialect to use on this day. That the creatures used and understood language was a foregone conclusion now. He had suspected for some time, but after studying the reports from the *Ilyovahtna* it was no longer in doubt. He had seen the holo log. He knew that the pandas huddled for conversation in some unknown tongue. He knew they had spoken a sentence to the tech ensign Yarvek-EZ. In a common trade language no less.

He settled finally on Strahlinvek. A little rough on the tongue; he'd had little cause to use it in the last few years, but it came back to him with a little practice. It was the only dialect he was certain the creatures at least understood a little of.

If his suspicions were correct, they were probably more fluent than he.

He took a deep breath and a final nervous step. The excitement was almost too much. He had waited for this day for so long—watching plan after careful plan fail—that he had almost despaired in ever reaching this grand moment. Yet here they were, the fabled Tchelakov thirty-seven. Well, thirty-five—but who was he to quibble? The future stood before him. How he handled this would determine how long it would take to unlock their secrets.

"I have been practicing what I would say to you when I first met you," he said in a strong, clear voice. "In fact I have said it over and over again to ease its delivery. Yet I find myself here with a complete lack of words. The greeting I had prepared seems completely inconsequential."

Barrett stopped and looked down at the ground, his hand coming up to touch his face. He rubbed his nose with a finger. He regained the pandas' gaze. "This place is known as Wyx. It is in a well-populated volume of space, surrounded by many thriving planets. It is a very safe place. But this you must know. You have known that you would meet me here on this day in this place, or at least I believe that you have known. My name is Hellius Barrett. I am the man that is responsible for bringing you here."

A low murmur resonated from the pandas. "You may have been told many things about me, and undoubtedly I have made your lives more difficult in these arduous months. For that, I apologize." He took a deep breath. There was no use to lie to these incredible creatures. He had decided on a course of absolute honesty in order to secure success. "I will not stand here and tell you that all you have heard is untrue. Nor will I tell you that you should forget all that you have heard. I state simply that there are truths left untold."

Several pandas glanced briefly at one another. "You will of course discover this in time. For now, welcome to Wyx. My home, now yours."

Behind Barrett, a giant slab of the tarmac lifted slowly up. Beneath the first meter of ceracrete long, black repulsor modules thrummed with energy. "I know it has been a long journey and you would like to rest, perhaps explore your new home, but first we must attend to your health. I have reason to believe that you are in physical danger. I have been informed that your last caretaker, Helen Tchelakov, may have implanted something dangerous inside each of you. This is the truth. I have assembled a team of the greatest Imperial doctors under my command who will help us discover the danger and find a cure. No harm will come to you, and I will personally stand by you through all the examinations."

Barrett stepped back and swept his arm toward the hovering slab. A stairway formed by blocks of ceracrete extended. "Would you please accompany me?" Though he remained outwardly confident and calm, Barrett's heart raced and sweat beaded along his brow. This moment would dictate months and maybe even years to come. Cooperation could make this the most wonderful of collaborations.

"He is afraid that we will not accede," Leusta clicked.

"His aura is a jumble of emotions: exhilaration, fear, anticipation, hope. Look how the spectrum shift sparkles," Archimedes added.

"But he speaks the truth."

Indeed, the green halo of conviction had gleamed through the blush of pale radiance as he spoke of the danger. "Unfortunately, yes," Leusta sighed. "Oh, Helen. I was so hoping the dreams were incorrect in this case."

"Do not trouble yourself with regret over her," Cabeus rumbled. "She has betrayed us all, just as the Elders foresaw. And worse still."

"But she will redeem herself. There is still hope for her."

"Perhaps. The Path is not yet clear on that."

"I know," Leusta whispered. "I know…"

"Should we follow this man?" Tulli asked.

"He could carve us up by force if he wished. He is offering us a gentle alternative. And he speaks the truth," the older panda Ell'han growled quietly.

"Agreed."

TO BARRETT'S GREAT satisfaction, the pandas began to walk slowly forward. One by one they swayed past and stepped up onto the slab. He closed his eyes as the last one passed and savored the feeling for a brief, glorious moment. Then he was all business once again.

"Commander Arnas, Captain Strom," he called back to the waiting officers. "Please join me."

The giant slab, filled with pandas, began to slide across the tarmac at a gentle pace. Barrett stood at the stern, near the operator, grasping a handhold. He turned to Arnas.

"Commander, have you ever sired a child?"

"My Lord?"

"A child, Arnas. Do you have a child?"

"No, my Lord."

"Pretend now that you do. That in fact you have more than thirty children."

Arnas glanced at the pandas and back to Barrett.

"Yes," the vice proctor nodded. "Your new family, Commander. A family more precious to you than life itself."

Arnas stiffened visibly. "With all due respect, my Lord, I do not have the—" he hesitated slightly, "—the *rapport* that others might have with the beasts. My patience with them is small."

Barrett smiled and tutted. "A reluctant father. You will have to learn patience."

"They do not trust me. They are visibly less animate in my presence."

"You will have to earn their trust, too." Arnas started to speak, but Barrett waved him silent. "No amount of argument will sway me, Commander. You and your men are now the pandas' surrogate guardians. They must be made to feel safe and secure here. They must understand that no one will ever take them away from this place again. That they do not have anything to fear, that they finally have a home."

"Are not others better suited to such… such *care-giving*?"

"You are a warrior!" Barrett bellowed. "Nothing is beyond your call. I will not have my new guests protected by doctors, or scholars, or scientists. They will have the best!" Barrett was shouting now, blood reddening his face. "They will have the greatest warriors in my command to guard them every day. You will *earn* their respect, their patience, their trust! You will not ever raise a hand to them. You will not carry weapons in their presence. Your men will learn to play. Your men will learn to nurture. Your men will *learn*." Spittle was forming around the corner of Barrett's mouth. He swiped the back of his hand over his lip and let the color drain marginally from his face. "Arnas, you will learn more from these *beasts*, as you refer to them, than you can possibly imagine."

The Vice Proctor turned away and straightened his tunic. "For now they are our guests. Make them feel at home. Treat them like your children," he said in a brittle tone. "Make them feel safe."

"Yes, my Lord," Arnas said in a subdued tone.

Barrett turned back to face the pandas and the commander. "Someday these pandas will come to know Wyx as the home they always dreamt of, as an impenetrable fortress of safety. They will rule alongside you and I. I can only hope that when that day comes, they will look at us fragile humans as their *friends*, as their equals." He cast a withering gaze at the commander. "All children surpass their fathers, Arnas. Treat these kindly, for all our sakes."

Arnas cast a wry look at the creatures. None stood in the center where it was safe. Instead, they all lined the front edges of the slab like curious mercats, staring at the troops below while they glided just overhead.

"Go now," Barrett said. "Report to Momuso. He will squire you and your men to your new quarters in the habitat. There will be a full protocol briefing before dinner. Have four squads ready for dinner tonight."

"As you will, my Lord." Arnas drew himself to attention, then launched himself off the lighter in a roar of jump jets.

Vailetta watched him arch away and then cocked a curious eye back at Barrett.

"Yes, Captain?"

She pursed her lips. "Why all the fuss today—why such a display?"

Barrett clasped his hands behind his back and stared forward. "If you hold the crown jewels, why keep it a secret?"

Vailetta pondered this silently.

"Not only will possession of the pandas command respect, but the fact that we control them in and of itself should be a remarkable deterrent. Think of all the systems that will bow to our wishes, knowing that we hold the future in our hands."

"Even if you have not yet unlocked the future's secrets..." Vailetta murmured.

Barrett smiled. "You catch on quickly. It will be good to have you back at the diplomatic table. Which reminds me, there is a banquet tonight that you must attend. As a guest of honor, of course."

"It will be my privilege." She started to add something but stopped.

"Out with it, Captain. You should know by now to speak your mind."

Vailetta glanced at the pandas. "As honored as I am by your generous invitation, I would think that inviting one of the pandas might be looked upon as a kind gesture. Having observed them for some time, I could suggest one or two who—"

Barrett waved her silent. "You needn't worry about the guest list, Captain. I'm quite capable of choosing who should and should not attend Proctorial functions."

"Yes, my Lord. My apologies."

"None necessary my dear. I told you to speak your mind and I didn't mean to denigrate your considerable insights." He smiled at her softly. "Just let Tholsen show you to your quarters, and have your assist stop by Officer Acquisitions—there should be a package there for you."

The giant slab slowed to a standstill and then began to settle back to the tarmac. At the point where the surface of the slab was once more even with the surrounding ceracrete, Vailetta was surprised to find their lighter-slab sinking further still. Four sides of a subterranean shaft rose around them and the daylight quickly receded. After sinking perhaps fifty or so meters, an opening on one wall appeared at foot-level and rose to reveal a brightly lit hall. The slab lighter halted at the hall's floor-height and Barrett ushered the pandas off.

"I'll take it from here, Captain. Go see Tholsen. And don't forget the package." The slab began to rise and Vailetta watched the vice proctor and the pandas drop from view.

9

THE FEAST

WITHOUT THE SIZE CONSTRICTIONS INHERENT TO NAVAL vessels, Vailetta found her new dirtside quarters positively enormous. There were two full rooms, and a 'fresher as big as her entire quarters aboard the picket. She took a good hour to scrub herself raw inside the facilities, working hard to remove the latent stench of living in close quarters with so many others. She emerged feeling like a lotus blossom. For a long period she lay spread out across her berth, wet and gloriously naked. She let her skin cool in the air, droplets slowly evaporating. Finally out of the confining uniform that she had worn for weeks on end, she was reluctant to put on clothes. The smartly cut Go-kazoku uniform, while commanding in its elegance, was not all that a woman might want. It was good just to lie here, nothing but skin.

The door chimed and Vailetta rolled to the edge of the berth. "Gany?"

"Yes mistress."

Vailetta skipped across the floor that creaked underfoot. She grinned; it was *real* wood. Barrett had put her in diplomatic chambers. She punched the door's manual access. The beaded form of Ganymede stood outside holding a large, flat box.

"Bring it in, bring it in," she said with excitement. The art followed her inside and carefully laid the box on the berth.

"What is it?"

"I do not know the contents. It is not particularly heavy for its size."

Vailetta knelt on the berth and eagerly spun the package around, looking for an easy way inside. "I bet I know what's in it," she said. "Barrett gave me these decadent quarters—he's spoiling me." She popped two catches and the package fell open.

Vailetta dropped the top half and reached slowly into the box, fingers rubbing the silken fabric.

"Oh my."

Vailetta drew out a carefully folded gown, standing to hold it full length. The translucent fabric unfolded and gently opened to the floor. It was a Reighblÿn shadow gown, a tapering blue masterpiece.

"Oh, I don't know, Gany. I'm not sure it's me."

"Nonsense." Ganymede walked over and grasped the delicate straps, holding it up to Vailetta's chest. "Pull your hair back."

Vailetta obliged, holding back her long dark hair with one hand.

"Just as I thought. It will be perfect."

She looked at her art with an innocent expression of doubt.

"Come now, we have just enough time to prepare. One simply does *not* turn down an invitation to a ball."

THREE ASYMMETRIC STRAPS of translucent material wrapped around her right shoulder, holding the gown just barely in place. The long tresses whispered against the floor as she turned back and forth for Gany to see.

"How do I look?" The lucent material shimmered as she twirled, alternately hiding and revealing the shadows of her form.

"Like a real princess," the art said softly.

"Hush now."

"It's true."

Vailetta blushed with excitement. *A banquet. In my honor.*

"You must go now—you turned down your escort."

"I wanted to walk."

"Well then, you have to leave."

Vailetta glanced at her gun belt lying atop a chest. Her hip and thigh felt strangely naked without their presence.

"You won't need that," Gany said, catching her hesitation.

"I know," she sighed.

"You're on Wyx now."

"I'm not used to feeling safe."

"Don't get used to it," Gany warned. "But enjoy it while you're here."

"Hmm—just odd being on a planet where you can walk unarmed."

"This is the safest planet in a hundred systems. No one dares to challenge Barrett's authority here. Besides, isn't there a complete weapons ban in the new Habitat?"

"That's the word."

"Well then, you're ready. Stop fussing with your face and go!" Vailetta finished adding color to her lips, a luxury she had not indulged since before she left Daulinbêres. Being a soldier often supplanted more whimsical practices. She'd had little opportunity to accent her femininity of late, yet here she was in a full gown. She gathered up the long tresses, gave Gany a quick buss on her cheek and dashed outside.

Her quarters faced a broad open-air terrace lined with forgontu oak and baby criscus. Her feet skipped over native stone pavers, glistening as if a rainstorm had just passed. Creeping baukla climbed the towering mesh louvers that stood at intervals between the buildings to control the winds, like giant, rigid banners. The fading light of the pink sky was caught in the gigantic glazings that hovered over the promenade at a rakish angle, further protecting the walk from the elements yet allowing the air to move freely beneath. Refracted through the cerasteel framework, soft purples and greens scattered over her path.

The lustrous Wyxian stone, used to great affect in the long sweeping buildings that rose beyond the trees, caught the last dying hues of the setting primary. The skyline twinkled like the lights of the craft that swam through the blustery twilight. The terrace became progressively wider as she walked, opening to a broad promenade.

Foot traffic was heavier here, with zips and roto'mo's flashing overhead. Restricted to the air-lanes further overhead, hurkaboys, flyers, and twirls moved at substantially greater speeds, landing on flyer pads on the thin towers that arched out from every building. There was a suspensor tube at the next intersection that would zip her up to the trolli-barge station, or there was a magrail carriage in this square. Both would get her to the

Naval Courtyard in plenty of time. She paused to look up at the jumble of steel towers and stone facades, aware of the gazes that lingered over her form and gown. Nice to be the object of attention, if even for a short while.

She decided the height and serenity of the trolli-barge would suit this night and ducked around the square into a side avenue. Slick-skinned sales clerks busied themselves closing up their shops and carried outdoor displays back inside their retail establishments. Most here could afford artificials, and there tended to be a great abundance of arts in all echelons of Jobaenz' workforce. Children spent more time in academies. Parents urged their young to specialize, to take advantage of the Imperial science, technology and service corps. As a result, proprietorships were passed on not to children, but many times to trusted and beloved artificials who had run the family business profitably for years and years. Arts took on family names and rose to prominence, just like in the Core. Vailetta smiled; it was a side of the Imperial presence she loved.

A line of fifty suspensor tubes glittered beneath blue glow globes that floated just over the pedestrians' heads. Vailetta stepped into the ticklish field of the first available tube and spoke the name of the station. She rose swiftly within the glazing, watching the promenade shrink below. A hurka-boy dipped to its landing pad, briefly in her line of sight, wings folding up like a butterfly before she zipped past it. Warning chimes sounded and the field hummed lightly as she was delivered to the station's height.

She stepped onto the open platform just as the barge floated in. She rushed across the station, flashing her ident-link in a reader and hopped onto the trolli just as the railing slid back into place. With its roof glazings pulled back in the mild weather, Vailetta could just make out the stars of Laidel and Stōka winking through the haze. The trolli-barge quickly gathered speed and sailed over the city. Vailetta walked up to the unprotected second level and let the wind run through her gown and pull at her hair. She released the pins that Gany had so carefully placed and let her hair flow freely.

In five minutes she was above the Naval promenade. She took the suspensor down and walked briskly through the square. The Naval buildings rose from the piazza like giant, inverted teardrops. Thin towers ringed the buildings, their lengths strung with ionic cable. Charged particles in the wind reacted with the cables' magnetic field, creating vivid, dancing colors. The aurora fields sparkled in the dusk, reflected by every building. Audible as well as visible, Vailetta cocked her head to listen to the crackle and rustle. The paper crinkling sound mirrored the commotion her gown created.

The first floor of Naval Operations was open to the street; the rest of the structure rose overhead on massive columns. The lieutenant in command of the watch stepped in front of the two guards as Vailetta approached, did a brief double take and then drew up to attention having recognized her face. Lord Barrett's Captain of the Guard was not someone easily forgotten.

Vailetta smiled demurely and swished by. A door irised open for her in one of the columns. Inside seven heavily armed guards surrounded a central suspensor tube.

"You're late, Captain. I'm afraid they've started without you."

"You try getting into this thing," she said. The guard did not smile.

"You will be scanned as you descend, ma'am. You might as well give my any weapons you might have forgotten."

"That won't be necessary. There's nowhere left to hide anything in this."

"Yes, ma'am." To his credit he kept a straight face as he stepped aside.

Vailetta descended. She was curious about this new "Habitat." There had been talk about a new, secret facility beneath Naval Ops, but nothing short of rumors had surfaced. Barrett had certainly been provided ample time to prepare for the pandas' arrival, with their capture dragging out far longer than he'd planned.

The suspensor slowed and without stepping out of the tube, Vailetta found her feet standing upon solid ground. *The bottom of a suspensor tube?* She didn't think she'd ever been to the bottom of anything in Jobaenz. She stepped out into a cold, dark hall, so large that she could not see the wall in any direction, nor the ceiling overhead. A single glowstrip in the floor led off in one direction.

Vailetta's curiosity was piqued, however. She walked in the opposite direction; she had to know. After twenty paces, with her hands held up to fend off any abrupt appearance of a wall, she stopped and removed her left shoe. She threw it as far as she could. It clattered against the floor in the distance.

"Oh great," she murmured. Then as an afterthought she barked out: "Lights!"

"Captain of the Guard, Vailetta Strom, identity confirmed. Command accepted." The hall was bathed in yellow lights and Vailetta could begin to see just how large a space she was in. The circular chamber extended nearly a hundred meters in all directions from the central suspensor tube. The walls were carved out of the white limestone and left with the rough scars of the laser ax. An immense door stood at one end of the hall. Huge lifters and cargo lighters were parked in the shadows nearby along with thousands of stacked cargo pallets. It looked like a construction site that had shut down for the night — perhaps the detritus of the finished Habitat? At the opposite end of the hall lay a smaller, but no less substantial door with neo-markers in the floor leading to the suspensor tube.

Vailetta collected her shoe, still some sixty meters from the wall, and hustled back to the smaller door.

"Lights," she called, and the chamber fell to darkness once more.

A lone glow-globe hovered over the door's access. Vailetta flashed her ident-link and the door split in two and trundled slowly aside. It revealed a brightly lit passage twenty meters wide and ten tall. She proceeded inside the sterile environ, feeling small and slightly silly in her formal gown. The hall ended in another identical door. She stepped to the panel and once again the door's two halves scrolled aside.

Another hall greeted her, as antiseptic and empty as the first. The door at the end was smaller this time and split open after she flashed her ident-link. The hall beyond tapered to more human proportions. She reached the fourth door, this one deep burgundy, and frowned, looking back over her shoulder. This must have scared the pandas to death. Unless there was something spectacular in the next room, the creatures would feel like they were being lead to their prison. She hoped that the "Habitat" was not as sterile and lifeless as these halls.

The door scrolled upward and gave access to another hall, this one smaller still. The ceiling was now five meters overhead. She walked slowly through the passage, staring at the walls which glowed brightly and then faded to near darkness every few seconds—like they were breathing. A low hum resonated around her. She halted in front of the fifth door; there was no access panel. *Very odd.*

She searched the smooth surface of the wall on either side of the door, accustomed to the standard ident-link reader necessary to reach any secure area. The walls were precisely machined and offered no hint of a hidden panel.

"That won't be necessary, Captain Strom," a smooth voice announced.

"Excuse me?"

"You are among the guests I have been allowed to grant access," the door said with an almost childish enthusiasm.

"Ah, marvelous," Vailetta said with just a little exasperation—why hadn't the door just let her in then? "Let's have it then."

"How's that?"

"Access," she said flatly. "Let me in."

"Oh, yes, of course," the door gushed as it rose upward. "Don't get many to talk to down here you know. 'Course now there's the guests, but Dr. Sartok told me 'no talking to the guests' which doesn't really seem fair—"

Vailetta walked slowly through the doorway, enchanted by what lay on the other side.

"—Oh, yes—well then, there you go. Glad to be of service. Got to close up now behind you. See you when you leave then? Yes then, better be off." The door slid shut.

Though she had judged the first darkened hall to be large, this space dwarfed it by a substantial measure. She stood upon a grassy knoll, the ground soft and mossy underfoot. An incredible forest valley spread out below her. Tall, full-gown pines rose in all directions obscuring the ceiling which was invisible in the darkness, the far wall which was either too far away to be seen, or masked by the dense copse of pines. A meandering dirt path wound down through the carpet of pine needles, lit by open torches that flickered and burned every few meters.

Vailetta turned and looked at the door. The walls around it were the same roughly carved limestone—the only reminder that she was in fact *indoors*. Off to one side, twenty meters up the wall a balcony could be seen, but there was no visible access to it. *An observation platform?*

A long, low hoot caught her attention and she twirled back to the forest. The flutter of wings heralded a bird that burst out of the canopy in a flush of beating wings, circled overhead and disappeared back into the black sky. Vailetta listened carefully. The steady croaking and throaty screech of insects, toads, and the like punctuated the ambient spectrum. Somewhere in the distance she thought she heard the gurgle of water.

A broad smile stretched across her face. *Why should she be surprised? She should have expected no less from Barrett.* Gathering up the hem of her gown, she trotted down the dirt path, soon following the sound of laughter and boisterous conversation. A hundred meters in, the forest was dark on all sides of her and the illusion was complete. The path continued to wend its way down, growing steeper and rockier as she continued into the bowl. Twenty meters further she stopped in wonder.

A gigantic circular structure constructed solely of wood rose from the hollow below. Massive timbers set one next to the other supported a domed roof that reached a solitary peak forty meters above her. It was like a fantastic temple of wood. Flaming sconces ringed the outer walls, sending sooty smoke up into the night.

Vailetta hustled down the embankment and stopped just outside the one massive opening. A bonfire lay in the center of the interior and torches lit the rest. Vailetta marveled at the amazing construction. It was just like the lyceum found by the Shock Troops on El-Bouteran, though done on a grander scale. It was large enough to accommodate a hundred pandas. The amphitheater was filled with pandas and humans and dozens of other creatures—all except the pandas in various forms of formal dress.

Five magnificent mahogany tables were set near the bonfire. The round tables had place settings for two-dozen apiece with rough wooden benches as seats. As she stood in stunned disbelief at the entrance, Momuso strode toward her, a goblet in each hand.

"Welcome, Captain! You're just in time. Dinner is about to be served!"

Vailetta numbly accepted the goblet and let Momuso lead her into the interior.

"Marvelous creatures these pandas, don't you think? Not quite as big as our vokoba, but then these are ever so much more clever!"

"Let go of the poor woman, Momuso. She doesn't want to hear you blather on." Riikesarh stepped up to greet them. He raised his own goblet in toast. "Drink up, Captain. You look like you've seen a ghost." Both men laughed heartily.

Vailetta took a look at the wine in her cup and decided that wasn't such a bad idea after all. She tilted back the contents in one gulp.

"Well now, there's the spirit!"

"Don't let the dress fool you," Torg murmured as he drifted into appearance. "She can drink you under the table, Momuso."

"Excuse me," she demurred politely and turned to the assassin.

"By all means." All three men bowed effusively.

"One will, Captain," Torg said softly.

"One will, yours," Vailetta said.

"Let me refill your goblet. You look like a woman in need of a drink." He poured her more dark wine from a wooden gourd.

"Thank you." She emptied the goblet and held it back up for him. Torg refilled it and his without a word.

"This is quite a spectacle," she said.

"The Vice Proctor has outdone himself."

"Indeed."

"Lord Barrett has surrounded himself with the very best. Should we be so surprised that he is one step ahead now?"

Vailetta took another hasty sip. "No, we shouldn't." She looked over the rim of her goblet at the large man. "Will it work?"

At that moment a large drum strung vertically between two posts was struck repeatedly by two Troopers until the crowd had silenced. Barrett walked to the bonfire in the center of the lyceum.

"Once again, let me offer you welcome. To our new guests, let me say that I am disappointed that you have not honored us with your thoughts. Please, let us not pretend. I am aware of your intelligence, of your capacity for language. I speak many languages myself. Perhaps there is one that we both speak." He slipped into Strahlinvek. "Perhaps a simple trade language — not too complex, easily derived from a hundred other dialects — hmm? It would allow an easier give and take here. This banquet is in your honor. It is not a disguise, it is not a sham. This habitat is my best educated guess as to what would make you feel most comfortable. It is underground, I admit. But it is infinitely more secure than your previous environments. No one will land here to take you away. This is a protected environment. And if this place is unsatisfactory, then we will create another. If you tell me what you need, what you desire, we will accommodate you. When times become less volatile, when no one dares chase you any longer, an entire world will be found for you."

Barrett circled the bonfire, looking at the pandas scattered throughout the chamber. "Please. Tell me what you desire. Tell me what you need."

Vailetta watched the vice proctor. She'd never seen him look so benevolent. *Would the pandas think likewise?*

A whisper went up among the Imperials as a large panda stepped forward. The giant creature lumbered up to Barrett at the bonfire.

"I am Ell'han, Elder within the Tchelakov Tribe. We do indeed understand you. Since you have allowed the masks of duplicity to fall, we shall allow you the same respect. You speak truth when you offer us sanctuary and safety. We have seen this. And this is not a small thing to us. We have never been *safe*. Know though, that this is a Path we have not chosen lightly. Your Path, Barrett of the Imperials, is not the same Path that we follow. It simply has crossed at this point."

Barrett nodded carefully. "That is enough for now, Ell'han, don't you think? That our 'paths' have crossed? Come, let us have a feast and discuss the future. Perhaps our 'paths' will change. Perhaps your *safety* is just the first step of many great things. Perhaps *fate* has brought our paths together."

A low rumble circled the fire from the older pandas. *The Imperial's use of* fate *and* path; *was it conscious? Or coincidence?*

Ell'han spoke once more. "We will dine with you, Barrett of the Imperials. Though when we tell you what we *need* you may not like what we have to say. You have offered us an open hand rather than the closed fist we were led to expect. We will listen to your stories. We will see how long you speak the truth."

"That is all I ask," Barrett said. "Come. Let us feast!"

THE SHOCK TROOPS under Arnas' command had received just one briefing about their new duties, and as such, there was some degree of confusion about exactly who was to do what and when. But Arnas was determined to handle the evening like a military exercise. The marines were to be the pandas' sole guardians. There would be no other handlers. There would be no artificial servers—too impersonal for Barrett's wishes; he wanted everything handled with a human touch.

Therefore, all the needs of the great banquet were attended to by Shock Troops. It was like the first day of culinary basic training. Platoon one was busy in the new mess buried beneath a section of forest near the central lyceum. Fleet sergeant Krass was in charge, and to his trained eye, it was not pretty. He didn't believe he'd seen worse carnage in twenty-six years of military service, and he let the men know it.

Meanwhile, Arnas had squads two and three in the bamboo thicket, hacking through the thick stalks with plasma machetes. It had been chilling when he'd first stomped through the mud to find the tall green stalks. He'd had to steady his breathing and remind himself that this was not El-Bouteran, that there was no Byrethylen Wraith awaiting his men. The irony of having to chop food for the creatures that had cost him so many made it all the worse. The pandas, now his *children*.

He shook his head and gripped the machete tightly as he carved through the base of the resilient grass. *It was Médeville, not the creatures who unleashed the wraith. It was Médeville.*

Squad one dragged their loads of bamboo back to the underground mess, while squad one had orders to haul theirs straight to the lyceum. At first the thought of this detail grated on his nerves, but the more he thought about it, the better it seemed. By the time Barrett had finished outlining their duties in the first briefing he knew exactly what he would say to his men.

No one would die in this tour of duty. That was the bottom line. The 41st marines were in dire need of a dirtside rotation. Time to train replacements, time to heal old wounds—emotional as well as physical. And they would still be in the thick of it: assigned to the vice proctor's most important project. So they had to haul a little bamboo. He'd had worse details. Much worse.

EVERYONE FOUND A place at the round tables. Six or seven pandas sat at each one, situated between humans and T'chell and others alike. Several of the cubs insisted on sitting next to their parents, but this was easily accommodated. A continuous stream of Shock Troopers in simple green jumpers hustled inside the lyceum carrying trays of fresh fruit, wooden gourds filled with spring water, and bushels of bamboo. Like a precise military drill, the men and women split off and began piling their wares on each of the five tables. The bamboo was stacked in the middle like overgrown and unkempt centerpieces. Wine and spring water were poured in goblets and bowls.

Several pandas sniffed uncertainly at the bamboo, reaching paws into the jumble of stems to inspect the selection. It was good stuff. Leusta recognized several strains familiar to worlds they'd hidden on in the past months. And not just any shoots—this grass had been culled from the heartiest stock, the most inviting strains. Someone knew what they were doing.

Encouraged by the smell and fortified by the Elder's acceptance, the pandas began to select shoots from the middle of the tables. Green stems stood straight up on many tables like leafy banners hoisted in the flickering light. Many an Imperial dignitary was smacked upside the head by stems handled with eager but less dexterous paws. Wine was spilled, hats were knocked askance, and noses were tickled by the slender leaves. But it all added to the general good nature of the feast. Laughter echoed up into the raw timbers. Goblets were righted, more wine was poured.

Several braver diplomats began tearing smaller shoots off the stalks of their neighbor's meals and began fruitlessly chewing on the tough reeds. This continued until teams of two Troopers carried steaming cauldrons to the diners, and ladles of steaming bamboo shoots were poured for the guests with less powerful jaws. Bamboo was the order of the day, and whether cooked, steamed or raw, it was feasted upon by all.

Vailetta watched the Shock Troops bustling in and out of the smoky darkness. With amusement she spied Commander Arnas pouring soup into Riikesarh's bowl. He looked up to see her, eyes flicking once over her blue gown with a nod and frown of approval. He gave her a good-natured wink and hurried off. She giggled — the wine was pretty good actually.

A panda was seated between Torg and Vailetta. Though most of the table had introduced themselves to the seven pandas seated amongst them, Torg had remained silent and watchful. The panda to his left was staring carefully at the assassin while chewing on a stalk. Vailetta leaned forward to try to catch Torg's reaction. After several minutes of politely ignoring the panda's examination, he turned slightly to face the giant creature. His eyes glowed faintly in the shadows.

"I recognize you," the panda said still chewing. "From the dreams."

Torg leaned forward, golden eyes narrowing ever so slightly. Vailetta could see the fascination behind them.

"You are the *chagrig-la*. The *man of many*." The panda sniffed. "Those are iabont tear ducts, yes? Like the raptors of Gregstone? Keeps the eyes flushed without lids, yes?"

Torg drew back, his pale face more ashen than usual.

The panda nodded. "Thought so. Smelled like it." The panda set down his meal and leaned close to the assassin, his nose inches from his face. "It is good to know that you are here among us." The creature's breath was hot and moist. "The Elders will be wanting to speak with you." The panda leaned back and reached for a new stalk of bamboo.

Vailetta had never seen Torg look surprised before. The expression was absolutely priceless. She reached across the table to pour wine into his cup.

"You look like a man in need of drink," she called with a grin. Torg pushed his goblet toward the proffered gourd without a word.

AT A SEPARATE table, Leusta paused between bites of her delicious bamboo to gaze at the Elders across from her. "This man, this Barrett, is not like the dreams," she rumbled, the clicks and growls lost in the boisterous noise.

Cabeus nodded. "The events of the Path unfold just as we predicted, and yet—"

"—The context is different."

"Yes. These Imperials are not at all what they seem. After the escape there were no reprisals."

"And Desi's claw was repaired immediately—replaced in fact. Have you seen it?"

Cabeus wrinkled his nose wryly. "Yes, I think everyone has. He's quite proud of it." The big panda leaned back and chewed on his third bamboo stalk; quite good in fact.

"This Barrett has been straightforward with us."

"A first for a human," Archimedes interjected.

"Did you hear tell of his instructions to the warrior-male? Poli overhead them on the floating ground."

Archimedes groaned loudly, "I heard that the warrior-male will be with us *every* day."

"To ensure our safety," she said.

"To keep us in line," he countered.

"No, that was not the gist of the conversation."

"No matter," Cabeus interrupted. "Better to have a known quantity here with us, than a new surprise each day. Besides, he has a steady aura. The gruffness is part of his nature. Remember the *Griffin*? When we first encountered him, he was similarly disposed towards us."

"Ah, yes," Archimedes drawled, smacking the table with a paw. "A warrior himself."

"And remember," the older panda continued. "This new warrior-male lost many of his brethren in his pursuit of us."

"That is not our fault!"

"No. But it will take him time to forget, to see us as individuals instead of a vague menace."

"The point I was making," Leusta growled, "was that this Barrett has ordered his 'greatest warrior' to drop everything else and do nothing but nurture and protect us."

"You could make the argument that we foresaw this as well," Cabeus observed. "*Beneath a sky unbroken / Despite the break of day / The warriors will surround you / With you they shall lay.* We took it to mean that they would be our captors."

"Instead they are to be our guardians?" Archimedes asked skeptically. "What's the difference?"

"Do you see a weapon on any of the humans?"

Archimedes looked briefly around the lyceum. There were many men and women eating and drinking, talking—offering bamboo across the tables to pandas. None were armed. He drew back his whiskers. "It could be temporary."

"I don't think so."

"Either way, we're still captives."

"Yes. But isn't it curious that nothing but the green aura of trueness has surrounded all of Barrett's statements?" The old panda resumed munching on his bamboo stalk.

Leusta watched Archimedes' ears flick thoughtfully as he, too, began chewing again. This was all very curious. She wished that Sid were here to experience the strange reality of this Path they had all chosen together. *These Imperials were nothing like the stories they'd been told. Could it be that they had been trusting the wrong humans all along?*

10

DESCENT

GARRAND KNELT IN THE RICH, AROMATIC SOIL THAT COV-
ered the amidships hold. Row upon row of bamboo flourished
in the fecund loam. Were it not for the steady thrum of the reactors that trembled up through his hands and knees he might
have been on any of a dozen worlds adding to his collection.
It has been too long, he thought as he turned the dirt with a
simple spade. His fingers scrabbled through the rough chunks
to find the roots. Laid out on a cloth beside him was a pile of
carefully harvested seedlings. There was a certain solace working the soil deep inside the bamboo grove. It gave him time to
ponder his last few sessions with Sid.

Garrand hummed to himself as he worked, the lyrical visions swimming in and out of his thoughts.

The Thief of Ships
Has little time
Her place in the stars
We're bound to find

A rosy pall
The dark of night
The Thief is bold
Puts up a fight

Before the bell
And death's disgrace
She'll take his hand
And accept her place

Her fate now in the Griffin's hand
Like his before in hers as well
Safely plucked from a warrior's stand
Before the silence of the final bell

He raked through the moist dirt with fingers splayed. The images fell apart like petals dropping from a dying flower and came to rest in new places. Fresh divinations floated up and burbled out as he worked the dirt.

There was a rhythm to the words, a simple majesty that underscored each thread that Sid plucked from the future. Each night they sat by the fire and contemplated the paths. It was now a cherished ritual. Sitting on the cold, steel plates, two friends staring into the dark abyss. Trying to see things a little differently, reaching out to unravel fate's careful mess. In the process, he saw a lot of where he'd been. He could see what each piece of his life meant to him now. And every so often he caught a glimpse of where it was all heading.

He turned the dirt and sang the words.

> *Death himself*
> *Has found a place*
> *The Man of many*
> *You will have to face.*

The rough tapestry of the Path of Fate was being delicately woven into place and here he was, a simple soldier, peering over the shoulder of time itself. Supping at the table of the gods, privy to the unknowable. He laughed as he worked the soil.

Strangely enough, it was beginning to make sense. It was clear why Sid felt so strongly about finding the archival world. The panda believed that they would find the one who would help them rescue the tribe, the Thief of Ships. It was believed that his help alone would not be enough. Nor would finding the location of the tribe be enough. They were all pieces of a puzzle. And Sid insisted that the only way to discover this woman, this 'thief,' was to first find Archiva.

Could the Archives still be active after all these years? The problem was all the more compelling because there was no telling what they would find once they got there. More imperative at this point, with the Glaplōs system drawing near, was determining the identity of the Thief. How could they locate her if they did not know who she was? He sighed and stopped digging, allowing his weight to settle back on his calves.

The Thief of Ships will fall from grace
And dangle from a slender thread
The Griffin's fate she has to face
A crown upon her lovely head

If she reaches for the Griffin's hand
Above her shattered wings
Their union will forever stand
Of this the tribe will sing

A crown upon her lovely head. Royalty? Or merely symbolic of her willingness to help? Or a misinterpretation of Sid's vision? *A past alliance / A warm embrace / The Thief's defiance / Like a mirror's face.* Past alliance? Mirror's face? Something niggled at the back of his reckoning, a wretched feeling of familiarity that he could not quite place. *Fate be pinned / To the Griffin's* arm */ A fall from grace / Unlike a fall to harm.* It was there, he could almost grasp it.

"What are you doing, Garrand?"

He jerked in fright, surprised that he had not heard anyone approach. He twisted his head around to find Helen standing behind him.

"These shoots are coming up too densely here," he muttered as he rocked back to his knees. He stabbed the spade back into the loose dirt around the roots. "They'll never survive here. Ship's hold doesn't afford enough light to support such dense regrowth. Need to be replanted elsewhere."

"You're right," she said softly.

He squinted up at her. "Of course I'm right. That so hard to fathom?"

She smiled at his gruff facade. "No." She bent to finger some of the seedlings. "Just didn't know you cared about this particular part of your cargo. You put up such a fuss when it first came aboard."

"They've got to eat, don't they?"

"There's plenty of harvested bamboo for Sid and Alexander."

Garrand grimaced and pulled up another root. "The rest of them—they're going to have to be fed too."

Helen closed her eyes and bowed her head. *Garrand Médeville would be the death of her*. She reached a hand out to touch his back but stopped just short. Her hand wavered, then fell back to her side. "Yes, of course," she mumbled and rose to her feet.

He looked back up at her. "Did you come here for some *reason?*"

She stared at him for a prolonged moment—half sad, half angry. She fought the impulse to lash back at him and pushed aside the sadness. "We're there," she said flatly.

"Well then," Garrand stabbed the spade into the dirt and brushed his hands together. "Let's go see for ourselves. It's not every day we get to visit a mythical planet."

GARRAND STUDIED THE floating sartographs from the nav pod. The flitting colors of the display washed across his face, underscoring the lines of concern that stretched away from his eyes. The data all pointed to the same incontrovertible fact: the sixth planet in the Glaplōs system was a fourth stage gas giant. The upper atmosphere was composed of turbulent clouds of hydrogen, helium, and ammonia, with traces of methane. There was a high level of energetic particles trapped in the magnetosphere that extended millions of kilometers away from the planet. Gigantic storms raged through much of the visible upper layer of gases. Lightning streaked through the clouds every few seconds, stretching across thousands of kilometers.

"Strange that it's not radiating energy at a high level," Garrand murmured.

"Why should it be?" Helen asked.

"The slow gravitic compression of such a huge volume of gas usually radiates more energy than it receives from its primary."

He shifted in the acceleration couch to look at Bailey. The art returned his gaze wordlessly. The planet loomed huge through the crystal glazing, its albedo casting a blue pall across the artificial's skin. Alexander and Sid sat staring out at the growing orb. Even *Destiny* was uncharacteristically silent.

"We are, however, picking up gravitic readings appropriate for a giant," Bailey warned.

Garrand frowned and ran a finger over the edge of the console. *How could he ask her to descend into that massive gravity well?*

"Sid, if it's not what the instrumentation says it is, then what is it exactly? An illusion?"

"No, it's real enough. I don't think the world-ship's sensors could be so easily deceived. However, I do believe that it is not as deep as it appears."

"Meaning what?"

"I think of it like a crust. Like an outer shell, a husk around a completely different inner volume."

Garrand looked at the readouts uncertainly. "If you're wrong, the pressure of the atmosphere will crush us no matter how gentle a glide slope we take."

"Captain," Bailey interjected. "I would not recommend taking too cautious an approach. I'm reading extremely high turbulence in the upper cloud layers. If we spend much time in a shallow descent, the wind sheer will tear us apart."

"If we go in too steep through such resistance we burn, too shallow and we get ripped to shreds, and somewhere in the middle we get crushed. I don't like this."

"There's calm beneath those clouds, Captain." Sid said. "I am certain of it."

"Bailey?"

"It's possible, theoretically. Our sensors cannot penetrate more than ten thousand kilometers into the upper cloud layers. What's beneath that is anyone's guess."

"But all your readings point to what?"

"More storms, denser atmosphere, crushing gravity."

Garrand looked at Sid. "And you think this is all a sham? A smoke screen to keep everyone away?"

The panda sagged drearily.

"Well it's working."

Helen rotated her pod down to Garrand's level. "Do we really have to do this?"

"Sid thinks the answer to our questions lie down there somewhere."

"In the Archives."

Garrand nodded. "If they're down there, and if they're still working as Bailey believes."

Helen frowned. "And there's someone down there who just happens to know what happened to a group of pandas so secret that only a handful of people even realize they exist?"

"Someone or some-*thing*. It sounds crazy, I know. But not with everything else." He rubbed his shoulder and grimaced.

Helen spoke softly. "It's your choice, Garrand. But we're running out of time. If Sid's strongest dreams tells him to be on that planet then…"

"Either I believe in Sid or I don't."

"And if you don't there's not a compelling need to save the tribe because Barrett will find out soon enough whether they are real or not—and he won't hesitate to use them."

"So I just hurl us into what appears to be certain death."

"The answers are down there, Garrand."

The Captain took a deep breath and made up his mind. He brushed past Helen and stepped onto the command pod. The railing slid close behind him and the hemisphere spun away from the rest of the crew.

"Better web in," he called down to them.

Helen and Bailey looked at each other for a curious second and then scrambled to secure the two pandas.

"Hold still," Helen said to the squirming cub. "This is going to be rough." She tightened the web until the cub could barely move.

"Too tight!" he squealed.

"Stop wiggling or I'll have to cinch it down another notch."

"Come on, miss." Bailey said nervously. He ushered Helen to a couch and made sure she was fastened tightly before webbing himself at the nav board.

Garrand took a deep breath. "Okay sweetheart. Take us in along the equatorial axis, just below that big storm."

"You're not really serious," the ship replied caustically. "You're going to go through with this madness?"

"Afraid so. If I just have to trust Sid, then you just have to trust me."

"Trust is not really the issue, Captain Médeville," the ship replied in a very formal tone. "Simple survival is."

"Well, if we're going to go out, might as well go out with a bang."

"More like a brief, fiery plunge," the ship countered.

"Take your pick," Garrand said. He still had not touched the manual controls. He wanted *Destiny's* acceptance first.

"Somehow, rats don't seem like such a bad problem anymore."

Garrand smiled. "That's my girl." He reached forward and grasped the control node. "Bailey, give me a projection of the best approach beneath that storm front." He tapped a swirling eddy on the navi to indicate which storm he meant.

The artificial fed the parameters into the core and a sartograph sparkled into the hollow of the bridge. A tangle of colors representing the overlapping currents of wind bent over, around, and through one another, a kaleidoscope gone mad. The most dangerous turbulence was represented by a fat, yellow knot that twisted along the trailing edge of the storm that they would try to slip beneath. Their parabolic course through the maelstrom blinked red, the ribbon shifting every few moments as the conditions changed.

With his left hand, Garrand spun his pod in a lazy barrel roll around the bridge, watching the ribbon jump and bend, getting a feel for the course. He settled on a gentle roll and set *Destiny*'s Needle rolling in the opposite direction, preparing to approximate the ribbon's coil.

The ship accelerated toward the planet, becoming a tiny speck before the massive atmospheric disturbances. The planet was so large that it exerted an almost inexorable pull. Would there be a point of no return? Would *Destiny* fall like a meteor drawn helplessly into the gravity well? How deep was the atmospheric layer? There could be some ultra dense core of molten material—liquid metallic hydrogen maybe—at the very center of the gas giant, or there might not. How long could they survive, descending through the thick gases before crushing gravity imploded the hull?

"Sir, I'm picking up signs of an intense magnetic field."

"A planet this size should have quite a belt," Garrand replied.

"No, this is more unusual. The field is highly concentrated just beyond the outermost layers of gas."

"A concentrated magnetic field?" The ship was approaching fast, nose turning gently to assume the proper angle of attack. A slight vibration shook the consoles. "Like a containment field maybe…" Garrand frowned thoughtfully. He could feel the ship begin to buck through the control node as she entered the upper fringes of resistance.

"Perhaps, Captain."

"Give me full shields along the forward quarter."

Bailey complied, adjusting the spread. "We're passing through the magnetic field."

Destiny's Needle bucked through the upper layer of atmosphere and plunged into the thick, gaseous welter. Turbulence began to immediately shake the ship despite the inertial dampers. Visibility was zero out the glazings but the sartographs displayed the four hundred kilometer winds in vivid detail. Crosscurrents created massive wind shear in the wake of the storm that roiled overhead. The ship's superstructure began to make strange moaning noises, sounds Garrand had never heard before. Everything shook. Garrand's fingers bounced over the command board.

"Inertial dampers are beginning to fail," Bailey reported.

"Keep those shields up."

Instrumentation began to falter as the sensors were unable to penetrate the noxious clouds. Numbers winked out from the sartograph, the cascading colors representing the winds and the glide path and the storm all disappeared.

"Keep holding your last known course, *Destiny*," Garrand barked over the growing din, trying to picture in his mind the twisting path of the red ribbon.

"Following last approximate projections, Captain."

"Stress exceeding factory specs by ten percent. Eleven percent. Twelve. Thirteen…"

Garrand no longer had a feel for their rate of descent. He began to wonder if Sid had finally made a mistake, a mistake that would crush them all.

"Dampers failing. Shield buffers at maximum. Hull stress critical."

"Try dumping the buffers through the particle cannon."

"There's no physical link," Bailey protested.

"Reroute it through the storage coils."

"Not enough time; dampers have failed."

"Keep those shields up!"

"Reading a second magnetic field dead ahead."

A second field? Garrand's mind raced. *The bottom of a containment field?*

The turbulence was so bad that his vision began to blur. He feared he would pass out soon. The noise was unbearable. Instinctually, Garrand reached down and slammed the power node through the safety catch, increasing the thrust past the firewalls. The sub lights screamed under maximum power. *I'm sorry, I'm sorry,* was all he could think to say.

And then a supreme calm gripped the ship, as if some archetype of benign goodness had reached out to steady them. The ship roared out from beneath the clouds and into the smooth vacuum of space once more. A fantastic volume lay beneath them, lit with a purplish glow. The turbulent clouds curved up and away from them on all sides, like an inverted horizon. They were within a spherical shell. At the center lay a grey planet, small within the vast shell. Three glowing moons were visible, orbiting well within the great layer of clouds.

The bridge remained in reverential silence until Garrand spoke. "Distance to the far wall?"

Bailey glanced down at his navi. "One million kilometers."

"*Destiny*, you got an estimate of the depth of that layer?"

"Sensors failed during penetration. Your guess, Captain, is as good as mine."

"It took forty-seven seconds to navigate," Bailey said. "Given our velocity and angle of attack, it could be as much as thirty thousand kilometers deep."

"Any idea what's holding it in place around the planet?"

"Some sort of amplified magnetosphere. We passed through a top and a bottom. I'll need time to study the data."

The size of such a containment field was staggering by itself, but another thought struck Garrand. "Any idea how that much hydrogen, helium and ammonia was collected in the first place."

"Unknown, Captain. But whatever intelligence came up with a way of suspending such a veil of clouds in an orbit that far out from the central gravity well could probably come up with a number of ways of collecting the gases necessary to fill it— particularly given enough time."

"Hmm. Enough centuries, you mean."

"It's amazing," Helen said.

"I'm getting incredible power readings from all three moons," Bailey continued.

"That must be the source of light and radiation for the planet," Helen said excitedly.

Indeed the surface of the moon facing them on the far side of the planet was a bright, purplish-yellow glow.

"You could be right," Garrand said. "There's plenty of life on the planet. In fact the readings are off the scale."

"What could be producing that much power on those moons?"

"Another mystery," Garrand grumbled to his crew. Inside, though, his heart soared. It was beautiful, the three moons suspended over the grey planet like purple ornaments. The planet itself was still a half million kilometers away and seemed strangely small within the great shell of clouds that enveloped it. Garrand patted his hand on the command board and whispered to his ship. *Thank you.*

"Take us into orbit, Bailey."

"Aye, Captain."

"Let's take a good look before we try to land." Garrand finally stole a glance at Sid. The big panda sat webbed to his couch, staring at the planet that rotated gently below.

"Welcome to Archiva, my friend."

11

ARCHIVA

"WE'RE GOING TO TRY TO SET DOWN TWO OR THREE KILO-meters from what *Destiny* tagged as this rock's most flagrant energy signature," Garrand said. "Something's generating enough juice down there to leak through all the shielding and show up on orbital scans."

"So you are getting power readings?" Helen asked.

"Yeah, they only registered after we broke into the interior."

"And you've found a likely source?"

"We haven't just been circling around for nothing. Whatever's showing up on such a broad spectrum is probably powering this whole chicanery."

"You'd think it would be shielded."

"Oh, it is. But there's so much power down there, no shielding is going to mask it all. Look at this broadband reading."

Helen peered up at the floating readouts. She whistled. "If these readings are correct—"

"—They are."

"—Then there's still massive activity on this planet." Her eyes darted over to Garrand.

He smiled darkly and reached over Helen's shoulder to shut down the display. The bridge was illuminated by ghostly radiance from the three moons, all of it reflected inward by the shell of clouds. Lightning strikes punctuated the purple wash from above and below. "It looks like Sid and Bailey were right—this place is still active," he said in a low tone.

"After all these centuries," Helen murmured. "Where do we land?"

"As close to those energy spikes as possible."

"Any other signs of life or activity?"

"Massive life readings—but none look to be organized. There could be whole cities down there, but if there are they're covered by six or seven hundred years of native vegetation growth."

"It can't be that bad."

"In this moist hothouse? Look at the readings on all the temperate zones—prime jungle conditions. It's had a chance to run wild for a thousand years."

"If it's uninhabited."

Garrand cocked one eye at her. "All of Sid's dreams showed it to be deserted. He walked through abandoned ruins. Everything else has turned out just the way he foresaw. Going to start doubting him now?"

"Then what's running it all? Automation?"

Garrand shrugged. "If it is, then it's unlike anything I've ever experienced. Everything I own breaks down sometime or other," he pursed his lips and looked around the interior of the bridge ruefully, "and usually right when I need it most."

"Maybe that's just your touch," she said wistfully.

"Well, Bailey did say that the Archives were turned over to machines. Maybe they run everything else as well."

"Even after the Migontus moved on?"

"We'll see," he said. "There's only one place anywhere close to the energy spikes viable for landing. It's a rock promontory—everything else is unbroken jungle, rainforest, what have you."

"When do we make planetfall?"

"Two of the moons are coming into view of the bluff within the hour. I guess you could call it daybreak when that happens. We'll do it then. There's plenty of storm activity within the planet's natural atmosphere, but nothing like what we went through earlier. We'll keep an eye on it. In the meantime, we should all try to get some rest."

❖ ❖ ❖

"BAILEY! DID I SAY TO START?" GARRAND JERKED HIS ARM AWAY and squinted.

"Sir, you're being very difficult. You know as well as I this must be done."

The art patiently grasped his wrist and extended the arm again as he continued the physical therapy. "I'm sure you'll want full use of this."

They were seated around the mess table. In defiance, Garrand had his feet up supporting the cub, who lay in his lap chewing a mouthful of bamboo. He reached up and ran his tongue roughly over the captain's face, leaving bits of half-chewed green behind. "Alright, kid, that's enough. Time for business." The cub scooted off his lap and joined Sid next to Helen's chair where the unconcerned elder was sorting through a stack of fresh-cut bamboo.

"Where are we exactly?" Helen yawned.

"As far as I can make out, we're parked on a promontory about eleven hundred meters up, and this is as close as we can get in the ship. I've set us down within two or three kilometers of the largest energy spike, but that's a lot of jungle." He grimaced as Bailey pulled his arm again. "Unlike my first mate though, the planet isn't predatory itself. There's definitely something mechanical out there. How about it Bailey?"

"Between the shielding and the heavy vegetation there's no way I can pinpoint the location of the field generators without getting down there."

"That's going to be easier said than done."

"Why not use the suits?" came a muffled interruption from Helen, who rested her head on the table, her hair fanning out in a tempting red-gold shimmer. Garrand pushed off from the table with his feet, balancing on two legs of his chair before rocking forward with a thud and a grunt.

"The Trioxins?"

"Why have them if you won't use them?" She reached up to massage her neck.

"She has a point, there, sir. I was thinking maybe a suit would be your best bet, especially in your condition."

"My *condition* is just fine." He thumped both his thighs.

"If I may interrupt," Sid broke in politely. "Which suits would these be?"

"Trioxin suits, Sid. Like the Imperial Shock Troopers wear."

"I see." He inspected another stalk and began methodically stripping it. "Then that would explain it."

"Explain what, Sid?" Garrand leaned forward expectantly.

"Just a dream. I had this nagging image of Helen standing with a Shock Trooper on the surface of Archiva."

"What?" Garrand and Helen exploded simultaneously.

"It all makes perfect sense now, of course."

Garrand scooted his chair closer. "You weren't going to even mention this?"

"You understand the nature of dreams, Captain. Much of what is seen never comes to pass. Just random threads never woven into the tapestry of the Path of Fate."

"Any other *threads* you'd like to mention?"

"No," Helen cried out, sitting up abruptly. Garrand squinted thoughtfully at her. "No," she repeated softly. She paused, biting on her lip. "You can't interfere in the interpretation process. It has to come from within him."

Garrand sighed with frustration. "Look, any other little surprises—like you with a Shock

Trooper—I want to hear about it."

"Like *what*?" Helen pushed back from the table, exasperated. "There're hundreds of threads to sift through. Sid can't tell you all of them. He has to fit them together himself."

"I know *that*. That's what we've been working on: *inter*pretations. He said it himself. We're all part of a tribe now. We all have to help decipher the dreams." He turned to the panda. "So, Sid, any other threads fit with that one?" He watched the panda swallow another mouthful of chewed shoots.

"There might have been a *dreighon*äis," Sid mumbled.

A bad feeling crept up Garrand's spine. "That's not what it sounds like, is it?"

Sid's eyes shifted away from the man.

"A dragon?" Helen asked in disbelief. "Here?"

"Maybe."

"Maybe?" Garrand's voice cracked with disbelief. "And you'd just let me go down there not knowing?"

"Captain," Bailey said soothingly, "Cheqlund Varz was a long time ago."

He lashed back, voice thick with venom: "That doesn't make it any less awful."

"Garrand," Helen said gently, trying to head off his anger. "If you wear the suit you probably have nothing to fear."

He rolled his eyes and mouthed the word *probably.* "And what's going to keep *you* safe?" he countered.

"There are three suits, after all."

"No way. It's not like putting on a dress."

"I've worn armor before, Captain "

"It's a weapons platform. You have to train for months to even be able to walk in them safely. I put you in one of those and you'll be a danger to yourself and to me. You're likely to blast off my leg before we're out the lock."

"So what do we do, just sit here and hope Sid can see everything before we make a move? Meanwhile the tribe gets farther and farther away."

"Hey, this little detour wasn't my idea in the first place."

"This is your ship, isn't it?"

"We're following the Path the Elders foresaw!" Garrand shouted. "We had to find Archiva. We have to find the Thief of Ships!" He turned away furiously and braced his arms against the cold bulkhead. *Listen to yourself, old man. Even you're saying it now: Elders, Path of Fate, Thief of Ships.* He shook his head. *What had he come to? Faith over reason?*

"You two are like a pair of wailing lopers," Sid grumbled.

Garrand turned to find Helen fighting off a smile behind her cross expression. He tried to stay angry, but Helen sidled up to him and whispered, "We have to find the Thief of Ships?"

"Shut up," he whispered back, but not meanly.

She ignored him and brushed up against his chest. "We have to follow the Path…"

"Okay, you've made your point," he said starting to get a little uncomfortable. She grinned up at him, undeterred. He retreated, sliding back onto the acceleration couch.

"Let's have another look," he said. A map of the jungle rose from a projector and rotated slowly between them. The mottled greens danced against the walls. "Here. Where the trees appear denser in the middle of old jungle could be where new growth is fighting." He indicated the region, a lush green smudge in the projection.

"Where a city could have been covered?" Bailey moved closer to look over the captain's shoulder.

"That's the idea. What do you think, Helen? You're the plant expert."

"It's a possibility. But I'm not letting you go down there alone. I'll take my chances in a suit."

"No. Once I scout the area and lay a base camp down I can burn a trail back to you."

"Raze the area just for me? That doesn't sound so good. Sid, tell him. Sid?" Helen twisted in her chair. The panda was facing the other direction, deftly turning a short stalk of bamboo in his paw and stripping the tender shoots away. "Would you please pay attention? You can eat later. We have a real problem here."

Sid turned, his black-ringed eyes dreamy.

"Sid?"

The panda rolled to his feet and padded over to Garrand's side. "I think you've chosen well, Captain, but the dream showed Helen in a suit."

Garrand sagged visibly. *How could he argue with someone that had already seen what would happen?*

"And as I'm built for jungle travel, I'll come along too."

"Wait a minute, Sid. We don't know what we're dealing with here."

"No harm will come to me."

"Can I go too?" Alexander piped up.

"Absolutely not," Sid said before Garrand could. "You are to stay here and work on your studies with the Turkle Sphere. You have been neglecting them of late and I allowed it while the captain recovered but now you must press on."

"Yes, Elder." Alexander lowered his head.

"And you're not going anywhere either, Sid," Garrand said. "You stay on the bridge and monitor our progress. We may need a dream or two before this is over."

"So I get to go?" Helen asked eagerly. Would she finally get out of the ship, have something to do besides hunt rats?

Garrand glanced at Sid, "I guess so."

"Thank you," she reached forward and kissed him impetuously on the cheek.

"I'll secure Sir Sid before we depart, Captain," Bailey said, turning to leave.

"Wait a second. I want you on the ship."

The artificial halted and turned to argue. "*Destiny* can lift if she needs to, but you are not up to shape yet. The suit will aid you, but tire you as well. And you have not trained in one for months. I could not live with myself if I allowed you to go it alone."

Garrand shook his head. "No way."

"Captain, your stubbornness will not serve your best interest in this case. You cannot go alone."

"I'm not going alone." He jerked a thumb over his shoulder. "She's going with me."

The art's amber eyes dimmed. "You need me as well."

"Yes, here." Garrand gazed at his silent friend. Bailey was right—he needed him. Just the conversation was tiring. But Helen would have to do. "Look, I'm not going to keep you inside very long. Once I find a closer landing site and clear it off, I'm going to need someone to pilot *Destiny* in. After that, I'll need you to help me explore the interior of whatever we find. Helen has the necessary knowledge to keep me out of harm's way for now."

"Very well, Captain. I will prep the suits."

IMPERIAL GUARDSMEN TRAINED in all manner of combat, even in the Trioxin suits meant only to be worn by marines. Back in the Académe, Garrand had thought it great fun to go bounding along in the Trioxin suit, his youthful energy tripled by the suit's machinery. But as Garrand stepped outside *Destiny's* Needle in the suit and looked back at his ship he felt a chill pass up his spine. It had been a long time. It felt strange to be encased in the old gear again.

The enormous sphere of the ship's bridge gleamed through the mist, its crystal glazings reflecting a hundred dark, twisted shapes around it. The long sweeping neck that passed overhead, supporting the cantilevered bridge mimicked the climbing vines that looped and draped from tree to tree. The precisely-machined hull plates glistened with condensed moisture in the humidity, like a cold beverage glass sweating in the heat. He turned reluctantly away from his ship.

Helen stood at the edge of the ship's stern, studying the strange, little trees that somehow managed to survive atop the craggy bluff. Her helmet cradled in one arm, she stared into the shadows as if mesmerized.

Garrand flexed his quadriceps, trying to gauge how his injury would affect the suit's accelerated musculature. He took three careful strides and then a cautious leap. The suit responded smoothly, and he landed without pain.

"Captain?" Bailey queried the suits comtab, the voice drifting up from the helmet in his hand.

"No problem," he replied and waved reassurances up to the glazing where the art and panda were undoubtedly watching him. The continuation of movements—like an exaggerated follow through—came back to him readily. With relatively little exertion, he bound down the length of the ship and stopped at Helen's side.

"What do you see?"

"Elfin forest," Helen whispered. The sight begged a reverential tone. The gnarled dwarf trees were frozen in subjugation, as though supplicants had been enchanted into wood, their misery left unchecked. A light drizzle intensified the effect. The spattered drops collected in his lashes, accumulated on the tip of his nose. He remembered not to brush them off; he'd broken his nose once with a power gauntlet trying to satisfy an itch.

"How far off is the stretch of new growth we targeted?" he asked, looking out over the jungle below.

"A click and a half that way," she pointed down into the valley. "Too far away to see in the mist."

A tendril of vapor curled over the ridge. Garrand flared his nostrils and sucked in a deep breath, his last fresh air for the foreseeable future. The drizzle stung his face. A stiff gust of wind brayed through the tangled of trees. The sound was unrelenting. He closed his eyes and let the drops pummel his face. His arms felt stiff and uncomfortable in the suit. He flexed his shoulders and felt the whole suit rise up, expanding a couple of centimeters. Relaxing his neck muscles, the tiny overlapping plates eased back to their normal position, servos winding down with baby sighs.

He had used the Trioxins many times before. But each time reminded him of the most important: the time he'd suited up, grabbed a steel fitting, and dropped like a stone to the ocean floor. The time that he'd used the Trioxin to gain entrance to the *Stanzer* on that fateful day twelve years ago. And now he was back inside one — the wind demon's voice crackled through the sting of drizzle. *You gave up everything once while in one of these. Will you do it again?* The ashen sky lit up briefly as lightning struck the valley below.

"It's like one of my nightmares," Helen said softly.

Garrand shook his head clear of the remembrances and blinked at her. Her face was small in the huge suit. Her hair was damp, loose curls dangling over her ears. Beads of moisture ran down her cheeks but her chin was held high. *So, she had them too.* It seemed fitting for hers to finally come to light on this grey afternoon in a place no one had set foot on for generations.

He hoisted the helmet up over his head and felt it lock into place. The forest seemed even more alien now that he was cloistered away from its whispers and moans. They trickled through the speakers in the suit, but without the cold touch of wind and rain he felt removed, like watching a holocube from a warm acceleration couch.

"Come on, lock it down," he urged her.

"You don't have to do this, Garrand."

"We both know that isn't true."

She studied him briefly, but it was impossible to gauge his expression through the faceplate. She swung her helmet up into place and felt it lock into place. Garrand flipped open her stasis panel and checked all the readouts.

"Reading all green, *Destiny*."

"I'm getting a good feed," Bailey replied. "You're clear to descend."

Garrand punched up tactical and the bluff became a colorful, wireframe rendering. As he turned, Bailey appeared only as an icon for artificial assist.

"Your readings look good, sir. How do you feel?"

"Old."

Despite the suit's strength, Bailey had stripped it of heavy weaponry and armed him with only a plasma machete and burner. The art saw no reason to have the captain tiring from unnecessary weight. The ground-to-air rockets and their ilk had been left behind and the suit newly balanced with a few counterweights and sensors attuned to the energy spikes that betrayed the presence of field generators in the jungle below.

Garrand clomped forward in the heavy Trioxin boots, sending out sparks from the shale. He unstrapped the plasma machete and gave it a few experimental whacks, then returned it to the makeshift shoulder holster and looked up.

"All set?"

"Green across the scopes."

"All right then." He flipped his view screen back to visual display. He'd always done his landings by eyeing them, not quite trusting the datacore to be accurate enough. He looked out over the rocky promontory.

Unlike the gnarled growth behind him, lush jungle stretched out below as far as he could see, broken only by one great line that he took to be the river they'd flown over earlier. At the edge, the rock was loose and crumbled underfoot. He took a long look at the bunched tree canopy before he took a string of impact grenades from his belt and popped them over the side. The grenades opened up during descent, releasing a host of tiny explosives that fanned out and erupted as they hit the upper branches of the trees.

A hole opened up, a dark maw amid the dazzling greens. A burst of birds broke from the branches, flying to safety, their angry screams trailing behind their colorful plumage. Missing were the territorial calls of larger animals that should have met the challenge were they there. Or maybe they were just waiting for him, a new and interesting meal of exotic flavor. *Shock Trooper suit? Hey, crusty outer shell, soft red insides.*

"Stop it," he commanded. "You didn't come this far to be on the menu."

"What was that?" Helen's voice had an edge of worry to it.

"Nothing."

He walked back up the slope, kicking his boot toes into the shale to create some footholds, turned, and began running to the edge. In three bounds he pushed off, leaping from the face of the cliff. He fell in silence for three long seconds before his jump jets fired. The thrust wracked the suit, shaking his bones miserably as he struggled to guide himself to the smoking hole he'd created. For a moment it looked as though he'd overshot, and he bit down hard on the controls in his helmet. Then his world turned green, and he began a slow descent down the fresh tunnel, burning limbs casting a spectral glow.

The suit's external lights ignited automatically as darkness enveloped him. He glanced off a branch and jolted to the ground, feeling the spongy jungle floor give. He fell weakly to his knees at the impact, his body not up to form despite all the physical therapy. He ran his gauntlets over the thin reddish-yellow topsoil and brushed the few centimeters aside to reveal a tight mass of white threads, that intricate connection between tree rootlets and fungal mycelia that kept a tropical rainforest alive.

"What are we seeing, Garrand?" Bailey asked tensely. "Your lights are too low."

"The ground!" he growled, pushing himself to his feet and increasing the intensity of his illumination. "I'm reading five percent daylight down here—it's hard to see."

"Of course, Captain. It's bound to cause problems."

Helen watched him drop on the pillar of fire and noted where he disappeared into the trees. She backed up three paces and took a running start before leaping off the promontory.

Garrand watched her flames singe the tree limbs above. She maneuvered through the outreaching branches awkwardly, but managed to set down on two feet.

"Not bad for a rookie," he muttered sarcastically. He knew that only a great deal of training could have allowed for such precision, despite the jerky movements. He'd never doubted that the Nralda had given her ample time in Trioxins, despite his protestations aboard ship. He smiled to himself. Sid had his little surprises, Helen had hers.

"Thanks," she said evenly through the com. "I got the hang of it pretty quick."

"Yeah," He punched up the full visual spread and his helmet faceplate brightened to tactical display. The jungle switched to a three-dimensional graphic rendering. It would be easier this way to pick his steps. A directional icon marked the bearing to the suspected area of fresh growth.

"Getting a good feed Bailey?"

"The uplink is a bit garbled."

Garrand wacked a gauntlet upside his helmet. "How's that?"

"Better."

"What about you, Sid? Any of this look familiar?"

"Not as yet, Captain."

"Of course not." He checked his bearing in the visor and took out the plasma machete. There weren't any natural animal trails here, but the underbrush was not too obstructive. They proceeded toward the trickling blue representation of the river.

"What will we be looking for when we get there, Helen?"

"Things that point to deliberate habitat disturbances. Things that allowed native growth to rush in and take over. Places that were once clearings or roads will have the most aggressive growth. Like after a fire, all the new foliage fights for the suddenly abundant light. Daylight reaches parts of the jungle floor that has never seen it."

"So it grows up thicker than the surrounding areas. I see."

"Or you're looking for something so perfect and commonplace that it covers up the entrance to an underground lair."

Garrand clomped over a fallen tree. "There's a puzzle like this on the captaincy boards."

"Really? How did it go?"

"It was a complicated scenario—a test of character."

"They must have liked your solution, they made you a captain."

"I was creative."

"You use that word often. Does that mean you like to break the rules?"

He laughed lightly. "More like I like making the rules work for me. The universe is a strange place. It doesn't always follow the reality we impose on it."

"Is that why you have faith in Sid?"

"Let's just say I believe in relying on your gut feelings. Sid's got a pretty big gut."

Helen wrinkled her nose at the bad joke, then her face flattened into a serious expression. "The puzzle—how *did* you solve it?"

"Same way I solved it in real life."

She thought for a moment. "The *Stanzer*?"

"Yep."

"Figures."

His voice bristled. "You obviously got hold of the Imperial record. What, you don't think much of my creative spontaneity?"

"They didn't exactly reward you for your 'creativity.' You'd still be a Captain of the Guard had you failed the test."

"Yeah, but not a very good one."

"Then the test doesn't make sense. The only way to be a good Guardsman is to act in a manner which gets you kicked out of the caste?"

"One of life's little ironies." He hacked through a thick lianas vine. "Just think though: if I hadn't gotten kicked out, I'd never have met *you*."

"So," she said wryly, "it was worth it in the end."

He stopped mid-swing and pondered the flippant supposition. *Actually, it was worth it, Or it could be*—but only if he could pull it off. He continued slicing ahead. *Cheplus, it was one big* "if." He was stomping through the jungle on a forgotten planet while the tribe was hundreds, maybe thousands of light years away. *What if this wasn't even Archiva?*

He shifted away from a tangle of vines toward a slight clearing.

"Avoid the light gaps, Garrand. They're beautiful but attract lizards and slinks and rodents like pacas and agoutis—and *those* attract pit vipers."

"Avoid light gaps. Check. Stick to darkness. Helen we have a million hectares to search. Doesn't this seem a little impossible to you?"

"Not with Sid."

"This is quite a test. I've never had to stretch the odds this much. It's been a theme since I met you."

"You like a girl with a little challenge to her. Besides, it's not so impossible. Sid just needs more input. He'll narrow the search once we get close."

Garrand pressed ahead, trying to create a workable rhythm of hacking through the vines and nettles while hopping over dead falls and massive twisting roots that shot out like stanchions in all directions. Everything was stop and go. Bound over a colonnade-sized tree here, slog through chest-deep marsh there, and hack through vines everywhere. Though the plasma machete made this relatively simple he found himself tiring rather quickly. Despite the physical therapy his arm was not ready for hard labor.

The jungle pressed in on all sides. The suit's cooling system could not keep up with his need to perspire and condensation rolled down the inside of the visor. His nose still itched. In school, Trioxin suits had been fun. But here he longed for some light armor and, after much hacking, a repulsor sled to rest on. His visor filtered in the sounds and smells of the jungle. Over his heavy breathing came the amplified burn of the machete and the stench of singed leaves. Spiny leaves flapped against his visor, obscuring his real vision at every step. Slashing one line away only left another.

Marching through the soft, dense undergrowth he began to feel as though he moved underwater, his feet sinking into the silty bottom, the view murky and obscured by swaying sea fans.

He thought about fighting his way upward again through the canopy and trying to ride the jump jets to the river and starting from there but blasting out of the canopy and back in again was too risky. They were both down in one piece now — better to slog it out on the ground.

By the time Bailey's voice crackled through the com suggesting he rest, Garrand immediately sank to the ground without dispute. Exhausted, he trusted the suit to warn him of dangers he would never see.

"Bailey, are we at least going in the right direction?"

"Affirmative, Captain."

"What does Sid think?"

After a moment Bailey responded: "Sid has had another dream. He sees a veil of water and a doorway."

"Good. We'll keep heading to the river."

"Sartographs are updating. Your new bearing is 47.2 degrees." The orange icon shifted slightly east in his visor.

Garrand and Helen took turns burning a path through the jungle for the next two hours. Garrand sipped on water and power solution from tubes in the suit's neck. When his readings dropped too low, the suit fed him adrenaline. He fell into a slow-motion reverie as he stumbled over thick liana vines, his nerves so strained and pumped with adrenaline that the exertion was like an exaggerated sleep-dance.

Helen bit down on the private channel. "So what happened at Cheqlund Varz?"

Garrand stopped suddenly. He swung his helmet around to look at her, eyes large behind the fogged glazing. He appeared startled, as if the two words had frightened him in and of themselves. "Cheqlund Varz…" he said very quietly. The name triggered gruesome images in his head.

"Well?"

"Dragons," he said, as if the one word was sufficient explanation. "Lots of dragons. Fokathenais and Bour'lin—" he caught himself and turned away. "They filled the sky. Screams everywhere. Ate three of my men."

"You mean killed them?"

"No. Ate them."

She looked at the back of his helmet, horrified.

"It was gruesome." He swung the plasma blade at a young golan oak, cleaving the trunk in two. "Emperor didn't chose them as his symbol for their timidity," he said with another powerful swing. "Those myths you hear about dragons being old and wise? Don't see it myself. They were chosen for their ferocity—" he swung again. "For their savagery. The only thing noble about dragons is that they'll do anything to protect one another." He stomped through a smoldering thicket of severed vines. "Which is great if you're another dragon. Is it my imagination, or is this getting thicker?"

"We must be getting close—the shores of rivers are often walled by a tangle of vegetation."

Vines burned as the machete carved an opening. Garrand emerged from the jungle with green tree frogs clinging to his visor, their slick bodies pressed into the glazing. Their yellow eyes peered into the helmet, pupils bulging out as though surprised to find a warm predator-free perch.

He stood on the spongy bank of a green river. Its current was swift and loud. The water disappeared over a cliff fifty meters downstream. The waterfall was a dull roar. Garrand unlocked his helmet and lifted it off. The breeze cooled his face as he flicked the frogs off the visor. Helen stomped through the opening and stopped beside him, cracking her helmet open too. Her hair was dark with sweat. She looked tired.

"We're close," she said peering across the river. "There's regularity to that growth."

Garrand studied the far bank. It didn't look any different to him.

"It's not natural. Look there's almost a right angle there where that jetty juts out."

"Like the trees took root on something manmade?"

Helen nodded. "Migontus-made at least."

"Bailey, how close are we to the nearest energy spike?"

"432 meters. And you're standing approximately sixty-two meters above the source."

"That means we have to go over those falls."

Helen followed his gaze and looked back at him uncertainly.

"Lock it back down," he ordered, hoisting his helmet back into place. He tested the firmness of the ground. "There's not really a good place to get a jump here." He eyed the green waters.

"Wait. You're not going to—" but it was too late. Garrand fell face-forward into the river and was drawn quickly downstream.

"Fire your jets after you fall over the edge," Garrand's voice said in her com. "Just follow me down."

Helen hastened to lock down her helmet. She took a last look at the murky water, swallowed hard, and allowed herself to fall in. She was immediately disoriented as she twisted in the rapid current. She fought to get her bearing and then alarms rang through the suit as she tumbled over the falls. She suppressed her panic, fired the jump jets, and allowed the suit to automatically right itself. A flashing purple box outlined Garrand's position in the visor and she nudged the suit over the rising spray that thundered from the bottom of the falls.

Garrand hovered just over the surface of the much calmer basin in front of what appeared to be a wall of water. Steam boiled off the surface. Helen maneuvered her suit next to him, the steam and spray obscuring the impossible wall. Garrand reached out a gloved finger and poked through the wall. Water dripped off his gauntlet when he withdrew it.

"This the sort of unnatural growth we're looking for?" he cracked.

"We're wasting fuel," she said. She didn't know how they'd get out of the water without jump jets.

Garrand tilted slightly forward and dipped into the water wall. He was completely immersed in the water for a moment and his jump jets whined and sputtered until his momentum carried him through.

"Garrand?"

"It's okay. It's only about a meter thick."

Helen bent forward and passed through the veil of water landing beside Garrand on the other side. Garrand had already removed his helmet.

"I think we're here," he said softly.

They were standing on an immense round platform three quarters of which was surrounded by the water wall. The stone platform was covered with beautiful inscriptions. Fifty meters away a doorway wide enough to accommodate a platoon abreast led into darkness.

"What's holding the water up?" Helen asked.

"I don't know. Some sort of magnetic containment field," Garrand replied. "Same sort of technology that keeps the shell of clouds in place I would bet."

"Nice that it's all still working."

Garrand started across the platform. "Bailey, you getting this? I think we've found Sid's doorway."

"What do you think this was?" Helen asked, matching him stride for stride.

"Loading dock, wharf? I don't know. It's definitely the beginning of a city."

"Where are you going?"

"Let's find the roof of this thing. See if we can't clear off a place for *Destiny*."

12

NIGHTFALL

GARRAND STOOD AT THE PARAPET OF A GREAT STONE TER-
race and watched the purple moon setting over the jungle. It
had taken nearly three hours to fell the trees and hack through
the roots which had grown up the sides of the ruins over the
centuries and gained purchase on the roof of what he had
dubbed "the wharf." They had burned clear through to the
stone itself and gathered up the debris into giant piles that
burned black and sooty in the twilight. All that remained of
the jungle presence was the twisted mound of roots that disappeared over the rounded rim of the roof.

Garrand finally picked out *Destiny*'s landing beacons that
twinkled through the haze as she approached. He felt like an

explorer from olden days—the first man to set foot on some undiscovered shore. He watched the silhouette of his cruiser slide over the canopy with pride. Bailey did a full orbit of the roof and then slipped into position allowing the ship to descend with a gentle yaw. The great boomerang shape swung lazily overhead, the fires reflecting off the bridge's crystal glazing. Bailey set her down on the center of the roof, landing skids scraping over the stone then groaning as they accepted the ship's full weight. The jagged leading edges of the superstructure jutted well out over the edge of the roof, and the ship's stern hung precariously over the opposite end.

Sid lolled down the ramp as the repulsors wound down. Garrand walked over to greet him. "Welcome to Archiva."

"Thank you, Captain," the giant panda rumbled. "Thank you."

Alexander scampered down ramp, followed by Little Bit.

"Keep an eye on him," Garrand ordered the art. "I'm going in to get this suit off."

The tech art acknowledged the order and rolled after the cub.

"Helen, it's amazing," Alexander called. "Look, there's a white bird eating flocks of blue butterflies." The panda chased after the fluttering insects.

Helen laughed as she walked up the ramp. "That's a hungry jacamar after morphos." She followed Garrand to the armory, eager to get out of the heavy Trioxin suit.

Bailey met them at the entrance. The artificial assisted in extricating both humans from the Trioxins and locked the suits into the ready mount racks.

"What's the plan?" Helen asked.

"We hike in as far as we can tonight and set up camp. Tomorrow we'll search for some way into the archives."

"If the Archive is even in this city," Helen said.

"This place had the largest energy signature," Garrand snapped. "Besides, Bailey said the Archives were planet-wide. There should be a way to access the information from *any* city."

"That's true," Helen conceded. "Like a library or repository."

"Bailey, you have the gear ready?"

"Yes, Captain."

"Okay, get a couple of lighters and hover it out to east edge. There's a doorway there leading back down to the surface."

Garrand ran his fingers through his drenched hair.

"Why not just sleep on *Destiny* tonight?" Helen asked. "You look tired."

"No," he said flatly. "We're under a deadline here. We go as far as we can tonight."

THE WHARF OPENED up onto what appeared to be another stretch of dense rainforest, but when Helen looked carefully through the vines and leaves, she could see the straight lines of buildings beneath the foliage on both sides. "This used to be a street."

"Yeah. A big one—promenade or something."

"A marketplace for the Migontus to sell all their fish from your 'wharf.'" Helen said with a wry grin.

Garrand led them down one side of the former promenade close to the vine-encrusted buildings. Upon closer inspection, some of the structures were just crumbling ruins with trees growing up through their roofs.

The humans, pandas, and artificials made their way slowly down the ghostly street, lanterns sweeping the rough stone structures.

"Any of this look familiar, Sid?"

The giant panda looked particularly alert as he lumbered over logs. "Yes, quite familiar. I've seen this place in its heyday, in all its former splendor."

"Must have been something," Garrand said.

The party made its way into the city almost a full kilometer before Garrand stopped them in a relatively clear area.

"Why don't we camp there, under that big tree?" He hoisted his gear to his good shoulder.

Helen shook her head, wiping her hands on her pants. "Bad idea. That's a matapalo."

"Four hundred or more tree species and you know them on all?"

"That one I do. It's a strangler fig, a tree killer. It hosts amblypygids at night."

"Nasty things, are they?"

"Whip scorpions."

"Why don't you pick the campsite? 'Bout time you pulled your weight on this trip." He lowered the gear and stood a respectful distance behind her preparing to sit on a fallen log and watch.

"Don't sit *there!*"

"Scorpions?" He looked with doubt at the inviting seat.

"*Parponera clavata.*"

"Spiders? Jumping spiders?" He began brushing the seat of his pants at the imagined legs of salticids.

"Ants." She faced him matter-of-factly, waiting for his outburst.

"Ants?" he stopped swiping his pants with a look of disgust. "Is that all?"

"Believe me its one of the most painful things you might live through. Worse than being branded. But if you don't want to take my word for it…"

"Okay, so don't sit. Don't go near trees — fallen or standing. I'm beginning to miss the suit."

"I told you the suits are preferable."

"I thought that was the appeal of a jungle, the lack of rules. The chaos." He watched her begin dusting her jumpsuit with a fine powder. "How do you *know* all this stuff?"

"I spent my whole childhood doing this. I've gone from planet to planet with these pandas. You learn quickly when you have to live in a new forest or jungle every few months. Here, you need some of this," Helen proffered the can. "It's sulfur to repel chiggers. That repellent you're wearing is only going to vaporize in this climate." Garrand grunted at the smell but took the can.

"Some paradise this is!" he said, raising a noxious cloud between them. He clapped his hands together, sending out white puffs from his fingers. "So you did a lot of field work?"

"My entire life. Dad never believed in anyone staying inside and watching holocubes all day. He expected me to do my fair share — and that meant plenty of learning the hard way. See this?" She pulled the zipper on her jumpsuit and lifted the pantsleg back to reveal her left thigh and the white jagged line of an old scar.

"On a night expedition I ran into a black caiman — it's like a dragon — and one of the largest predators around."

Garrand grimaced. "How old?"

"Early juvenile."

"And you?"

"Both of us. Darstin was right beside me when it happened. It's the only time I've ever seen him afraid. For just a moment he lost his cool composure when that reptile burst between us and snapped down on my groin."

"Didn't he help you?" Garrand stared at her hard through the dispersing sulfur cloud.

"He didn't have the chance. One of dad's assistants, Erundori, took a plasma machete to it. Took the jaw clean off. I never knew a man so skilled with a blade. Didn't even nick me. I'll say one thing about that caiman, though. We were free to go into the field out of Darstin's watch after that."

She knelt and lit a pyrethrum coil. "More insect protection. Better check your blaster. It won't keep its charge so well out here."

He felt a sense of begrudging respect for her, following her lead in setting up camp.

"You're doing the cooking?" Garrand folded his hands behind his head.

"You needn't be so amused—Darstin's aide taught me to cook. It made the time pass."

"What will we be having?" he peered into the pan.

"Vîlo de fungi," she announced. At his doubtful expression she amended, "Mushrooms in butter vîlo sauce." She seemed to know what she was doing, scooting the mushrooms across the pan by deftly turning the handle.

"Should you be adding so much salt? I like my taste buds to do a little work."

"You need to perspire. It'll cool you off."

"I must be hungry—that looks edible."

"I haven't killed you off yet," she laughed, but the joke fell flat and they lapsed into a stale silence interrupted only by the sizzle of mushrooms and herbs.

She turned the contents onto two plates and handed him one without looking. He set it down and politely waited for her to start. She sighed softly and raised her fork to her lips. A spindly arm shot into view and ripped it away.

"How dare you! After refusing to cook me anything," she stood indignantly. Garrand rose as well, suddenly furious.

"Jean-Wa, I told you to stay on the ship!"

"Capítän it is lucky for you I do not obey as you are about to be murdered!"

"That's quite an allegation," he said soberly, looking at his plate with doubt. Helen's face looked pinched as though she could barely keep from crying. "That's a lie. Am I never to be forgiven? They're just mushrooms, harmless mushrooms."

"Not these mushrooms, my dear," said Jean-Wa with soft compassion as he gently took the plate away. "You are tired and mistaken. The most deadly things do not always seem so. These mushrooms are far more dangerous than a wraith." Garrand's face darkened.

"Is that so?"

"Yes, Capítän, I am afraid these are toadstools. I picked up their scent from just outside the ship where I was doing but a bit of foraging—"

"No, I meant, Helen, is that so?" He raised her chin and looked into her eyes. "Do you really want to be forgiven? *Can someone with such a hunger and need for revenge have a place left for friendship?*"

She looked steadily back at him. "Yes, I need more than just vengeance now. I need you to—to like me again, like before."

"Is that before when you first came on the ship and I intensely disliked you or before when you had the upper hand and I disliked you?"

She pulled away. "If you're just going to joke about it then forget I said anything."

"Couldn't you take a little teasing if you were forgiven?"

"You don't mean it—you think I tried to murder you just now."

"If any of us thought that you'd already be dead. But, no, if you'd wanted to kill me you've had ample chance. I think you really do want some reconciliation."

"I do."

"It's not easy to forget."

"I don't expect you to. Just… give me a chance."

"I could do that," he said slowly. "But only if you leave the cooking to Jean-Wa." She gulped a laugh, halfway between mirth and sobs.

"I think I could agree to that. After all, I was about to take the first bite."

"I'll remember that," Garrand murmured, looking at her with fresh eyes. Jean-Wa bustled over, despite the coltish unsteadiness of his rarely used legs.

"Don't worry about supper, Capítän. I'll soon have some broiled trogons served up for you."

"Trogonds?" Garrand looked ill at the suggestion.

"Just little birds is all. Not the beasties with the tusks and small brains. No, that would not please the palate, not at all. Then we have the tarts with semi-wild fruits, the pepinos and the pochotes, the granadillas and the naranjillas, the carbolas and the spondias, the guanabanas and the zapotes." The artificial whistled as he walked away.

Garrand lay back on his nest, freshly prepared by Sid and listened to Jean-Wa's enthusiastic rambling that soon put him asleep. He awoke to darkness, a cacophony of lusty amphibian noise and an insistent, delicious smell that immediately brought his stomach to attention. He sat up quickly and found his arms entangled in the tubing of an IV bag.

"What is this?"

Jean-Wa rolled up to him in the darkness, his eyes glowing like a coatimundi's.

"Not to worry," he clucked, plucking the bag away expertly. "Just a snack."

"Don't be so bossy. You can always wake me up when a meal is ready."

He rubbed his arm, feeling the slight pucker in his skin where the IV needle had been for several hours. He rolled the sleeve over other welts that told him the insect population was snacking as well. "Where's that sulfur powder?"

"Right here, Garrand." Helen emerged out of the darkness, her arms filled with spectacular white flowers smelling like jasmine. She dropped them into his lap.

"Hawkmoth flowers—they bloom at night."

"Nice," he grunted.

A series of snaps heralded a loud crash in the distance. Garrand sat up with a painful start.

"It's just a tree," Helen said. "They can't stay up in these heavy winds. They're weak. It's a new treefall. Go back to sleep, it's safe."

But that was the problem. It never was.

"How can anyone sleep with all this noise?" he grumbled convincingly, though every fiber in him strained to see past the darkness, to witness the danger that hid from him. "I might as well string up a hammock in the reactor core. You go to sleep. I'll keep watch for awhile." He sat tensely on the edge of his nest of leaves.

He flinched as he felt an injector wand shoot through his shirtsleeve. Chemical sleep gripped him; as he faded into an internal darkness, unable to resist, he heard Helen reassuring him as she eased him back on the nest. "I got it from Jean-Wa. To make you sleep. To keep you well. I'll keep watch. I promise."

13

THE RUINS

GARRAND AWOKE TO FIND HELEN SURROUNDED BY A
swarming flurry of butterflies. He blinked and sat up. Her
arms were outstretched and some of the insects had alighted
on her bare arms.

"What are those?" he asked.

"Clear-winged ithomiid butterflies," she said happily.

"They're beautiful," Garrand said, "they must like you."

"Not really," she laughed, "they just want the potassium in
my sweat."

"Hmm." He extricated himself from his itchy nest of leaves
and brushed himself off. Bailey appeared out of nowhere and
began picking leaves and twigs from his hair.

"Enough!" he groused. "I'm not in need of a valet."

The artificial stopped fussing with him, but remained.

"What?"

The art extended a cup of steaming janda and a clipscanner.

"Oh," Garrand said sheepishly. "Thanks."

Bailey retreated wordlessly.

"Knows your moods, I see," Helen said.

"Knows enough to leave me alone this early in the morning."

Helen brushed off the butterflies and turned her attention back to inspecting equipment laid out on a log. She picked up a piece of her disassembled blaster and resumed cleaning it.

Garrand took a deep gulp of the scalding stimulant and turned slowly in place to get his bearings. They had camped at the edge of a broad avenue. Here and there he could catch a glimpse of the order the street had once imposed, but mostly the straight lines had dissolved into a jumble of overgrown vines and roots. The stone walls of the buildings were covered in creeping moss, and doorways lay dark and open. The fabulous ruins struggled to rise above the jungle that had grown up between their ordered symmetry. The streets were filled with rows of beautiful cypress, bothai, and golan oaks. The trees stretched off into the darkened tangle. The native growth was so thick that it appeared as if the buildings had risen miraculously from the jungle itself.

He stepped up onto the trunk of the tree that had fallen during the night and scrolled through the ship's status on the clipscanner. Satisfied that all was well, he looked around for Sid and found him sitting nearby, carefully licking Alexander's head. Morning bath; he could use one himself, but there were more important things at hand. He gulped down the rest of the janda.

"Let's get this expedition underway," he called out from his vantage point.

Helen's head snapped around at the commanding tone. He sounded for all the stars just like the Imperial Guardsman he once was; strength, confidence, and just a hint of urgency ringing in his voice. It wasn't like the soft, suggestive tone she had grown accustomed to aboard the ship. With a crew so eager to please, he hardly had to raise his voice, much less order them around. But now there was a definite sense of 'there are things that need to be done, and they need to be done now.' *Was he feeling the crunch of time, the same sting of knowing that Barrett had access to the pandas that she did?*

Bailey stood at the captain's side, long barreled burner slung across his back. Sid and Alexander sat on either side of him, staring back at her.

"You ready or not?"

She snapped out of her reverie. "Don't wait on my account." She hastily reassembled her weapon and snapped her gear back into place on her belt.

Garrand and the two pandas started down the avenue, but Bailey waited for her. "Hurry up, Miss Tchelakov."

She was dismayed that Bailey had reverted to a more formal way of addressing her, but she could expect little else from the artificial. With a sigh she remembered a day not so long ago that he had kissed her in the bamboo grove.

Sadly, she accepted his hand and let him help her over the uprooted tree. Beyond, lay the moss-covered streets of a city forgotten centuries ago. Under the strength of the purple moons that burned like soft primaries seen through a thick haze, the buildings glowed in a rich palette of yellowed stone and greenish-blue vines. The flowering creepers softened the rough edges as they grew up the sides of the city structures. The textured stone facades glimpsed beneath the greenery revealed delicately carved patterns and intricate features.

Above the reach of the tenacious growth, towers stretched a hundred meters above the canopy of golan oaks—defiant reminders of a time of civilization. As she walked, Helen stared up into ruins that had not seen inhabitants for hundreds of years.

She caught up to Garrand. "Where are we headed?"

He tapped his datapad. "Toward the largest energy spike. It's about a kilometer off. Bailey thinks he can make out a building at the end of this big promenade—something big and prominent, like a public repository."

Helen squinted through the dark snarl of trees and vines that had replaced the street. With her unaided eye she could see nothing.

"What do we look for?"

"The Archive, of course."

"You think that's the source of the spike?"

"What else would be using power down here?"

Helen shrugged.

It took an hour to traverse the overgrown promenade. A large building rose out of the jungle like an enormous granite block at the end of the avenue. Twin stairways swept down from an elevated gallery, widening as they neared street level.

Garrand paused at the foot of the curving stone stairway. He wiggled the sole of his boot through the vines to find the edge of the first step. The first riser came up nearly to his knee and the balustrade curved up well over his head. He glanced back at Bailey. "What'd these Migontus look like, anyway?"

His thigh, already aching from the long hike, protested painfully as he made the long, exaggerated strides necessary to climb the broad risers.

"I'm afraid I did not access visual files on the Migontus species," Bailey said from the bottom of the stairs.

"They are thin, elegant creatures with beautiful curving backs," Sid said.

Garrand grunted with exertion as he pushed up the last several steps. He bent over panting, hands on his knees and stared down at the giant panda.

"They're covered in short, soft fur," the panda said with a dreamy look as if he were looking at one at that very moment. "They have long, delicate legs and short arms and they favor brightly colored silks and tellas which they wear wrapped around their chests. And hats, they love hats. Wonderful, elaborate headgear to shield themselves from the hot, midday suns—well, now we know them to be moons."

"How do you know all this, Sid?"

"I've seen them walking along this very promenade," he replied. "In my first dreams aboard your noble world-ship I walked to this very spot as we see it now. I also saw it as it was before, with all the marvelous creatures and beautiful buildings. You tell me they were called 'Migontus,' so that is what I must have seen."

Helen started up the great staircase, moving more deliberately than Garrand, one slow step at a time. "Well, long legs would explain these giant stairs."

"And the tall doorways we've seen," Bailey added.

The two pandas galloped easily up the steps, followed by an equally swift Bailey. Garrand still stared at Sid as his breath came back to him. The giant panda walked up and sat down right in front of him, as was his habit, nose just a few inches from his own.

"What is it, Garrand?"

The puzzlement in the man's eyes gave way to a wrinkled nose and a smile. "Your ability to *see*," he shook his head ever so slightly. "I just wish I could see what you do. I wish

I could see long-limbed Migontus with they're tremendous hats. I wish I could see this place as it once was, like it was meant to be seen. Not like this." He took a deep breath and pushed upright. "All I ever see is my own little twisted version of the past."

"That is because I dream of my hopes and you dream of your fears."

"Sure sign of a small mind, eh?" he said half-seriously.

"Not at all, Garrand. My concerns lie with the future, and yours with the past."

"Hmm. More like I'm afraid of repeating the mistakes of my past."

"As soon as you realize they weren't mistakes, you'll stop having dreams of the wind demon."

Garrand shook his head. "He's as much a part of me now as your visions of Archiva and the Thief of Ships and the Silver Beasts are a part of you. I just can't imagine closing my eyes and not seeing him."

"Need your nightmares, do you?" Helen spit sarcastically.

"No, I just need my past." He tugged at the amulet's thong with the crease of his forefinger. "It's what got me here."

"And what propels you forward," Sid agreed. "No one is denying your need of a personal barometer, Captain." The panda looked at Helen crossly and followed after the man. "We all dream what we have to dream, just don't be surprised if your dreams change as you grow."

The elevated gallery offered a panoramic view of the promenade they had traversed. Stone walls, browned with age, jutted up through the trees. Great flocks of birds roosted on partially collapsed domes, their keens echoing across the city. Garrand could see *Destiny's Needle* perched on a rooftop back by the river almost two kilometers away. She looked dark and deadly and from this distance. He turned back to the building's weathered facade. It did seem to be an architectural focal point situated at the end of the long avenue, broad ceremonial stairs leading to this expansive veranda. Garrand halted before the green, encrusted wall and surveyed the way the vines had grown up around the windows. There seemed to be just one entrance to the building.

"This it?" Helen asked.

"The spike's coming from in there."

"Well it looks impressive enough to be a repository."

He stepped back. "Bailey, burn us a hole so we can get at that door."

The artificial hefted his burner and carved a precise line around the doorframe. Smoldering growth dropped neatly away from the iron framework."

"It's not wood or it would have rotted away long ago," Helen observed meekly, sorry that she had upset Garrand once again and trying vainly to make up for it.

"Yeah, steel of some sort. It's got hinges, so it shouldn't be too hard to get into."

Bailey returned the burner back to its over-the-shoulder harness. "Should I attempt to work the lock?"

"Let's see if a little low-tech solution works." He stepped forward and before his first mate could protest gave the door a solid kick. The frame buckled with age and the door opened several centimeters. He kicked it again and then set to it with his shoulder. "Give me a hand here."

Sid, Bailey and Helen added their weight and the door yielded with a groan.

"Easiest door yet," Garrand muttered.

"Don't get used to it," Sid warned, thinking of their joint interpretations of what lay ahead. *A veil of tholas guard the prize.*

"Ah, I'm accustomed to stubborn doors. By the way, you'll have to tell Humhal all about those hats. He loves hats."

Inside, the hall was broad and open, like a passenger terminal. "Which way do we go?" Helen asked.

"Toward the center, I should think." Like the rest of the city, the building was not immune to the aggressive native growth. Vines and creepers had grown in through the windows and up through cracks in the stone floor. Tangled trees and prickly bushes fought for the available light, leaning toward windows and stretching up toward skylights. Garrand unhooked his plasma machete and began to cut a swath through the interior jungle.

Further in, the hall branched and divided with tunnels leading off in different directions through arched doorways. Garrand chose the centermost tunnel and pressed forward. Slick with rotting vegetation, the hallway ahead curled down a wide flight of steps. Helen walked with one hand resting on Sid for balance. Garrand motioned them to stop.

"Bailey, we need a better luma in here."

"Something's wrong?" Sid asked.

"Yeah," Garrand scratched his neck. "You know, there shouldn't be any working walkways—I'm not reading any energy usage here."

"Where? I can't see anything," Helen said tensely.

"No, I'm sure it's moving," Garrand insisted.

Sid grunted, "I must agree."

"Bailey—get in here with that luma!" Garrand strained his eyes against the dim haze his low-powered luma provided. Soon a haphazard light swung past his face, filling his vision with popping spots. "Not on me, over there. On those big leaves covering the walkway." He could just make out the movement beyond. "See?"

Helen squeezed a fold of Sid's fur. She saw an orderly mass of meter long leaves marching on end in one direction across the adjacent corridor. "No," she said softly. "They're being *carried*."

"Bailey, increase the intensity." The brighter light revealed shiny, black insect bodies beneath the moving leaves. Garrand clenched his teeth. "More life."

"Cheer up, Captain. They're not big enough to carry *you* off," Helen said, examining the insects over his shoulder. "Don't worry, Sid will protect you."

He pushed her away and stepped carefully over the procession of leaves. Sid followed him with less regard for the insects. The line parted and continued around his legs.

Garrand found himself humming as he picked his way through the overgrown corridor. "*The Thief of Ships / Has little time / Her place in the stars / We are bound to find.*" The little riddles bounced around in his head, annoyingly obtuse yet strangely compelling.

"We haven't met anyone that has stolen a ship, or tried to steal a ship this whole journey," he griped. "How am I supposed to figure out who she is?"

"You are speaking as a temporal dolt," Sid growled, shoulder rocking into the captain's hip as he ambled beside him. "You're always thinking in terms of the past. 'Where were we? What have we seen? What have we done?'" He bumped more forcefully into the man with his next stride. "Never do you think: 'where will we *be*?' Our fair Thief of Ships may steal something in the future, in our future. There are other clues in the vision. Do not always look for the obvious."

Garrand bumped him back. "I don't always look for the obvious. But you're not helping with the interpretations."

Sid reached down with his jaw and snapped at Garrand's heel. "What do I know?" he asked with a throaty growl. Garrand spied the attack coming and skipped ahead. "I'm just a mindless predator." He loped after the human.

"That's right," Garrand called over his shoulder, picking up speed. "And you're as slow as you are predictable!"

"Wait, slow down!" Helen called out. "You don't know what's down there."

But Garrand had no intention of slowing down, not with a giant panda at full bore chasing him down. He crashed through a tangle of ivy and vines and slipped and skidded down an inclined ramp, arms groping the air for balance. He stumbled forward at the bottom, regaining his balance and pulled up to an abrupt halt. The sound of Sid careening down the ramp forced him to turn around, but he was too late. The giant panda slid right into his knees and he fell to the ground hard. He was surprised to find that something soft and yielding had cushioned his fall. He pressed his palm down on the plush surface of the floor. It didn't feel organic. A flurry of clickety noises in the darkness ahead caught his attention.

"Get off of me you clumsy fuzzhead." Sid had the captain's neck between his jaws in a tender hold. He licked the back of his neck. "Eww. Stop that. There's something here. A lot of something." Sid released him and sat up. Garrand rubbed the slobber off the back of his neck and rose slowly as well. "You see? Look at that." He pointed across the room.

Sid sniffed cautiously. The floor across the room was alive with activity—he could see dim shapes moving along the ground—but it didn't smell like anything alive. It was more like the oily machine smells aboard the world-ship. Tick-tick clacks echoed through the shadowy interior.

Garrand switched on his luma and swept the beam across the floor. A thick, deep red carpet covered the entire room. It did not look age-old and threadbare, but rich and thick. He sniffed delicately, to Sid's great amusement. "It smells like soap. Someone has freshly shampooed the rug."

He stepped carefully forward, trying to make out the dim shapes that jiggered across the floor at the other end of the room. There was nothing organic in the room, no organic material seeping through the cracks, no ivy climbing the walls. Garrand swung the luma back around behind him. The ivy and roots stopped abruptly at the foot of the ramp, sliced neatly off where the carpet began.

"Where are you?" Helen yelled from the top of the inclined access.

"Down here. Mind the ramp on your way down," he warned. Helen skidded down the steep ramp and fell to her knees on the carpet at the bottom. "Nice landing," Garrand cracked.

He kept the light near her until she was back on her feet.

"What's down here?" she asked, brushing leaves and debris off her chest.

"Not sure yet," he started to swing the luma back around and froze. Something was weaving its way toward them, skittering along the carpet on two sets of opposing legs. Sid backed uneasily away.

"Hold still," Garrand commanded.

"Eee," Helen yipped. "What's that? It looks like a big bony spider."

"That's no spider," Garrand said. "Hold still."

The jittery thing scuttled right between the three of them, ten legs on either side of its polished black casing pumping up and down producing a clicking noise. It was not quite knee height and clearly mechanical. It stopped at the foot of the ramp and began kicking the tiny bits of leaf and dirt that had been knocked down the incline into a precise little pile. The ten legs were amazingly adept at the activity, flicking the flotsam ahead while the opposing set scrunched the machine slowly sideways along the carpet.

Two more machines jittered along behind the first, ignoring the intruders. One began working at the uneven edge of the ivy at the ramp, little legs removing the offending tendrils with officious snips, while the other sat down on the rug and began spinning around. Frothy suds emerged beneath the edges of the machine's shell as it scrubbed the carpet.

Helen giggled with pleasure. "Captain you could use a couple of these aboard your ship."

Garrand shot her a glance. "Could use more than a couple after your little 'bio transport mission.'"

Helen made an innocent face like Alexander caught on the baba pillow. Sid growled at the nearest one as it got too close.

"Ah, leave it alone Sid. It's just a maid."

A half dozen more clicked into view, observed the progress of the first trio, then retreated quickly the way they had come, almost bumping into each other as they zigged crazily back and forth but never quite hitting.

"Come on," Garrand said, hooking his luma back to his belt. "Don't let 'em get away. They should lead us to whatever is running this place."

"What are they?" Helen asked as she trotted along beside him.

"Primitive artificial intelligence of some sort. Who knows, one of 'em might be Bailey's great, great grand daddy."

"But who are they working for? Who's telling them what to do?"

"They're probably partially autonomous. You know, like low-level tech arts. It's a good sign that we're getting close to the repository."

"I didn't expect the automation to still be running," Helen confessed.

Garrand gave her a reprimanding glance as if she of all people should have more faith in Sid's visions. "It would have to be to some degree, or Sid and *Destiny* and Bailey never would have tracked down the data relays. Something's working down here."

"But who's working it?"

"That's what we're going to find out." Garrand paused as they brushed past a long counter at the far end of the room. The surface had a pleasing sweep, and stood just to one side of a large doorway. "It's like a desk in a big foyer."

"A foyer to what?"

Garrand checked the indicator at his belt. "To the archives. We're almost right on top of the biggest power spike. Whatever's still running in this place, it's running right inside there.

The little scupper machines darted under the partially open door, and then the door began to scroll back down. "Sid, quick, help me." Garrand put his shoulder under the door and braced himself. The door didn't slow much. "Get under, get under," he wheezed to Helen. "Go!"

Helen and the giant panda ducked under the door. "Garrand, come on." He released his hold and rolled under the door. Unlike the foyer, the floor here was cold and hard. Not steel, but polished marble of some sort. He got up slowly and joined Helen and Sid who were staring up at the ceiling.

Long delicate strands of feathery material were draped in webbed patterns from the distant ceiling. Each strand emitted a beautiful golden glow, bathing the whole room in a rich, delicate tapestry of light and sinewy shadows. The room was very wide, but not very deep and had the look of a large public space. Spaced at regular intervals, outsized doors lined the broad far wall, wide enough to admit large numbers of citizens. All of the milky, translucent doors were closed. The entire far wall was itself translucent, though more greenly opaque than the giant doors.

Garrand walked up to the central-most door and pressed his face up against the hazy glazing. There were lights on inside, but he could see little else.

"Wow," Helen said, still gawking at the ceiling. "Quite an entrance."

"Yeah, but the entrance seems to be locked. I don't see any access panels."

Helen walked down the length of the far wall. "You're right. None of the doors seems to be accessible from this side."

Garrand pressed gingerly on the translucent door. "You'd think the thing would just open up for us."

"Who wishes me to open," a voice thundered out.

The voice gave Garrand a start. "Whoa. That just took a year off my life. Who is that?" he called out loudly.

"I am an emissary of the Great Senii Vilne Markks. Who wishes to disturb the Great One?"

"We are— " Helen started to reply but Garrand waved her quickly silent. This was an important moment.

Helen stared at him with frustration, her expression demanding explanation. "*There hasn't* been anyone down here in hundreds of years," he hissed under his breath. "*How we answer will determine everything.*" Something was nagging him as well, something at the back of his consciousness. *Wh*at was it about that name? Where had he heard that before?

Helen walked up close to Garrand's ear. "Why don't you just tell it who we are and why we're here."

"Because, sweetheart. Whatever's still running down here hasn't had any interaction with other intelligence for centuries. It sounds like it's gone a bit loopy. You heard it. It called itself 'the *Great* Senii Vilne.' We better go along, or we'll never get in."

Helen blinked up at him suggestively and pursed her lips. "So just call yourself 'the Great Garrand Médeville' and we're in. It's sort of an unspoken title for you anyway," she added with a playful smirk.

"No, that won't work. We have to go the other way. If it has delusions of grandeur then we had better be humble. Besides, I think I know who this is." *Senii Vilne Markks? Could it be?*

Helen furrowed her brow. "We discover the lost world of Archiva, hack our way down to the center of forgotten ruins, untouched for a millennia, get to the bottom and you think you know who's running the place?" Garrand was rubbing his temple hard, eyes shut. *Like a genie rubbing a lamp,* she thought indignantly. *Trying to conjure some miracle out of his head.* "Talk about delusions of grandeur," she muttered.

"Function of having the greatest chef in all Carinaena's Shell," Garrand replied wearily.

"Yeah, right," she said, slightly confused. "You pull this off and I *will* call you the Great Garrand Médeville."

Garrand opened his eyes and grinned mischievously as if very pleased at that prospect. "Excuse me." He pushed past her and spread his arms wide. "Great Senii Vilne Markks," he called out loudly, making a lazy circle as he spoke. "We are humble pilgrims come from a far distant star. We are here to bring tribute to your greatness."

"What tribute do you bring?"

"We bring riches from across the galaxy," Garrand proclaimed. "Fresh bor-bor fruit from Kess, marvelous tannerelos from the distant Eemon Nores, kelt crabs from—"

"What is it you seek?" the voice boomed back impatiently.

"We seek nothing but a few moments of your time so that we may bow before you and perhaps learn something from your greatness."

"What do you offer in return!"

"We bring recipes," Garrand cried.

Helen looked at Sid and mouthed, "*Recipes?*"

"Recipes from the furthest reaches of the galaxy…"

"The Great Senii Vilne Markks has all the recipes he needs," the voice bellowed.

"These are new recipes your greatness. From cultures beyond the great one's reach. Recipes for him to examine, so that he may expand his greatness."

"You dare suggest that the Great Senii Vilne Markks does not have enough recipes?"

"Of course not, your greatness. But these recipes are beyond our meager understanding. We need you to show us their flaws." Garrand cast a wry look at Helen just before he buried the hook deep. "We need to know why they are being proclaimed as *greater than yours!*"

It would be his greatest bribe yet, and the prize greater still: all the knowledge collected and intercepted for a millennia. Silence filled the golden entrance hall while the voice mulled this. "The Great Senii Vilne Markks doubts that you have any recipes worthy of his attention."

"But how will he know unless he looks at them, unless he *shares with us* his knowledge?"

"You must prove that you have a recipe *worthy* of his wisdom."

Garrand clenched his fists. This was worse than the *shai* ceremony with all its airs. Plus, he hated having his bluffs called. So he raised the stakes without blinking.

"Very well, then we challenge the Great Senii Vilne to a cookoff! One of our fresh recipes against any of his. If we lose we will depart without further troubling his greatness. And if we win, then he must let us in and share all that he knows."

Garrand held his breath and waited.

"Challenge accepted."

"Very good," Garrand said. "I volunteer to judge the results of the cookoff."

"Unacceptable."

"Well I'm not letting one of those —" he waggled his fingers at the ground, " — those scupper thingies judge it either. We need an unbiased third party." He was thinking he could foist Bailey as a completely unbiased judge, being somewhat akin to a machine himself.

"There is a suitable subject here in the city."

"There is?" Garrand frowned; he hadn't expected this. "Who?"

"The Chief Grower will judge."

"Who is this 'chief grower?'" he demanded.

"We will have a guide take you to him." One of the little scuppers appeared from a slot and skittered across the marble floor toward them.

"The competition shall commence in one day. That should allow you time to prepare your *recipe*. Follow your guide. He will show you to the Chief."

The scupper jiggered past them and to a side door that dutifully scrolled open. The machine did a nervous circle waiting for them, as if it could not come to a complete stop.

"Come on," Garrand said. "We'd better find out who this 'grower' is."

"Wait a minute," Helen said, hurrying behind him. "Who is Senii Vilne Markks? And how'd you know who he is?"

"He's a chef. Jean-Wa prattles on about him incessantly. He died something like six hundred years ago," Garrand said as he passed. "His essence was probably picked up by the Archive a long time ago."

"His ghost essence?"

"Yeah. Some cultures preserve all their famous members as electrical entities. Once he's a ghost, he could be sent anywhere, just like a quantum relay. It was picked up here like everything else I guess."

"But that doesn't explain what he's doing running the place."

Garrand shrugged. "To hear Jean-Wa sing his praises, he was the finest chef ever to live. Sounded like an enormous pain in the ass to me. Artists, you know. The great fop probably had such a tremendous ego that it dominated all the other poor slobs locked up in the Archive. Eventually it rose to the top. If it's into the automation, then it's picked up the Archive's directives to keep things going. It's got the scuppers runnin' around, keeping things clean, just like a fastidious chef. It thinks it's running the place, and now we have to prove that we're worthy of his greatness just to get inside."

"But we don't have any recipes," Helen objected, hurrying to keep up.

"I *know* that. Jean-Wa will have to come up with something." *Something good*, he muttered under his breath. "First we'd better have a look at who's judging this fiasco."

"Garrand, I don't like this."

"That's 'the Great Garrand' to you, and cheer up. When's the last time you got a guided tour of a ruin?"

"Not since you first showed me your ship," she fired back.

The scupper led them quickly through a series of passageways. At each intersection its little legs danced up and down impatiently as it waited for its charges to catch up and then it zigged down a new aisle.

"You keeping track of where we are?" Helen asked.

"Yeah, I think we're about to the edge of the building again."

The scupper climbed a gentle ramp, turned to make sure they were following and then disappeared into another room. Garrand felt a breeze on his cheek as he entered the new chamber. The stone walls were stark and unadorned. A large lifting crane hung motionless between rusted tracks overhead. Ceramic crates were stacked floor to ceiling along two walls.

"Loading dock," Helen murmured.

A big door lay open to the weather and wind stirred the chains that hung from the crane. The scupper made one lopsided circle around the party and then dashed up the loading ramp and out the open door.

They followed it outside. Two of the moons had already set, and the light was growing violet. The scupper darted down a carefully manicured path, stopping once to snip an offending bit of vine that had dared creep into the open. There were shallow ruts in the dirt and Garrand bent to examine the indentations.

"Something's been dragged through here," he announced.

"Yeah, but what?" Helen asked.

Their guide led them through the leaning golan oaks and to a small clearing. Small, careful furrows were carved into the dirt. Rows of vegetables were growing.

"How'd they clear this ground?" Helen asked.

Bailey knelt to pick up a blackened root. He held it up for Garrand to see. "It's burnt."

"Clear cut with fire, huh? Interesting." He followed the scupper around the edge of the garden.

Helen frowned in annoyance. "What does a ghost need with food?"

"Every chef needs a vegetable garden," Garrand called over his shoulder.

"But he's a *ghost*! What's he do with it?"

"Makes things, I guess. He's got the scuppers for hands, and a whole city to grow things in."

"But those things can't have done all this." She pointed at a plant that was carefully tied to a stake. "Look, that's almost a meter tall."

"No, but that could."

Helen looked up quickly. "What?"

"That," he pointed at a hip-high, green *something* that was oozing across the path.

"What in Haven's name is that?"

Garrand turned around and looked at her with an of-all-the-stupid-questions incredulousness wrapped around his smile.

She skipped forward, grabbed his waist and peered down at the pyramidal blob from over Garrand's shoulder. She wrinkled her nose at it.

"This would be the 'chief grower,' I'm guessing."

The scupper pranced around beside the creature and chittered at it. A single eyestalk rolled around the upper half of the wilting pyramid and looked at the scupper as it squawked and then at the humans.

"Recognize this, Bailey?"

"No sir."

The green blob oozed forward, like a fleshy lump that had lost its skeletal structure, and pulled itself toward Garrand and Helen with slow determination. Garrand resisted the urge to step back out of its way. It was almost touching his boot when it stopped and rolled partway on it's back. A hard beak was exposed on its underside.

The creature opened its beak and produced a clattering series of consonants and chirps.

"Oh, dear," Helen sighed.

"Bailey?" Garrand asked hopefully.

"He says he would be happy to be of service, Captain," Bailey interpreted.

Garrand felt the tension ebb from his shoulders. "Good. I thought we were going to have a problem there. What's that he's using anyway?"

"A bastardized cross of two lakto dialects as best I can make out. Mostly Lakto'lahnse, though there's a little Juiib in there."

"I don't speak Lakto'lahnse, do you?"

Helen shook her head.

"Well, Bailey, you're our mouthpiece then. Tell him we appreciate his generous assistance and that we are honored to be here."

Bailey stepped up to the blob and did a fair approximation of the same clattering chirps that had spilled out of the creature's beak.

"We'd better go tell Jean-Wa what's going on. He's going to want to meet our chief grower friend here."

"Meet him?"

"Yeah, he likes to interrogate his diners. Didn't he corner you when you came aboard?"

"As a matter of fact, he did."

"Told you. Sid, Alexander: come on, we're going back to the ship. Bailey you stay here and talk to the chief. I'll let Jean-Wa home in on you when he comes."

The artificial nodded briefly and continued chattering with the green, fleshy creature. The scupper, satisfied that its task was completed, gathered a carefully tied bundle of green stalks and began dragging the vegetables back along the path. The chief grower followed the scupper's progress with an eyestalk while still conversing with Bailey. The stalks made little ruts in the dirt as they were towed along.

"You're awfully flowery in your expression today," Helen nee-
dled him as they began to hike back to the ship.

"Got to know how to grease the locals," he replied. "We
didn't come all this way for nothing."

She stole a sidelong glance at him. *Indeed.* She hooked her
arm in his and let him lead her through the settling twilight.
Purple shadows masked all but the brightest of the flowering vines. She took a deep breath of the heady pollen and let
her concerns slip aside. Tree frogs croaked all around them, a
soothing cacophony that drowned out all but the sounds of
their own footsteps. She let her head loll against his shoulder.
For just a few minutes, the ruins of Archiva were the most ro-
mantic place in all the stars.

14

JEAN-WA

SOMETHING WAS AFOOT, AND JEAN-WA KNEW IT. THE LITtle chef could assess the Capítän's moods with a simple visual inspection. Today his face was flushed pink like a slow roasting taro beast and his eyes would not settle on any one thing in the kitchen. They flitted from rack to oven to pans and back again. It was a telling sign when the man did not come directly to the point the moment he entered the kitchen. There was silence, and that was not good, not good at all.

Jean-Wa tried to focus on his preparations for dinner, but could not keep his arms working with the Capítän standing silently behind him. He swiveled his head round to check the human's temperature every few seconds, but finally could stand it no longer. He turned fully around and waited expectantly, one pair of sheers idly snipping the corners off a towel.

"I need your help," Garrand sighed.

"Do not fret Capítän, Jean-Wa is always ready and able to assist."

"Wait till you hear what I have to say before you jump to the ready."

"What is it? There is not a casualty, no? Not one of the great furries? Quick show me to him, I will make it all better."

Garrand stopped him with his palms. "No one's hurt, it's nothing like that."

"Well what then? Please, Capítän, I am a busy soul."

"You know what our mission is now?"

"We seek to recapture our lost cargo, do we not?"

"Exactly. And we've come to this place to obtain information which is vital to the pandas' recovery."

"The location of the furries and the identity of the woman-bandit who will aid us," Jean-Wa said matter-of-factly.

The art's plain grasp of everything broke Garrand's solemn humor; he smiled. "Yes, that's right. This afternoon we came across a being, an *entity*, who controls the information we need. He is blocking our entry."

"Who? Who is blocking our entry, Capítän?"

Garrand held his breath. "The ghost of Senii Vilne Markks."

"The Great Senii Vilne? He is here? Oh my, I must speak with him. There is so much to learn—lead me to him at once!"

"You are not surprised that he is here?"

"I had heard he was still lingering about."

"Well there is a problem."

"Oh?" Jean-Wa rolled to a halt.

"He is blocking our access to the Archives and will continue to do so unless you are able to defeat him."

"Me?" the art's head rose in surprise. "Defeat him how?"

"In a cookoff."

Jean-Wa's eyes narrowed as he came to the crux of the matter: "He challenged *you* to a competition?"

"No Jean-Wa, he is in the position of power. I challenged him. I told him we had recipes that he had never seen, and he told me to prove it."

"In return for access to the Archives?"

"Yes, if you can out-cook him."

The artificial seemed to take this as a matter of course. "I see." He snipped off two more pieces of the towel. "I shall have to speak with him of course," the art said softly.

"Of course."

"And I will need to speak with the judges."

"Just one judge," Garrand said.

"Very well, I will need to meet with him briefly."

"I thought as much. I left Bailey with the Chief Grower— the judge. Turn on your locator and follow his signal."

"Capítän, there is one thing I must know." He fingered the tattered scraps of the towel. "Did you challenge the Great One out of desperation for our mission—for the stolen furries—or because you had faith that I could defeat him?"

Garrand rubbed the whiskers that were taking hold on his chin. "Jean-Wa, in all my travels across the stars, in all the thousands of meals I have eaten, none have been finer than what you have prepared for me day in and day out."

The artificials eyes deepened to an almost burgundy hue and his head rose up with pride. "That is all I needed to hear, Capítän. It will be my pleasure to uphold the honor of *Destiny's Needle*."

❖ ❖ ❖

"SO HOW DID IT GO?" GARRAND ASKED FROM THE DOORWAY. TWO hours had passed since Jean-Wa had departed for his visit.

"Eh? How did what go?" Jean-Wa was pulling down pots from the overhead rack and shoving aside utensils.

"It's not every day you get to meet your idol, what did you think?"

Jean-Wa snorted with indignation. "He is a sniveling apparition, surly and rude. He is *not* the lover of all things edible I was led to believe."

"Can you beat him?"

"How do you mean—he is a ghost—dead already, kaput! My shears would do nothing to him."

"I mean—can you *out cook* him!"

Jean-Wa grunted with haughty arrogance. "I shall thrash him like a volin-teppi salade whose hearty leaves must be shaken a hundred times before they ripen under my watchful eye. Have no fear Capítän, Jean-Wa will not fail you now!"

Garrand leaned back against Humhal's slot, appeased by Jean-Wa's confidence. The door opened marginally.

"So you didn't get along well?"

Jean-Wa threw up a pair of arms. "Aigh, who knows, Capítän. It could just be the result of being a ghost for so long. I find them, how do you say? Desperate? So sad. And who can blame them, with no mouth to eat, and no stomach to fill. One could argue that there is no existence without such simple pleasures. The poor souls—nothing to do but skulk about. Such a horror! They had best grind me up for scrap before I would suffer such a fate."

"Did you get to actually see him, or just talk to a disembodied voice?"

"I saw him all right. The little leggy ones drug out his shell like a great polished clam and he appeared—twice normal size, mind you. As if that alone could intimidate me. Let him pile on the size, see how far that gets him with the Chief!"

"What'd you and the Chief talk about?" Garrand asked, trying to imagine the encounter.

"I took a sampling of the basic flavors for him to taste," Jean-Wa said in a distracted tone. "And, more importantly—of course—I saw where he lives. Personal space says so much about a person's appetites. I examine the accouterments, the pantry, the kitchen—or in this case, the vegetable pit—and I poked an arm or two through the rubbish. Jean-Wa sees much. I think I have an idea about this one, yes."

Garrand relaxed, arms crossed, against the partially open Humhal. He watched Jean-Wa with a dubious expression as the busy artificial shoved aside four bowls of some concoction he'd been working on all morning. Two of the big silver bowls tipped over the edge and clattered messily on the deck. With uncharacteristic aplomb, Jean-Wa did not even swivel an eye around to look.

Garrand drummed his fingertip on Humhal's steel surface with a casual urgency. The door slid open another half meter.

"You've got to see this," he muttered out of the corner of his mouth.

"What?" the door asked. He took stock of the freshly upturned batter bowls and the lids that were scattered across the deck. "Another guest loose in the kitchen?" he asked with hopeful earnest.

"Nope. He's doing it himself."

"Do not tease me, Captain."

"Look for yourself!"

One pair of Jean-Wa's arms were pulling out cases of vacuum-sealed vegetables from the coolers while the other four were ripping the lids off the tops and throwing them over his shoulders.

Air hissed into the containers as the seals were broken and lids flapped and twirled to the deck plates.

Humhal warbled. "This is too much, I can't stand it."

Jean-Wa scooped a pair of hands into one bin and withdrew some leafy heads out into the light. "No, no, no!" he moaned. "This is no good. Terrible, terrible—look how the edges have browned and crinkled." He dropped the offending vegetable and dug his arms into another bin. "Aigh! What was I thinking? No, these are not fresh enough—I sealed these too late!"

"What are you going to make?" Garrand asked.

"Not now, my Capítän. You must wait like all the rest." He shoved aside the bins and dipped four arms into another. "No, no, no."

He wheeled to the end of the kitchen and back, shears snipping with agitation. He spun a bright red eye around and pointed at Humhal. "Help me remember, my friend." His whisks rattled as he tried to remember what he was thinking about. "The greens!"

"What greens?" Humhal asked.

"The greens, the greens," Jean-Wa nearly howled. "The ones I sealed immediately after Bailey brought them aboard from the grand market on—oh, where was it? Not Eemon Nores. Not Kess. Do you remember? The ones I was so pleased to have found—err, that we found, that he found!"

"Oh."

"I vacuum sealed them the moment they were brought aboard—oh, where was that? It matters not. What did we do with them?"

"Did you try the *special pantry*?" Humhal offered.

"Of course! A despensa especial!" Jean-Wa cried. He wheeled back down the aisle and set to a new set of bins.

"The 'special pantry?' What's that?"

"For the *occasion*," Humhal said proudly.

"Never you mind, Capítän. Hush now, door."

"Oops, sorry."

"Keeping secrets from me now?"

"It is a surprise for you, Capítän, and you are going to spoil it." More apparatus clattered to the floor as Jean-Wa made room for the new bins as he pulled them from the cooler.

Helen poked her head around the door. "What's going on in here?" she asked nervously.

"Jean-Wa is in a state."

"Why such a commotion?"

"Inspiration has hit our chef. I'd stay out of his way if I were you."

Helen's brow changed from wrinkled concern to confused interest. She stepped all the way into the kitchen and leaned back against the opposite doorjamb, joining Garrand in watching the feverish preparations. "This is fascinating."

"Better than hunting rats?"

"Oh, you know *nothing* can top that, Captain."

"And to think you used to make fun of me."

"Well that was before I *knew*," she made it sound alluring.

Jean-Wa had pulled out a whole new set of vacuum-sealed bins. "Are we sleeping aboard ship tonight?"

To her surprise, Garrand shook his head. "Sid and Alexander don't want to. They really enjoyed camping outside last night."

"I bet they did."

"So I told them we'd sleep out there with them again. Is that okay?"

Helen smiled kindly. "Of course."

"Good. Sid promised he'd build me a great nest."

"Same place as last night?"

"Half a click west, in the ruins. Sid said he found the perfect space, underneath an old atrium. Roof's all caved in, don't think it poses any danger."

Helen nodded. "It probably reminded them of the lyceums they were used to. I'll find you."

Garrand left the chef to his business and hiked out to the campsite. Sid was putting the final touches on the sleep nests and Alexander was gathering wood for a fire. With his leg aching fiercely, Garrand eased himself to the ground and leaned back against the bole of a tree that towered up through the partially destroyed roof.

"I was thinking about what you said earlier," Garrand said softly. "About what you said about the Thief dream—about other clues in the interpretation. I think you're right, I don't think she's stolen anything yet. But I do think I've already met her."

Sid sat up straight and concentrated on what the captain was saying.

"Several passages stand out: *'A past alliance / A warm embrace / The Thief's defiance / Like a mirror's face.'* Defiance like a mirror's face: okay so she's a pain just like me. And a 'past alliance.' That got me thinking about the next passage."

"Fate be pinned / To the Griffin's arm / A fall from grace / Unlike a fall to harm," Sid recited.

"Right, that one. Her fate rests in my hands. I have to save her somehow. Remember the newer verses we came up with, where she reaches for my hand?"

Sid licked a bent whisker back into place and bowed his head, remembering. He recited the dream song, the words resonating heartily from his tongue:

> *The Thief of Ships will fall from grace*
> *And dangle from a slender thread*
> *The Griffin's fate she has to face*
> *A crown upon her lovely head*
>
> *If she reaches for the Griffin's hand*
> *Above her shattered wings*
> *Their union will forever stand*
> *Of this the tribe will sing*

"Yes," Garrand exclaimed. "I save her from some sort of flying vehicle—something with wings."

"Unless she has wings herself," Sid pointed out. "She may not be human."

Garrand shook his head. "No, I think she is. But that's not the point. I have to save her—just like *she saved me*! Her fate rests in my hands, like mine did in hers as well—which is the same thing as saying 'like mine did in hers *before*.' Don't you see? She saved me once in the *past*, so now I save her."

"There you go with the past again," Sid grumbled.

"You're usually right about this time thing, but you're just as predisposed to thinking about everything that is *yet* to happen as I am about things that have *already* happened. Who's to say some of it isn't in the past and some of it in the future. We are not looking at this from a static temporal point. It's unfolding as we go along. Who's the only woman on this journey who held my fate in her hands and allowed me to escape? I'll give you a hint, it isn't Helen."

Sid looked uncertainly at the captain. "The guardian woman, the one that made Helen so angry," he said softly.

"Exactly. The Captain of the Imperial Guard aboard the Imperial frigate. The one who had me dead to rights in her sights and let me go. I felt something then and I didn't know what it was."

"You felt something? You didn't tell me that."

"Yeah, like I knew her or something — or like we'd someday meet again."

A ticklish chill went up Sid's spine. "You may actually be right this time, Captain."

"Haven knows, I'm right! A past alliance? Like a mirror's face? All the clues point to her."

"You knew she was a part of your future before I even had the dream about her."

"She has to be a part of our Path of Fate," Garrand said excitedly.

"But who is she? You still only have a face and an occupation."

Garrand smiled broadly. "Just let me at that Archive. I can find out who she is."

"How?"

"She had two daggers encircled by a band of gold stitched at her collar, just like the drops of blood sewn on my jacket years ago."

"Drop of blood? What does that mean?"

"I was Griffin, Brotherhood of the Princes of Blood. Beneath the five-clawed dragon there were two drops of blood on my jacket. But there are many hallowed castes within the Guardian Order. You are sworn into one when you are selected. Our Thief of Ships had two daggers, thus she is Gokazoku Kaigi, Brotherhood of the Silent Blade." Garrand relaxed back onto his elbows, satisfaction spreading across his face.

Sid settled down beside him, chin resting across the man's thighs. "I'm impressed."

Garrand grinned silently, as pleased with that compliment as any he had ever received.

"I just hope that Jean-Wa gets us a chance to get in those Archives tomorrow," he murmured.

"That little chef can do anything," Helen said as she dropped a bag of gear near the bonfire. Garrand stood up to help her but she waved him off. "Just lie down," she said standing in front of the flames to warm her hands.

Garrand collapsed into his nest of leaves. "Let's hope so," he mumbled.

Far overhead, beyond the crumbling buttresses, the purple glow of a setting moon cast the dark stones awash in pale blue radiance. *Like the light of creation,* he mused. *Like the Hall of Guardians.* The crumbling ruins did resemble that hallowed hall. He was lying in a ghostly shrine to Brotherhood of the Princes of Blood. An unsettling nostalgia gripped his chest. All too clearly, he recalled standing within the dark, forgotten hall after his induction, proud and tall, his mates by his side. Worse, he remembered walking down the slick floor beneath the grand vault for the last time in exile.

He scrunched deeper into the pile of leaves, trying to shake the memory. The air was still and cold. Nothing whispered in the pale luminescence, no wind, no cloying doubts. But it was exactly the somber stillness, the reverential quiet that reminded him of the Hall of Guardians. It was as if he were perched on a ledge, a great stone wall, tall and thin, with his past lying on one side and his future on the other. Each side strangely mirrored the other. The hall on the one side—a life of honor, adventure, loyalty and—in the pursuit of all that was dear to him—eventual disbarment. And the quiet rectitude of this ruined atrium lay on the other side of the precipice. A fitting symbol for what his life had become—he lived in the hollow shell of a life once grand and majestic, but now slightly shabby, time-worn and tired, but still filled with a curious sort of honor.

Once more he was faced with a predicament whose consequences would be felt well beyond these walls, well beyond his own selfish desires for honor, glory, or survival. And like before, one misstep and all that he had carefully and painstakingly rebuilt would be lost again. He worried little about 'disgrace,' for he was far from a state of grace at this point in life. However, the shame of a failure now would be echoed across the Shell, reflected in the cries of a billion souls butchered under Vice Proctor Barrett's vision for the future. He grimaced and rolled onto his side.

Helen watched the man shift restlessly. *What could bother him so?* It was one thing to hear about his insomnia, it was quite another to see it in person. It bothered her to see him unsettled. And worse, it bothered her that she was bothered.

"What's the matter Garrand?" she asked crossly. "You can catch a wraith, but you can't sleep at night?"

He grunted. "Maybe that's why I can't sleep."

"Am I going to have to sneak up on you with a sedative wand again?"

Garrand guffawed lightly—neither an affirmative nor a negative, just a bare acknowledgment, as if he didn't know either, not yet at least. He wiggled deeper into the pile of leaves.

The glowing embers burned low, casting just enough light for Helen to see the silhouette of Garrand lying back against the nest that Sid had prepared for him after his afternoon foraging excursion. The residual heat from the fire was still sufficient to take the sting out of the cold air within the cavernous chamber and Helen almost found herself feeling comfortable, almost safe. The pungent, smoky aroma of burning wood triggered childhood memories buried deep within her heart. Memories of camping expeditions with her father, searching for kindling, collecting sticks and twigs, piling them up and waiting for father to dump the heavier logs on top. Striking flint, sparks, and dancing flames that warmed the night long ago. She leaned back and stared at the buttresses that rose up the stone walls and disappeared into the blackness above feeling a tingle of warmth in her toes. Odd feeling: warm toes, feeling a marginal sense of security, belonging. And all of it, what? An illusion? A brief respite from a harsher reality, harder truths?

Barrett was out there. He had the pandas. And he was in a better position than Darstin to make use of them. She sighed and rolled over. It didn't matter. They would all be dead soon… wouldn't they? Her knees drew in to her chest and she wrapped her arms around them. Somehow she didn't believe that—not completely, not anymore. Sid had such faith in the captain's abilities. Absolute faith that Garrand would save the tribe. She was almost starting to believe it herself.

Garrand stirred slightly, his pallet of leaves crunching as he shifted his weight. Helen stared at him, unable to discern the features of his face or his expression or even tell if his eyes were open or shut, but unable to tear her eyes away from his glowing silhouette. She tried to remember the last time she had felt this secure, had even dared rely on anyone besides herself. The man, like the darkened features of his face was impenetrable. A shiver ran up her back and she reflexively tightened her shoulders and shuddered.

She cursed him silently. *Garrand Médeville, how dare you bring warmth and hope to my life now.* Helen shut her eyes and shook her head violently. She mustn't forget her purpose here. She mustn't let a brief instant of light blind her to a lifetime of darkness and pain. Her misery, her father's misery, and her mother's death roared back through her head. Gruesome images of torture and pain, the memories of a thousand indignities flashed cruelly through her mind. Her mouth tasted coppery and sweet and she realized she had savagely bit her lip. The taste of blood sharpened the flow of hatred and bitterness, added piquancy to her overpowering hunger for justice, for revenge. Barrett would have the pandas, if only for a fleeting moment. But soon the Nralda would begin to pay. And they would pay and pay and pay. The mental image almost brought a smile to her red stained lips. And Darstin would pay dearest of all.

15

THE BUBBLE ROOM

Deep inside Wyx, beneath the capitol Jobaenz, Vice Proctor Barrett stood on the cantilevered balcony that served as an overlook onto the Tchelakov creatures' new habitat. The cerasteel platform jutted out from the roughly cut stone wall that began twenty meters below and arced well overhead, curving to form a tremendous dome above the canopy of trees. It was day cycle now, and the glow globes floating at the habitat's zenith burned white-hot and golden red before cooling to a soft blue. Several dozen drifted above the forest, heating and fading in alternating seven-minute cycles. The resultant rise and fall of light approximated the effect of clouds passing overhead. Light shifted and changed on the forest floor, brightness fading to shadows after a few minutes as globes cooled and floated off.

Barrett leaned against the rail and carefully watched the openings between branches, searching for signs of the pandas below. It was a difficult chore. The dome was alive with noise— barks, keeks and trills echoed through the warm air. A gurgling wash of water filtered through the aural backwash. Such a rich texture of sound masked any sign of what the pandas were doing. For all he knew, part of what he heard was the pandas themselves. Who knew what specific noises were actually coming from the creatures? He had to rely on his visual senses and he strained to catch a glimpse of the big black and white bears through the leaves.

Dr. Crevlin, chief of his medical staff, was rattling off the day's report behind him in a monotonous tone. He glanced over his shoulder at the ormedica: ramrod straight despite his obvious fatigue. Deep black circles ringed his red eyes. His face was an unhealthy yellow and muddy grime was smeared across his once white tunic. Barrett frowned at the doctor's appearance.

Crevlin caught Barrett's censure and looked down at his chest. He rubbed futilely at the embedded mud and pulled at the hem of his surgical gown that only served to make the wrinkles more pointedly obvious. "Commander Arnas has not yet had luck in bathing the creatures before their daily appointments," he muttered stiffly. "It takes four of us just to get them on the examination table."

Barrett waved a hand at the doctor and returned to studying the gaps in the canopy. "It's all right, doctor."

"They come to us with their fur covered in mud. Fresh mud on top of dried, caked mud. Their hygiene is atrocious. It's as if they take some perverse personal pleasure in showing up as filthy as possible."

Barrett smiled gently. He spotted a brief rustle of leaves and leaned forward over the rail, straining to see. A reddish vole skittered out from beneath a rotting log and stood to sniff the air.

"I've spoken to Arnas about doing something about it," Crevlin continued, his nervousness forcing him to continue speaking well after he knew he should have stopped. "But he said three of his men had been injured in an attempt to wash one of the brutes down by the stream. Can you imagine? They're hardly cooperative, despite what you've seen. They seem to reserve their nastiness for me and my team."

Disappointed that he could not see one of the pandas, Barrett turned away from the overlook. "And Commander Arnas?" he asked gently.

The doctor stiffened up another notch. "Yes, and Arnas," he allowed. "You should see his men. Bite marks, contusions, skin lacerations—and I'm not talking minor abrasions here, these are deep cuts. I spend as much time attending to the Shock Troops as I do the creatures themselves. But at least they're used to it. They're trained for combat. Imagine the damage they've managed to incur on my men. I've sent eleven to the infirmary already."

Barrett, hands clasped behind his back, listened patiently to Crevlin's grievances. The chief of his medical team had no one else to vent to. Barrett had pushed him hard. His team worked in a continuous wave of shifts to find what might have been implanted within the Tchelakov creatures to keep them from surviving if they fell into the wrong hands. Crevlin oversaw all the work. The time left to find a failsafe was drawing short. His life was on the line too, and he knew it.

"Concerns noted, doctor," Barrett murmured. "I have not changed my policy regarding the physical restraint of your patients, but if I do, you will be the first to know."

Crevlin drew the back of his hand over the corner of his mouth, wiping away a bit of spittle.

"Despite their appearance, they appear to be in good health?"

"Yes, yes. They *appear* to be quite robust—" he started to allude to his staff's injuries again, but thought better of it. "Apart from being mildly dehydrated from their voyage—a lack of environmental humidity—and lethargic, again, from captivity, they appear healthy."

"That is too much to expect: Helen Tchelakov turning them over to us with no biological failsafe. We're missing something."

"There, I concur. Their systems probably contain a sleeper virus of some sort. The good news is that whatever it is, it's still latent. There's time."

"And the bad news?"

"We may not know how to cure it *if* we—" Crevlin quickly corrected himself, "—*once* we find it."

"When it goes active, how long do you think?"

The doctor raised an eyebrow and shook his head. "A week? Two? Who knows what vile mite lurks inside their bodies."

"It won't be in their bodies," Barrett said softly, pacing slowly away. "It'll be in their skulls," he reasoned aloud. "In the most precious place."

"Their brains are enormous. It'll take years to even map the neural pathways, much less the specifics of Tchelakov's enhancements."

"Even in a full core-assisted postmortem?"

The doctor frowned. "That might make things easier. A cranial biopsy would be even better. I couldn't guarantee survival of the patient, though."

"They're too precious to waste…" Barrett sighed, "without good reason."

"Sacrificing one or two to find what ails the others might be the only course."

"I am counting on you to make that *unnecessary*," Barrett snapped, his patience evaporating.

"You have thirty-five of them."

"Yes," Barrett said much more forcefully. "*Only* thirty-five. In all of creation, only thirty-five of the beasts in existence."

"Besides the two that were not recovered," the doctor added.

Barrett clenched his hand behind his back past the point where it hurt. "Yes." He softened to a low whisper. "Besides the two that were not recovered."

Crevlin winced: he'd hit a nerve. Not a wise choice. He hastily tried to soften the impact. "You can't be afraid of two when you have thirty-five…"

"Two that may be *cooperating*? Two that may be spewing out the details of the future for a highly motivated soldier who has defeated Arnas and his Shock Troopers, that successfully attacked an Imperial frigate and escaped with his life? A man that has shown repeatedly that he was willing to risk his life for one of them? Afraid of that?" He snorted in derision. "You think perhaps those *two* are maybe feeling a little indebted to such a man? That maybe such a loyalty would be rewarded with a gift of the future?" Barrett whirled back to the railing. "*How can I be afraid of two when I have thirty-five?*" he asked the forest mockingly. "Just *one* of those creatures—healthy and cooperative—is worth all the sartographs in Carinaena's Shell, Crevlin."

"Of course, my Lord," the doctor stammered, sorry that he had spoken."

"Time grows precious, Crevlin. Even as we hold the harbingers of fate in our hands, time is slipping away. Médeville may already know what happens with his two, and thirty-five are worthless to me if they all die in two cycles. Worthless if we cannot divulge their inner workings or coax them to willingly tell us the future." He turned back, seizing the doctor with a cold, hard eye—a lifeless look that the vice proctor's minions knew and feared. His pupil so filled with hate and purpose that no light reflected back. "I am relying on you, Crevlin," he said slowly and darkly. "You must find what ails these creatures. You must discover how they work."

The doctor sucked in a raspy breath through his teeth. "As you will it, my Lord," he said formally. He mustered up the last of his ingrained arrogance. "You needn't fear. I will find the creatures' secrets."

Some of the dead, soulless anger drained out of Barrett's black gaze. A half-light returned to his eyes, and Barrett turned slowly away, the monstrous need for results briefly allayed.

Crevlin felt his knees almost buckle and fought to stay upright as he turned to hurry away. Three more pandas were due in the clinic in five minutes. He tried to concentrate on the upcoming examination, but could not shake the inhuman way the vice proctor had looked at him. His guarantee to Barrett was not idle—he *would* find the pandas' secrets—though he wondered to what lengths he would have to go to uphold the promise.

❖ ❖ ❖

ARNAS PATTED HIS TUNIC WITH THE FLAT OF HIS HAND AS HE rose in the repulsor tube. Puffs of dust and panda hair billowed up before him, clinging to the charged particles in the field.

He'd been summoned to the reactor level, and told to report directly to Vice Proctor Barrett without delay. He sneezed loudly and wiped his nose with a clean spot on the back of his sleeve.

The repulsor deposited him on a dim level. There were no doors on either side of the slick black hall. The ceiling disappeared well overhead. He shrugged and paced down the dark passage.

Fifty meters down the length, two guards stood outside a massive blast door. The men's silver chests were festooned with the crest of the Imperial dragon. Ashen helms with sharpened spires that curved down the back of their necks masked their expressions. Unlike most of Barrett's sentries who were armed with nothing more than tall Verkhi glaives, these held long-bore burners at the ready, their well-oiled mussels so long that they nearly touched in the center of the hall. The guards snapped the weapons upright as Arnas approached.

The blast door slid upward and he did not pause to await permission to enter. He slowed as the door rumbled down behind him however, surprised to be in a room whose function he could not immediately discern. The hall was broad and circular with arched buttresses reaching into the darkness like the internal ribcage of a gargantuan beast. A foggy mist swirled in delicate eddies just over the surface of the deck, and suspended above his head were twelve massive spheres arranged in a great circle. Each sphere had a burnished, coppery sheen, and the welter of wires and tubes that twisted up and away from them made them look for all the world like grossly exaggerated holo display nodes.

Even more surprising was the presence of two massive dragons that lay sprawled across the deck plates, bodies curled around a central, oblong bubble field. They were at least twenty meters from snout to tail. A jagged silver stripe sparkled down the largest dragon's back, marking it as a rare Fokathenais, a deadly hunter. Arnas had heard of the vice proctor's collection, but had never witnessed any of the specimens himself.

"Marvelous, aren't they?" Barrett asked. He stepped out from beneath the gangway that ringed the chamber, scarlet robe creating a wake in the fog.

"They don't look as fearsome as I'd come to expect," Arnas said defiantly.

Barrett snorted. "Wake them up and see what you think."

Arnas smiled and rubbed his jaw.

The Vice Proctor walked into the half-light at the center of the rotunda. "What do you think of my *bubble room*," he asked slyly, an undisguised pleasure evident as Arnas took stock of the magnificent copper spheres that encircled the rotunda. "This hall lies directly below the reactors that power the new E3 datacores that are about to come on line. Each of these," he gestured overhead, "channels a separate sartographic array from the vaults above. I will have the power of twelve E3's at my disposal when the prototype is finished with its test run. For now I make do with E2's."

"Twelve? You must be planning something big."

By some hidden command, sartographs leapt into existence one by one, filling the dark hall with bright three-dimensional displays. Whole systems rotated lazily around the circumference of the rotunda. Arnas looked at the nearest display more carefully. It was more than just an astronomic projection; there were hundreds of ships flashing into and out of orbits around different planets. Fleets of ships moved into attack positions in accelerated time frames. Waves of drop ships converged on planets, orbital bombardments cascaded onto cities in flickering split-second flashes and then the ships disappeared. The simulation reset and the attack began anew from a different perspective, with different tactics and all new configurations. Arnas strolled beneath the coppery spheres and looked at the same scene unfolding on each of a dozen different systems.

"When the E3's are on line," Barrett said, "and I understand the Tchelakov creatures, they will be used in conjunction with the pandas' foresight to select the proper scenarios. A panda will be linked to the array there," he pointed to the egg-shaped bubble field that sparkled in the center of the hall. "We will know what the defensive reactions will be to each attack. We will know what to do before it has to be done." Barrett paced around the outside of the rotunda, pointing out systems like an architect pointing out the proud features of his latest blueprint. "These seven systems will fall first."

Arnas noted the names that floated over the enormous displays. He recognized them all. "They are strong."

"The powerful will fall meekly to their knees before me," Barrett murmured as if reciting holy writ.

Arnas studied the Sartok readout, possible attack scenarios wavering in the half-light, and was suddenly frightened. It was a strange feeling, a ticklish chill that crept up his shoulders and tightened his gut. Shock Troops did not acknowledge fear. He had lived without fear for so long, had taught his men to defeat fear in its many guises, that it was particularly exhilarating when it hit him. He was sickened and aroused simultaneously.

He studied the planets and the hypothetical ships and attack vectors and probability projections with a practiced eye. Fear was alive here. It curled over every surface in the room, a paralyzing malaise that pooled around his ankles and crept up his body. The different attack plans were all good. Depending on the conditions and the enemy's response, one or two might even be considered brilliant. If Barrett knew what his enemy's reactions would be beforehand, they would be devastating.

His eyes skipped from system to system. There were attack plans well under way for each planet, each moon, each outpost. A heady parade of colors spiraled around the chamber, shimmering beneath the coppery spheres. Arnas felt a nauseous wall of bile well up in his throat. The sartographs displayed more than just a simple military expansion. This was not a strategic military annexation; it was not even invasion. It was annihilation. The systematic destruction of all who would stand in Barrett's way. His predictions aboard the *Ilyovahtna* had been far too mild when he had spoken with Strom. Mere billions were not at stake. A *thousand* billions would die.

Arnas stared at the vice proctor in stunned silence. Why was he being shown this? Was it a test? Words completely escaped him. The Vice Proctor was walking in a slow circle around the chamber, gazing reverentially at the floating readouts.

Barrett glanced at him as if he was surprised that he was still here. "That will be all, commander. I am expecting Miss Strom any moment."

The sartographs disappeared and the room felt strangely empty. But then he heard the deep, steady exhalations of the twin beasts before him. Arnas stepped carefully around the sleeping dragons and walked away, his stride quickening with every step.

The door opened as he approached and he nearly rushed into Captain Strom as she entered. He grasped her by the shoulders and met her eyes. The weathered lines in his face looked particularly hard, like deep cracks in his skull. He looked pale and angry.

"Commander?" she asked with concern, but he brushed past her without a word.

Vailetta continued in with a frown. She could feel the heat rising from the deck plates and noted the dragons lying curled around a bubble field in the center of the chamber.

"Lazy brutes," she observed.

"Torpor," Barrett countered. "They've just eaten."

Vailetta walked up to the very edge of one of the tapering tails. It was scarlet and shone with an ethereal radiance in the gloom. The scales were tiny at the very tip. She poked the edge with a toe.

"I've just begun to read your full reports," Barrett said. "Any opinions you'd like to share with me that aren't in them?"

"We should have brought her in," Vailetta said quickly.

"Tchelakov? With the full extent of her treachery not yet revealed?" the vice proctor asked, agitation creeping into his stride. He whirled at the steps to the observation platform. "I think not! Who knows what infamy lurks beneath those heavy pelts. My surgeons have not yet discovered anything in their initial examinations — but that, I fear, is asking too much. In time, some foul disease, some parasite or other such mite will turn up. And I will still have something to bargain with."

Vailetta grunted, "Darstin's head?"

"We wouldn't want to satisfy Miss Tchelakov's appetite for vengeance prematurely."

"She's helped raise these creatures since the program's inception. You really think she would jeopardize their lives — all of their lives with medical tampering?" Barrett stared at the captain of his guard stolidly. Vailetta sighed. "What honor is there in that?"

"It's easy for you to stand here and speak of honor. Raised in the heart of the Core, schooled in the finest bastions of the Emperor's knowledge, a member of the vaunted Gokazoku

Kaigi—nurtured and protected. Remember we're dealing with a Nralda agent. An *abused* Nralda agent. One without a home, a child that was skipped from planet to planet. A woman with vengeance in her heart and a nebulous position from which to extract it."

"But what does she gain by killing them?"

Barrett strolled slowly back toward her. "She keeps us from having them. She keeps *me* from gaining access to their secrets."

"She keeps you from betraying *her*."

He smiled. "I must continue to invite you to the diplomatic table. There's a decided political bent to your reasoning."

"But you've already broken your end."

"No. If she delivered the pandas to me on Groereh—at the scheduled rendezvous *in two weeks*—then I would be obligated to uphold my promise. There was nothing mentioned about me *taking* them from her beforehand."

"It's a fine point at best."

"Hmm, yes. I'm aware she's not likely to see it quite that way. Negotiations, I'm sure, will resume."

"After you discover exactly what failsafe she has in place."

Lord Barrett resumed his pacing. "When her treachery is complete, when we discover exactly what foul surprise she has left for us, then I'll deal with Helen Tchelakov."

"If she's still alive at that point," Vailetta muttered darkly.

He turned. "Alive?"

"Would you let her live, knowing what she'd done?"

"Médeville wouldn't kill her—"

"—Wouldn't he?"

Barrett looked genuinely concerned for an instant. "No," the calm resurfaced. "No, she still lives. Master Torg is correct: the good Captain will not give up." He snorted, "Not now.

And if he intends to recapture his cargo, then he'll need her alive, like it or not."

Vailetta's shoulders slumped.

"Oh, but the tension should be exquisite," Barrett allowed an uncharacteristic grin to turn the corner of his lips.

"I wish to be assigned to the pandas," Vailetta said boldly.

Barrett's smile vanished.

"I grow restless with nothing to do. I would request that I be assigned to helping with the pandas."

"You are *my* personal guard, Captain Strom. The Tchelakov creatures are no longer your concern."

"The Tchelakov Tribe," she snapped testily.

Barrett spun back around. "What was that?"

"The creatures, my Lord. They are known as the 'Tchelakov Tribe.'"

Barrett arched a brow, momentarily overlooking her insolence. "The Tchelakov what?"

"Tribe." Vailetta stood her ground defiantly, unwilling to back down in tone.

The Vice Proctor studied her silently, secretly pleased, but retaining his outward air of stern exasperation. "And how did you come by this... title?"

"They told me, my Lord."

"Oh, they *told* you, did they?"

"*You* should read your reports, my Lord," she said slyly, alluding to her briefing aboard the *Shiva* weeks earlier and Barrett's reprimand.

Barrett acknowledged the barb with a flexed brow. The corners of his mouth bent back down. "What do you think of sentience?" he asked in a pliant tone, changing tacks.

Vailetta thought for a moment, tracing the air before her. "At times I'm not even sure of our own intelligence, much less that of the beasts. But we have come in contact with wisdom in strange forms. Most recently the salt lichen on Wyktol's fourth moon, for example. It saved an entire human colony, 'from extinction' it explained, by alerting them to alterations in the moon's orbit which would eventually result in the moon's being pulled into the planet's gravity well and impacting the colony."

"A speaking lichen?" Barrett was appropriately amused.

"Not speaking as we know it, exactly, but well-placed thoughts in the mentors of that outpost."

"And how do we know that these mentors did not in fact come up with the conclusion on their own? Certainly their astro team could have gleaned these facts from simple observation, as it were, with their navi instruments."

"If the team and equipment had survived the journey to the planet, indeed they could have, but their ship was lost and their skills with them."

"So no one knew?"

"The mentors called it divine intervention, and raised the lichen to prophetical status."

"And raised them from the planet's surface. Did it occur to you that the lichen conveniently 'saved' the colony in order to procure transportation to safety? That if one of the other moons had been aimed for the surface they would have kept their silence?"

"Actually, Lord Barrett, if memory serves, the salt lichen died in their removal. They could no more survive off their ill-fated moon than they could at its impact."

"So plants sacrificed themselves. A very pretty story, Captain."

"With something to say for other species. Our history has proven time and again that we use other creatures to our own end without any regard to their own considerations. We find thinking creatures and treat them as if they have no feelings or rights of their own."

"There's a place for everything in the universe..."

"A place beneath us, you mean."

"If you like. Besides, if these sentient creatures are so wise then they will find a way to outwit us."

"Maybe that's not what they're after. Not every species seeks the domination of all others. Perhaps they put up with our human foibles in hopes of teaching us."

"What do you suppose they have to offer in learning?"

"I'm waiting to find out."

"I never thought your were the preaching type, Captain. I believe you have written humanity into the role of villain. Domination is predominately responsible for the survival of any species."

"Survival to the exclusion of others is wrong, don't you agree?"

"That may be, but genetic coding is quite clear on one thing, the species must propagate and protect its own kind. There's something," he paused, giving her a curious look. "There's something fueling your fire here. It's as though you seek to redress. What have you done?"

Vailetta paled. "Nothing, my Lord. I have followed your orders to the letter."

She tried to keep her face blank and unreadable.

Barrett murmured, "To the letter?" There was something here, Barrett could feel the captain's unease. "That's hardly like you... Perhaps I *should* read those reports."

"As you will, my Lord."

He considered this ready acceptance. No trace of protest. Then there would be nothing to find in the reports. Unless it was glaringly obvious. He made a deductive leap.

"You met Médeville, didn't you?"

Vailetta cheek twitched.

"You did! He did not merely *escape,* you faced him and *let* him live! It's true isn't it?"

Vailetta remained at attention. "I did face Captain Médeville," she said defiantly. "You gave no orders to detain him.

"You let him live!" Barrett thundered. "Oh, my, Captain Strom," he shook his head, "your precious Gokazoku sensibilities have failed you this time. You've gone soft."

Vailetta felt her jaw tightening. "How else were we to find what Tchelakov's true plan was, unless we let him go as well? You ordered that she be left alone, why would this not apply to Médeville as well?"

Barrett thought for a moment, his mind quickly spinning the possibilities: how to turn a mistake into a boon. His finger tapped his chin. "You are now the weak link—"

Vailetta looked up sharply.

Barrett caught her look. "—Well, at least in Captain Médeville's eyes. After all: you let him live when he had no reason to expect such mercy."

"My Lord," Vailetta protested.

Barrett waved her silent. "It will be *you* he seeks out."

Vailetta sputtered indignantly, "Me?"

"Yes, you. From his perspective, you are the most likely to reveal where the pandas are hidden."

"Seeks out?" Vailetta was confused.

"Yes," Barrett murmured. "Our good assassin seems to think that Médeville will not give up so easily. I am inclined to believe him."

Vailetta glanced into the darkness, seeking out the hidden assassin.

"We digress. I have just the mission for you. You will be sent to New Haivello on a diplomatic task. Tholsen will give you a full briefing. You will depart in two hours."

Vailetta's shoulders sagged. She was being taken out of the picture, removed from any chance of keeping tabs on the pandas. "As you will, my Lord. I'll have the Gokazoku Kaigi prepared to leave."

"That won't be necessary," Barrett interrupted. "You'll have no need of the Guard on this trip. It is a simple mission. I am granting them two weeks leave. Well deserved, don't you think?"

Vailetta's heart raced. She was being separated from her men. Did Barrett suspect her hidden doubts? Or was he simply being careful? Had Torg told him of their conversation? That was impossible. She'd have been relieved of command already. No, he only suspected. She had let Médeville live. That was reason enough for sending her away. She was not nearly as dangerous without her men.

"Very well, my Lord."

Barrett rubbed his jowls with thumb and forefinger and stared up at the glistening spheres that hummed with energy overhead. "Arnas will have to be reassigned," he thought aloud. He glanced at Tholsen who hovered in the shadows. "Bring Arnas back to me."

"Why is Arnas being sent?" Vailetta asked with growing alarm.

"If Médeville can find you, then the Gambor can, too."

16

The Dragon's Price

GANYMEDE WATCHED HER CAPTAIN ANGRILY EMPTYING the storage lockers. Vailetta shoved the gear that the art had carefully unpacked back into her case. "What's the rush, mistress?"

"I've been sent away."

"On a mission?"

"Under the auspice of one at least." She was surprised to find her lip curling into a snarl, closed her eyes and tried to get hold of her emotions.

"I don't understand. You are being *punished*?"

"Not exactly, Gany. Just set aside. Put out of the way so to speak."

"But you captured Barrett's prize."

"Yes, and in doing so became a 'weak link.' The only safe place for me now is away from the pandas." She shoved a short rack of coil charges into the satchel and looked up pointedly. "And away from the Guard."

"The Gokazoku are not going?"

She resumed packing. "No."

The artificial pondered this silently. "Perhaps that is why General Shecut wishes to see you this afternoon."

"What?"

"You are to meet him in the Great Hall in one hour."

"You spoke to Shecut?"

"He came by personally."

Vailetta closed her eyes. She was closer to the truth than she dared imagine. Closer than she ever wanted to be. She wanted very badly to be wrong about all of this, but it was unfolding like a terrible dream.

"There's a mule lifting from the flyer pad above Great Hall in one hour. There's a standard transport waiting in orbit to take you to New Haivello. It's not all that far, you know. Better part of two days is all."

"From the Great Hall?"

Gany smiled. "Lord Barrett knows your routine, mistress."

"Hmm. I suppose he does. That doesn't leave me much time." She fastened the case and collected her weapon belt from the ledge. Gany knelt to tie the leather thong around her right thigh. Vailetta watched the beaded surface of her skin undulate as she moved.

She rested her fingertips on the art's shoulder. "Gany."

"I expect I'll see you in several weeks, then," the art said matter-of-factly.

"Gany," Vailetta said more softly. Her personal assist looked up at her. "If I don't see you in two weeks I want you to run the subroutine *Myshka One*."

"Mistress Strom, I am sure that won't be necessary. I'll see you in two weeks—"

"Gany. Subroutine *Myshka One*, the program we imbedded in your matrix two years ago. Do you understand?"

The artificial rose to her feet. "I understand, Captain."

"It will release you from my service. It contains instructions about where to go to have the free will process enacted, it—"

"I know what it does, Captain Strom," Gany said stiffly.

"Very good then." She picked up the case and gave the art a final look.

"I will see you in two weeks," Gany said firmly.

Vailetta wanted to say, 'Yes of course you will,' but said nothing instead. She turned and left, pausing only briefly when the door slid shut behind her. The Great Hall was only three kilometers away and Vailetta felt a strong need to walk.

THE GREAT HALL rose above the surrounding teardrop buildings like an ancient engine, with the flyer pads jutting out like oddly placed piston rods. The tower was so large that the mule perched halfway up its length on a landing platform looked small in comparison, a simple hurka-boy dropping off a passenger, not a lifter capable of carrying hundreds.

Vailetta entered the broad public antechamber and walked down the gently inclined ramp that led inside the stone hall. She often stopped here before leaving the planet.

The room was a giant cylinder, slowly tapering as it rose. Massive granite slabs formed a continuous ring around the walls. Row upon row of names were inscribed from top to bottom. Having filled the first ring of granite, the names continued on subsequent tiers stacked one atop the other. The result was like standing within some incredible smoke stack, the funnel for a terrible funeral pyre whose flames had left a residue etched into the walls.

The interior was a cold, grey space, devoid of any technology. No artificial warmth or light softened its somber pall. There was not even a simple datacore to assist in locating the names. Instead there was a staff of human archivists who knew the exact location of the hundreds of thousands of names inscribed within.

Vailetta glanced at the alcove where the archivist on duty usually stood, awaiting the need of his services. The flickering flame sconce offered enough light to show that it was empty.

Urqual Magester, the planet's finest stonecutter, spent all his waking hours here, carving out the names of the fallen. Despite his prowess with a chisel, his name had taken on a ghoulish infamy; when battles went sour, it was said that things had 'Urqualed,' due to the fact that the old man would be so busy the next day.

In just a quarter century, Urqual Magester and his team of stonemasons had worked their way up to the fifth tier. She could hear his hammer and chisel ringing out above as he carefully chipped away at the granite. Vailetta climbed the nearest of the stone staircases that spiraled around the room. She stopped on the fifth tier and walked around the half circumference that was still smooth and devoid of names. The fresh names only made it half way around this level.

She glanced upward. There were another five tiers untouched above.

Urqual set down his tools, carefully sliding the steel instruments into his leather case rolled out on the floor. He took out a rag and rubbed the stone dust off a finished name. He stepped back and inspected his work. There was no hint of pride in the wrinkled cracks that spread out from his eyes. He simply gazed at the letters as if he were unconvinced that he had chiseled them true and level. "Have another mission, do you lass?"

Vailetta stopped well short of Urqual's position. "Not really." She ran her fingers softly over the inscriptions. She let her fingernails dip into the tiny crevices, scratching at the break between the letters and the smooth granite. Without conscious thought she continued around to familiar slabs, her hand automatically sliding up the polished smoothness. She rubbed the granite, fingers gliding over treasured names. *Trakon Lowell, Coel Worthington, Dawson Lapeke, Molly Goernt, Trey Moluone, Bourswain Polth, Terril Lance, Kiana Dersh, Lane Crevett, Mia Burwell, Marc Davall, Piran Fostier.*

"You're going to wear out that wall, lass, rubbin' it the way you do."

"Just need something to touch, something that tells me they were really here."

Urqual folded his rag and tucked it into his pocket. "Oh they were here, lass. They were here. You're testament to that now, are you not?"

She walked across three slabs, finding and touching each of the twelve names. Her compliment of the Gokazoku Kaigi, once twenty-four strong fresh out of the Core, now down to twelve. The Guard would serve here until there was but one survivor. Then, by tradition, he or she would journey back to Daulinbêres and sing the names of the fallen to the entire caste of Gokazoku in the Hall of Guardians.

"You linger here too often," Urqual grumbled. "You should heed the Guardian's Lament. Know you not the creed?

The words drifted to her lips and slipped out unbidden:

Do not mourn my passing
Languish not for me,
Though my body lies beneath the ground
My soul is finally free

Do not mourn my passing
The Dragon's price I paid,
My brothers are still standing
Our chosen course is stayed

Do not mourn my passing
My name sung into lore,
Regale the Hall with tales of courage
Alight the souls of many more.

"Aye. That's the one."

"It's so hard," she whispered. "I can't always remember. I have to touch them."

Urqual shook his head and bent down to his tools.

"Their names shouldn't be here," she said.

"They fit onto the wall just as easy as the rest."

"Too easily."

"Paid the Dragon's price they did. A bargain, if you ask me. All they've brought us, all we've given." He continued putting away his antiquated tools, paused and looked up at the woman. "Have ya doubts about the Dragon, lass? That what brung you up here?"

"About the Dragon? No," Vailetta sighed. She tried to think of some way to explain to the old man, but couldn't. "I'd just like to put you out of work Urqual."

"Aye, it's high time for me to retire." He rolled up his leather case and tied it with a cord. He cradled the roll against his hip and took a final look at the latest name. "But I don't think that'll happen anytime soon, do you?"

Vailetta glanced at the unblemished facade that rose overhead. *Barrett put this in place years ago,* she thought. *And he left plenty of room...*

"Good luck to you, lass."

Vailetta blinked, "Eh?"

"On your mission—good luck to you."

"Oh, yes. My mission."

"Mind you don't bring any work to me neither," he warned her. He rubbed a calloused palm with his thick thumb. "My hands are tired..."

The old man shuffled down the stairway. A man in a sharply creased marine uniform stopped halfway up the stairs to let Urqual pass. The stonecutter nodded in gratitude as he went by. The man continued up, his robotic leg ringing on the stone steps. Vailetta heard the well-known step-click, step-click and turned to face the general. Shecut walked with no hint of a limp, his signature bone cane held under one arm while he carried a beautiful wooden box in both hands.

Vailetta glanced over the edge of the tier to the empty floor far below. They were alone and there were no recording devices here. She brought herself to attention, but Shecut would have none of that.

"Ah, Myshka it's good to finally get you alone."

Vailetta smiled at the familiarity; there were not many in the galaxy that knew her by that name.

"I have something for you," Shecut continued. He unlatched the box and opened it, holding it out for her to see. Vailetta stepped forward and peered into the box. Cradled in blue velvet lay a single shining pistol. "It's from you father."

Moisture collected in the corners of her eyes as she lifted the weapon out from the box. "A Cresbourin blaster."

"Handmade by Gui Cresbourin himself."

"You carried this all the way from Daulinbêres?"

"He insisted. It was for your twenty-fifth birth celebration, but I'm afraid it's two years late."

"It's quite a way to come for a simple delivery," Vailetta scoffed.

Shecut grinned broadly, the cracks around his pale blue eyes stretching upward. Vailetta caught a glimpse of the younger man she remembered from her childhood, the jovial soldier that her father had relied so heavily on in the early days, a man trusted like no other. "Well, you know your father, there's always a task within a task."

"Of course." She hesitated before asking: "How were things on Daulinbêres?"

The general cradled her chin between his rough, battle-hewn hand. "He misses you. We all do."

"My life is the Guard now. My home is wherever they send me."

"Can you blame Him for seeking out your welfare?" he asked gently.

"Never," she whispered.

"You're still winning at *go* I hear. That will please Him."

"That's no surprise, is it?"

He smiled again, the younger man shining out through all the cracks. "You are the fulfillment of all His dreams for you and then some. But you have wandered near a great danger."

Vailetta twisted away. "I have learned much here."

"Let us hope you will not need to unlearn it."

"I am no longer in Barrett's *tutelage*, nor his favor."

Shecut grunted his doubt. "You are most assuredly still in his favor — too much so for your own safety I'm afraid. It may appear that he is sending you away — "

"What else could this ridiculous mission be viewed as?"

" — But more likely he is using you as *bait*."

"I don't know, General. I just don't know." Her mind was a whorl of doubts and unsubstantiated fears. She looked hard at the old man. "You gave up a lot to be with me."

"The Emperor asked it. I could not refuse."

"But the lost years. All for a present that could have been shuttled, the origin disguised!" She frowned at the weapon's beauty and tucked into her belt.

"I treasure seeing you again, my dear. I would not have passed this opportunity for a world. And I have lost nothing in my service to your father. He is order and happiness in a tyranny of chaos and anarchy. I have lived in the time before his rule — you cannot imagine the suffering there was." The general glanced around at the names etched into the stone. "There's a reason all these men gave their lives for the Dragon."

"I just hope that they did not pay the Dragon's price for the wrong man."

"How like your father you are, more and more by the hour," he said softly. "The Emperor will know what is transpiring here."

A task within a task. Vailetta's eyes flashed with recognition and hope. Shecut nodded, "Best you go along with Barrett's plans for now. You may think that you are being removed from the playing field, but something tells me you're going to be right in the thick of things."

"On New Haivello?" Vailetta asked incredulously.

"Barrett is rarely wrong. And he truly believes Médeville and the Gambor will track you down, otherwise he would not send Arnas and Torg."

"Torg is being sent as well?"

"I must go now," Shecut said abruptly, "and so must you. The shuttle is departing."

"But wait."

"No arguments." The general grasped her hand tightly. "Mind yourself, Myshka. You tread now amongst a nest of vipers."

Vailetta returned his squeeze. "Are you leaving, too?"

The old man smiled. "I follow my words," he said cryptically. "Back to the Core."

Vailetta allowed herself a sigh of relief. Her father would learn, one way or another.

"Give him my words too," she said. "Tell him I endeavor to honor him."

"You honor him each day, little one. Go now."

Dasko met her at the edge of the flyer pad. The scarlet mule was rumbling to life behind him. She could feel its repulsors shuddering through the steel plates. He came to attention.

"The men send their best," he said, nearly having to shout to be heard.

Vailetta dropped her case and stared out over the city, her mind still thinking about the general. Would her father think that she had dishonored him by delivering the pandas?

"They're looking forward to their leaves," Dasko continued. "I myself was thinking about going down to Lelandis."

The duty officer at the foot of the mule waved his datapad over his head, trying to signal Vailetta. The lifter's engines began their slow whining howl.

"Captain?"

Vailetta suddenly stared at her officer. "Don't go far."

"What?" he yelled.

"Don't go far, Dasko," she warned.

His eyes searched hers, trying to discern what she was really trying to say. "I won't go far," he said uncertainly.

"Don't let any of them go far, Dasko."

He shook his head carefully, trying to imagine what she was afraid of. "I won't. There's enough to do right here in Jobaenz."

"That's my man," she said, obvious relief in her voice. She grasped his shoulder with one hand, held it for a moment and then gathered her case.

"One will, Captain," Dasko said.

Vailetta smiled. "One will, yours."

"One will, the Emperor," he finished.

We will see, she murmured as she stepped into the shuttle. She stood in the airlock after it sealed and watched Dasko shrink from view. Her view of the city expanded and the mosaic rippled out beneath her as the mule lumbered into orbit. She was alone, truly alone, for the first time since she was a child on Daulinbêres. No longer did she have the reassuring sanctity of her precious Guardsmen at her side. It was a kind of nakedness she had not felt in years.

17

The Great Ghost
Cookoff

The scuppers had been busy. All the hallways lead-ing into the Archive repository had been cleared of natural growth. Roots and vines had been pulled up, dirt and moss scraped off the floors, and a fresh polish applied to the aging stone. Senii Vilne had cranked up a few more generators as well; cracked sconces now glowed with light and neo markers embedded in the floor glowed with directions.

"Looks like the 'Great One' is expecting us," Helen said.

Garrand and Bailey walked behind a small lighter that car-ried Jean-Wa, his legs, his serving cart, and his carefully prepared meal. "Poor guy hasn't had company in a few hundred years, maybe longer," Garrand murmured. "He might be warming to the idea."

"Well, still nice of him to spruce the place up a bit."

"There eez *no* trouble too great for ze guests of honor," Garrand quipped, affecting the chef's melodic annunciations.

The art spun his head around. "Fun you have — at my expense, yes? You do not recognize the deeper social contexts of the foods, of the preparations, of the consumptions. The dinner time is an event that all species share. It is contact between vastly different members of the tribe for common purpose. It is a social contract bringing all together for one short time." The artificial spun his head back around to face the hall. Garrand and Bailey shared a glance.

"It is the handling of food that has elevated one species over another," Jean-Wa continued. "It is what separates you, Capítän, from the kiptst and the wotoii — they have not yet elevated *dinner* to such a high art. They hunt and kill, devouring their meals instantly rather than preparing ritualistic dishes and digesting them while discussing greater affairs. You laugh at the preparations that the Great Senii Vilne has made, but he is no fool. He knows the value of putting guests at ease. This is a diplomatic function, with the highest of stakes, yes? And whom have you turned to, Capítän? Your combat assist? Your furries with the dreams? No, you turn to your chef. It is the food, I tell you. It all begins and ends with the food."

Garrand sighed and let Bailey continue nudging the lighter down the hall. Sid ambled past him, but Alexander stopped to nuzzle his hand with his wet nose. Garrand allowed the cub a brief scratch behind the ear, listening for the telltale clicks of the scuppers.

At each intersection, the tireless machines could be seen working in the distance pushing back the ever-encroaching jungle. Garrand paused to admire a group who had stacked themselves one atop another in ascending order to create a stairway of sorts for their brothers and sisters. An upside down scupper clutched a burner nozzle in between his twenty legs while another carried him up the makeshift stairs on his back. Together, they were burning the stubborn vines off the walls. A lighter floated nearby, filled with canisters of combustible liquid to fuel the burners.

"Industrious lot," Garrand observed. One or two of the little critters really would come in handy on *Destiny's Needle*. He wondered what kind of side deal he could get going with Senii Vilne.

For a planet whose inhabitants had long since moved on, died off, or simply disappeared, the first city beneath the mountains on the second largest continent of Archiva was abuzz with activity. As they neared the broad entrance foyer more and more scuppers jiggered past them, pushing their way into the hall.

By the time Garrand and Bailey pushed their lighter under the golden strands of light, the foyer was filled end to end with hundreds of scuppers, all of them jostling back and forth and chattering with expectant energy. Like a wheel rolling through a puddle, an aisle parted for *Destiny's* occupants. Garrand maneuvered the lighter to the center of the hall and waited.

"We have quite an audience," Helen said nervously. She looked at Jean-Wa who sat stoically on the lighter, all six arms clutching a covered silver tray with firm resolve. "What'd he fix?"

Garrand shrugged. "He won't tell me."

"Aren't you nervous?"

He gave her a thin, tight-lipped smile.

This annoyed her. "Well, it's out of your hands now, big guy."

"That's why I have a capable crew," he replied calmly. "I don't expect to be able to do everything myself."

She hated how he could stay so calm; her stomach was twisted up in knots. "When are they going to get this show on the road?"

"Right about now…" Garrand nudged her and pointed at the far wall.

A long line of the green, fleshy pyramids oozed single-file into the foyer from the hall leading to the loading docks. The scuppers parted once again and the creatures slowly scrunched and pulled themselves to the center of the room.

"I didn't know there was more than one of them," Helen remarked.

"Of course," Garrand said. "A whole herd of them work for the Chief. Senii Vilne has gardens all around the backside of the Archives. The Chief Grower has a crew of dozens who tend them."

The Chief scooched out ahead of his brethren and stopped in front of Bailey. An eyestalk rolled around to face the artificial.

"Make him feel welcome," Garrand said.

Bailey greeted the Chief in the jarring Lakto'lahnse tongue. The creature shifted backward, exposing its beak, and replied.

Garrand winced as the beak snapped and clacked. "What'd he say?"

"The Chief announces his great interest in the First Annual Archival Cookoff and welcomes the noble entrant from *Destiny's Needle*."

Jean-Wa nodded once in acknowledgment.

The Chief clattered again and oozed toward the lighter.

"Further," Bailey interpreted. "He says he's hungry."

Garrand stepped in front of the creature. "Not yet, not until ol' Senii Vilne gets here."

The fleshy edge of the Chief's body drooped itself over the toe of Garrand's boot. After a moment he could feel the beak scraping against the leather. He pulled his foot back hastily. "Oh, no you don't!" he leaned down to push the creature away, but his hand nearly disappeared into the gelatinous folds of flesh.

Helen giggled: "If he likes the way you taste, then we've already won."

"I'm sure I'm not nearly as palatable as whatever Jean-Wa has prepared." He withdrew his hand and wiped it on his pants leg.

A commotion rose across the foyer as scuppers scrambled away from one of the giant translucent doors. The milky door slid open and a new procession of scuppers paraded through. A green, oblong shell sat atop one of the scupper's backs. A pinprick sparkle of light erupted from the shell and the shimmering image of a man leapt into existence. Just as Jean-Wa had said, Senii Vilne projected himself as twice normal size. He looked down beneficently at the scuppers that rattled into each other in a frenzy of excitement as he passed overhead. The ghost was done up in immaculate white robes and a tremendous hat which flopped down over the side of his head in a curiously effective artistic flourish.

"Welcome," he boomed, arms spread wide. "Welcome to Archiva!"

Behind him, a processional of scuppers deftly pulled a lighter piled high with steaming samovars and ornate silver platters. The ghost of Senii Vilne watched with arrogant pride as his offerings passed beneath him, his holo projector sputtering static as his shell was jostled.

The cart contained a broad range of dishes, enough for the Chief and a dozen of his growers from the look of it. Garrand chewed the fleshy tip of his thumb as he surveyed the fabulous feast. There was no doubt that the food *smelled* delicious. He wondered if the Chief had olfactory senses hidden on his body. The Chief's stalk watched the cart draw to a halt before him impassively.

Bailey carefully lifted Jean-Wa off the lighter and onto his serving cart. The artificial wheeled over, and presented his offering to the Chief. With dauntless grace he carefully lifted the lid off the platter with one arm. Garrand and Helen leaned forward to see what lay inside. With another pair of arms, Jean-Wa removed a single, delicate, china bowl and laid it before the judge. The bowl was filled with mustard greens.

"Is that *it*?" Helen whispered.

The Chief's eyestalk swiveled down to look at the bowl. Garrand felt his stomach tighten. To his unpracticed eye, Jean-Wa's dinner didn't have a chance against the incredible spread that Senii Vilne Markks had prepared.

The ghost seemed to think likewise as he beamed down at his spindly opponent. "*This* is the best you could do? You have traveled all this way across the stars just to fix a wee salade?" Senii Vilne's holo body shook with mirth, laughter echoing throughout the foyer.

Jean-Wa stood in defiant silence, a freshly pressed napkin draped precisely over one arm. He did not comment on his idol's incredibly rude behavior, but awaited judgment with noble reserve.

"Let the judging begin!" the ghost continued to laugh heartily, the noise echoed by the chattering scuppers. He shifted to Lakto'lahnse and repeated the command. The Chief Grower oozed forward onto the cart. "I have prepared a Hueneker ritual feast. He will start with a small appetizer—a Quini delicacy—and then move on to the soup." The Chief drug himself onto the first plate, a rough piece of pottery, and swallowed the two tiny triangular pastries.

"He will then be tempted with the raw varo fillets, the steamed kelts, one vinegary ta'tlōn, and then a simmered gobi." The hungry creature oozed onto each of the plates. His beak could be heard scraping the porcelain as he ate. He sampled a bit of two dishes, cleaned a third and made his way toward the steaming crabs that lay on red lacquered porcelain.

"Notice if you will, the use of different vessels for each course. It is very important to use the proper dish to capture the seasonality of the ingredients and carry the integrity of the dining experience."

Garrand glanced at Jean-Wa, who calmly watched the Chief finish the last three courses and slide unceremoniously off the cart. Senii Vilne seemed positively aglow with pleasure. "Very good, Chief. Well done citizen!" He congratulated the creature in Lakto'lahnse and then turned to look at Jean-Wa. "He doesn't eat like this every day in the gardens, eh?" He clapped his hands and a scupper scooted up with a bowl of water and lemon on its back. The machine ducked down and let the bowl slide onto the marble floor. The Chief digested the contents.

"Is that satisfactory?" the ghost of Senii Vilne asked. "A plain sorbet can be brought if you wish. Or perhaps some simple greens to cleanse the Chief's palate—oh, forgive me," the ghost said in mock horror. "That's what you've brought!" He howled with laughter.

The Chief's stalk swiveled to look at the ghost, as if in silent reprimand, and then swung back to Jean-Wa's plate of greens.

He oozed forward onto the plate and ate. The fresh mustard greens crunched as they were devoured. Jean-Wa ran one finger along the crease of his napkin, receptors downcast.

The Chief oozed off the plate and rolled over onto one side, flesh drooping away from his beak. He spoke in barking clacks and all the joy drained from Senii Vilne's face. He grew so pale as to become almost invisible.

"What! What did he say?" Garrand demanded.

"The Chief Grower thanks the participants of the Great Ghost Cookoff," Bailey said as he listened. "And he is pleased to announce that this year's winner is Jean-Wa of *Destiny's Needle!*"

Helen screamed with delight and kissed Garrand's cheek. Jean-Wa took the news with stoic aplomb, offering the napkin out for the Chief. The creature accepted the linen and began devouring it as well. Garrand bounded over to his chef and gave him a huge hug. The art didn't quite know what to do with his arms, and they floundered about before resting on the man's back.

"Capítän, please. Not in front of the runner-up! It is bad form."

"Nonsense. You beat him. By Haven, you did it!"

Four scuppers appeared and slowly pulled Senii Vilne's cart away. The ghost bowed effusively to Jean-Wa and then allowed his scuppers to drag his shell away as well.

"How did you know?"

"Know what, Capítän?"

"How'd you know what to fix?"

"I created a dish suited to my diner, not my own glory."

"Simple fare for a simple tender of vegetables, eh?"

"Precisely. It is not the Great One's fault," Jean-Wa explained. "It is too long he's been without a proper audience—a problem

I have recently faced," he said with a softened tone. "When he finally had someone to cook for, he let his excitement get the better of him. He was carried away, that is all."

Garrand grasped his chef with both arms and fixed him with his full attention. "Well done, my friend. You have done yourself, the ship, and all her crew proud."

"Capítän, thank you. You are very kind. But it is as I have always said, no? It all starts with the food, yes? All with the food."

18

CITY OF GHOSTS

GARRAND STEPPED UP TO THE TREMENDOUS DOOR WITH
trepidation. He could see shadows moving beyond the milky
translucence. Hazy shapes shifted across the field of view. "I
have a bad feeling about this."

"Now what?" Helen asked.

"What if they don't honor their end?"

"*They?* I thought it was a single entity, a 'him,' an 'it,' a ghost."

"It is, but there could be more. Think he's the only one
locked up in there?" Garrand asked.

"Oh great."

"It was more a general reference to the ubiquitous *they*," he
muttered pressing his face up against the glazing. It was hard

to see what was going on inside, but *something* was happening. *They* were busy.

Helen was still pondering the ghost situation. "You didn't say anything about more ghosts—how are you going to threaten incorporeal beings? It's not like they have the same fears as the living."

"I shouldn't have to threaten anybody; we made a deal, and I won."

"You mean Jean-Wa won," she corrected.

Garrand chuckled under his breath. He knew that Helen was growing comfortable around him once more, for she was growing increasingly affectionate—and increasingly irritating. "Whatever. They'd just better honor their end."

"Hey, it was your idea to challenge his greatness, Senii Vilne."

Jean-Wa, who insisted on being present for the opening of the Archives, rolled gingerly forward on his serving cart. "Capítän, the Chief assures me that Senii Vilne Markks will uphold the honor of his word."

"We'll see about that," Garrand murmured. "You said yourself he was petulant. No one likes to lose."

"Ah, but Capítän, for him it was not a loss, but a gain! What did he have to lose, eh? Access to a vault with which he has grown bored? In your boastful challenge, you offered him a new recipe. For a chef, a new recipe is a gift sent from the great beyond." All six of the art's arms swept upward in punctuation.

As if one cue, the door split open with a glass-on-glass screech that made Alexander's ears shoot up. The cub pressed his head against Garrand's knee to shut out the noise. The twin halves of the glazed door rolled back into the walls, revealing a great, darkened space. Dozens of scuppers rushed back and forth just inside the doorway, as if the curtain had been lifted on the play a few moments too soon. A half dozen still spun in mad little circles, bumping between each other as they polished the floor. One scupper sidled up to Garrand's boot and reached out to snip at his laces with three legs.

Garrand bopped it with the toe of his other boot and the little machine retreated hastily. The rest finished their chores and followed it into the shadows, leaving a marble floor polished to a high gloss. The black and white interlocking shapes of the floor reflected a pale glow and he glanced upward. Great strands of the golden lights that they'd found in the antechamber were strung in fantastic webs that stretched away into the darkness. The twisting fibers suffused the beginning warmth of light, but even in the partially lit shadows it was clear that the room was quite enormous.

Garrand stepped over the threshold, and entered the Archive. His boots clicked on the smooth stone, the sound causing more of the scuppers to stop working and scramble out of sight. Helen, Bailey, Jean-Wa, Sid and Alexander followed him as the draped filaments exploded with radiance, transforming the Archive from gloom to glory. The intricate loops of feathery material billowed down from inverted spires like the largest chandeliers in existence.

The last of the scuppers darted away as Garrand walked deeper into the interior. The first forty meters of the room was filled with rows of tables, desks, and other horizontal surfaces. Each table was a different height, and many of the desks had unusual indentations and slots, though there was uniformity to the length and style of all the designs. Garrand passed by the tables built to human scale and stopped in front of one that came up to his chest. Semi-circular indentations were cut out on all four sides. He positioned himself in one of the slots; the table came up to his armpits. He rested his arms flat on the surface of the richly oiled wood.

"What do you make of this, Bailey?"

His first mate walked around the far end of the broad table, one hand tracing the edges with delicate precision. "Both the Xensul and Migontus were endowed with legs that would be considered quite long," the art said. "Thus, the height of the table. However, their forelimbs were considerably shorter by comparison. I would say that this table would suit their anatomy with a degree of comfort."

Garrand stretched his hands toward the oblong lumps in the center of the table, but despite the benefit of the indention, was still unable to reach. "Easier to get at the controls, huh?"

"Precisely." The artificial walked down one aisle. "And I would say that this table would cater to the needs of a T'chell, and this one to an Ikuil or maybe a Larken."

Garrand strained to reach the lumps. "I wonder how you turn these things on?"

"Perhaps if you used a table more suited to your modest proportions…"

"What fun is that?"

Bailey stopped at a shorter table and passed his hand over one of the inviting controls. One by one, narrow cylinders rose up from the center of the table.

"Wait," Garrand exclaimed. "How'd you do that?"

Bailey walked over to the next table to show him, but it proved unnecessary. Finger-thin cylinders were arising from all the previously flush tabletops.

In one glorious moment, the tips of each of the now fully extended cylinders brightened to a deep reddish hue. The tubes produced bright ringlets of light angled in such a manner as to not be distracting to patrons. The tables were now awash in radiance, the fine grains of the wood gleaming with an almost liquid sheen.

"Lamps," Garrand said. He stared at the little green cubes and nodes that had risen up from the middle of his table. A bright capsule rose well above the other controls, the top splitting into eight pieces and opening like the petals of a metallic flower. He frowned and scratched the stubble on his chin. He walked between a row of tables toward the middle of the room.

Odd kiosks were clustered in semi-circular arcs further in, and as more lights winked into existence, multiple levels could be discerned further on, with suspended stairways and ramps leading to separate wings apart from the main floor.

"Captain," Bailey said, "the energy spike just took a leap off the scale." A groaning whine thrummed up through the marble as a reactor powered to life somewhere below.

At a table off to one side of the room, a sparkle of light caught Garrand's attention. He wheeled around as light sparked from the center of an open capsule. With a crackle of static discharges and a crimson flash of light, a holo image sputtered to life. Bathed in an emerald glow, the figure stretched up and cracked its back before settling back to a normal standing position. It patted its holo robes and took a look around.

Three more holos sparked and wheezed into existence in different locations and then with another floor shaking groan, holos began winking on all over the room. The holo standing on the nearest table turned to face them, the bearded face distinctly humanoid.

The holo cleared his voice. "Ahem. Grick un cavai luu t'ck viti emmo…"

Garrand glanced at Bailey.

"He said, 'please select language,' I believe, Captain."

"Ai, Strahlinveka," the holo said in the same thick accent. "Ase?"

The holo was human looking, but elsewhere the holos took on a wide variety of shapes and forms. Garrand recognized some, couldn't place others. Each seemed to be wearing some version of the robes that the nearest had on — to whatever degree their physique could accommodate a 'robe.' Some sort of archival uniform no doubt.

Each holo called out a greeting as it was awakened and then turned to look around its table to find who had asked for its services. Most seemed surprised to find the room nearly deserted.

"Tu és hruni lak?"

"Maik ki'ya tchuet vis-ta ller…"

"How may I be of help?"

"Grick un cavai luu t'ck viti emmo."

Voices called out from around the room in dozens of tongues. After untold years of silence, the Archive was active once more.

Helen turned slowly around in wonderment, trying to take in the whole spectacle. "Wow. I thought it was just going to be one surly old man in a dusty library."

Sid had his paws up on a medium-sized table and was poking his nose closer to the foot of one of the holos. The holo pulled up the hem of his robe and tried to back away from the panda, but of course, was stuck in place by the limitations of his capsulated projector.

"Are they just re-creations of some sort?" Helen asked. "Data-core projections, like a virtual archivist?"

"I don't think so," Garrand said thoughtfully. He walked around a table peering up at the emerald projection of a T'chell standing in the middle. The holo creature turned to follow his progress, eyes staring gently down at him. "If that were the case, they would all be uniform, don't you think? Why go to the trouble of programming in dozens of varieties?"

"Kriek el søj binghe, da traeki tom?" the T'chell asked.

"Strahlinveka," the bearded holo said from the next table. "Try Strahlinveka, Ukii."

The T'chell bobbed its head in acknowledgment and said in its stuttering fashion: "How help you may we?"

"Your syntax — it is all wrong, old fellow," the bearded holo clucked. He looked to Bailey and shrugged modestly. "It's been quite some time, you see."

Garrand continued around the table, still talking to Helen. "No, I think these are holo ghosts. Real people trapped here by the Archive, like Senii Vilne."

"You can drop the 'holo,' old boy," the bearded one said to Garrand. "Just ghost will do, if you must. Though it's a bit rude if you ask me. Don't see us calling you 'meat.'"

Garrand stopped and fixed an eye on the holo. After a moment he bowed gracefully. "A thousand pardons, sir. We meant no disrespect."

"No need for apologies, that's quite all right," the man said, though he was obviously pleased that he had gotten one.

"It's like a city of ghosts," Helen murmured as she walked down the rows.

With nothing better to do, the holo ghosts turned and watched her as she passed. More lights and more holos sprang into existence further down the room and on all the elevated levels.

"It's absolutely tremendous."

"Apparently Senii Vilne decided to crank up the whole works," Garrand said.

Jean-Wa rolled up to a table with a short, squat little archivist. Two green hands emerged from the big sleeves of the ghost's robes and the webbed fingers drummed back and forth like a steeple. A pair of eyes rolled around to look at the artificial.

"Eie chie viex grr ta-ley?"

"Good day to you, too," Jean-Wa said. "Initiate search. Consumption, foods, Wabila culture, stimulants. Index ceremonies. Index Wabi-sabi. Execute."

"One moment please," the ghost burped. It continued to drum its fingers together, but faster now. "Ah yes. Very good. Wabi-sabi. Here it is. I can help you citizen, but if you'd like a more complete index or a more thorough dialogue on the subject, you might wish to visit Kerkin Paule Vasto. He's the resident culinary expert, and, you're in luck here—he's a bit of a buff on ceremonies, too."

"Location please," Jean-Wa asked.

"Table one oh nine, recreational pastimes, east wing."

Jean-Wa snorted. "*Recreational pastimes*? Humph."

The ghost gurgled out a laugh. "Another chef, eh? I didn't name the section, friend. Just follow the floor markers." Soft green neo markers shone on the floor, stretching down one aisle.

"Good day, sir," Jean-Wa said as he snapped his arms to his side and lurched off down the row.

Leave it to Jean-Wa to find exactly what he was looking for right off the bat, Garrand mused. "So much for figuring out how to handle the interface," he chuckled.

"You just going to let him wander off?" Helen asked.

"Stop him from finding out everything he ever wanted to know about the *shai* ceremony?" Garrand asked incredulously. "No way." He glanced over at the giant panda who was still sniffing the holo. "No smell, huh?"

Sid sat back part ways and looked up at the ghost on his table. "Strahlinvek," he grumbled. "Search," he said in a flat tone, mimicking the *thola*. "Bamboo."

"That's a bit broad there, citizen. Care to narrow the parameters a bit?" the holo asked politely.

Sid clucked his tongue against the roof of his mouth, thinking. "Indigenous strains on this world. Possible locations and current forecast for yields."

"Hmm, that's a little better. Let's see... bamboo. Ah, yes. Here we go." Three little nodes popped up from the surface of the table and new images sprang up. A field of bamboo waved in a stiff breeze in a mountain pass. A text description scrolled next to the holo image. The next holo was a static blur.

A separate voice said, "Please choose level of rudimentary information. Juvenile, adult, or scientific."

"Sorry about that," the ghost said. "Not quite sure if you're full-grown or not. You want a quick overview, or a full history of the agricultural significance of 'bamboo?'"

Sid looked over at Garrand who shrugged at him. "Just ask him what you want. He'll lead you through it. You don't have to be so formal like Jean-Wa. It'll probably gear itself to whatever you need."

"Hmm, I'm not getting any response from agricultural affairs. That's odd." The ghost looked over at the next table. "Hello, Kim? What's the story over at Planetary Resources? I'm not reading a crop report listing for—well now, that can't be right! For 532 years? I've heard they're falling behind over there, but this is ridiculous."

The ghost at the next table frowned. "What's that now? That can't be right. I just pulled a soy report for the southern plains for a young man just last week, and it was current."

A woman on a table two rows over piped up: "Maybe it's a glitch with the reset. Chronometers could be off."

"Well that's ridiculous," the first ghost said. "Five hundred years out of whack. That just can't be."

The skin tingled at the back of Garrand's neck and goose flesh popped up all the way down his forearms. He walked over to Helen and grasped her shoulder from behind. "They don't know," he whispered in her ear.

She reached her hand across her chest and laced her fingers over his hand on her shoulder. "How can that be?"

"No one told them," he said.

Helen looked over her shoulder at him with big, moist eyes.

"They must have no sense of the passage of time when they're off. Five minutes, 500 years—there's no difference."

There was a murmur that was sweeping around the room as the ghosts talked amongst each other.

"Say there, old boy," the bearded ghost asked Garrand. "Do you know anything about the reset that happened yesterday?"

"Umm, yesterday?"

"Yes, you know, to bring the new reactors on line. They never shut us down except for that. Maybe once a decade or so. Technology being what it is, they always seem to make refinements in those engines. You can't possibly have not heard, it was in all the dailies."

"You just stay on all the time otherwise?"

"Goodness, you are a little thick aren't you?"

"Dylan Grier! Of all the rude behavior," the woman at the next table admonished him. "Have you ever thought that he might be an off-worlder?"

"Oh, my," Dylan said, stroking his beard. "I never thought of that. I mean, after all, how often does that happen?" He looked down at Garrand. "What with the protocols, our seclusion and all," he explained.

"He must be somebody important then," the woman urged him sternly.

"Oh, goodness. Well then, I must apologize sir." The ghost bowed.

"I apologize for him as well," the woman said.

"And I as well," the T'chell added.

"Me too," the little green creature burped.

Garrand was suddenly the center of attention.

"We get a little discombobulated after a reset," the woman explained.

"Yes. And to answer your question, we are always 'left on.' After all, the information never stops coming in," he said nervously. "Besides, old Senii Vilne would never let us rest. Not since he became Chief Archivist."

Anxious laughter echoed around the nearby tables.

"Say you're the only ones here this morning. The doors should have opened three hours ago. Where is everyone?"

"Was there a problem with the reset?"

Garrand shifted uncomfortably. Helen shrugged at him, when he looked for help.

"Oh dear, there was a problem, wasn't there?"

"Sir, you must tell us."

A troubled murmur rippled down the aisles.

"I'm not sure how to tell you this," Garrand began reluctantly, "but I'm afraid you've been 'turned off' longer than just overnight."

"Oh that can't be," the T'chell ghost said. "Senii would never do that to us—not without telling us at least."

"How much longer?" the woman asked.

The T'chell still prattled on nervously. "I mean I know there has been pressure to shut down some of the repositories with the coming evacuations and all, but please. They would have *told* us."

"Senii would have informed us if they were cutting back, wouldn't he?"

"*How much longer?*" the woman pressed.

Garrand pulled out a chair and sat down. "Years," he said wearily. "Hundreds of years."

A stunned silence fell over the holo ghosts.

The T'chell moaned and grasped his small head. "This is why Senii doesn't like us asking questions of the patrons."

Some of the ghosts seemed to agree, but they still stared anxiously at Garrand.

"Okay, I'll tell you what... Dylan, is it? We'll reverse the roles here for a few minutes. You ask the questions and I'll try to supply the answers, okay?"

"Ah, good." The ghost knelt down part ways. "Senii doesn't like us asking too many questions. But if you say it's okay, then he can't say anything."

"Well?"

"What year is it?" the T'chell blurted out. A murmur of nervous agreement followed.

Garrand sighed; there was no way to soften it. "By the Collistas Dynastic Calendar it's 35,355. You can probably convert that to whatever is relevant here—"

A collective gasp shot around the room as the information spread.

"My goodness. Then we've been down for..."

"532 years," Dylan said.

"It doesn't even seem like a day."

"That can't be right."

"I'm afraid it is," Garrand said.

"Oh dear," Dylan said.

"What is it?" the T'chell asked.

"He's right. Check your backlog files."

Another chorus of groans surfaced from different tables.

"I have 3 billion backlogged entries under 'food.'"

"Cheplus."

"Four trillion hits on my cartographic updates," another groaned.

Curses in dozens of languages began to ring out in the room.

"Now look what you've started," Helen said.

"Someone had to tell them," Garrand said defensively. "Old Senii Vilne told them they were going down for a routine reset and he left them off for half a millennia."

"But why?"

"Conserve power? I don't know. Sounds like the last of the Migontus were leaving about then, shutting things down before they left?"

Many of the holos were whispering amongst themselves in a host of tongues. Dylan looked down at him. "Thank you for your frankness, sir. I suppose we have you to thank for our being turned back on."

"Is that true?" the T'chell chirped.

"It is," Garrand said.

"You must have a specific information request," Dylan said. "How may I be of service?"

A deep sense of relief flooded over Garrand and a slow smile surfaced. He closed his eyes and rubbed his stubbly face, whispering thanks to Sid and his incredible gift, to Jean-Wa's genius in knowing just what to fix a backwater vegetable grower. *One step closer.* The Archive was his for the asking. *One step closer to recovery. One step closer to redemption.* He opened his eyes and leaned forward. "I need information concerning the Collistas Dynasty."

"Historical references?"

"No, current operations. Military personnel records of say, the last five years. Carinaena's Shell specifics. There'll be a reference to the Core Worlds and Daulinbêres, but I'm more interested in assignments in the Shell, specifically the Wyxian Proctorialship."

"Hmm. Norton Heywood handles all Collistas related input. He's probably the biggest expert on that empire."

"I need service records for Guardian caste members. And ship registries, too," he added.

"Imperial ship registry is Dia Prescot," the ghost said. "Norton will know better than I about caste records. You'd best start there. Everything that comes in concerning the Collistas Dynasty gets tagged to him. He shunts it off to his team."

"Where is he?"

"Just follow the neo markers—blue ones that is. He's over by north wing, with the important stuff," Dylan said with a laugh. "I'll let him know you're coming."

Garrand stood. "Thank you."

"Wait," the ghost called. "What is your name?"

Garrand didn't see any danger in revealing his identity. They would probably piece it together easily once the ship was detected leaving and they looked for cross-references. "Garrand Médeville."

The ghost bowed with a willowy shimmer. "Well, thank you citizen Médeville. I am pleased to make your acquaintance. But if you'll pardon me, I have a bit of catching up to do."

Garrand nodded: "Of course." He looked to Sid and jerked his head. "Come on. Let's go find our Thief."

"What do you want me to do?" Helen asked.

Garrand stopped. Could he ask her to do something important again? Could he trust her? She looked at him eagerly. His mind rang with the memory of seeing all her defensive measures stacked up inside *Destiny's Needle*, untouched. But his heart ached with something else. He remembered falling asleep beneath the purple moons, his head cradled in her lap, her fingers caressing his hair. *Second chances... third, fourth? How many do you get? You've used up quite a few yourself, old man. All that doesn't matter though. Only the tribe matters. We must rescue the tribe before it all tumbles out of control.*

He gauged her carefully and made a decision. "You see if you can track down the location of the tribe. I doubt you'll find anything, but maybe Barrett slipped up somewhere, left a clue. Use your imagination. See what you can come up with."

Helen's face brightened, and her chest heaved. Garrand's acceptance was a bracing relief.

Garrand hurried down the aisle, but called back over his shoulder: "This Captain of the Gokazoku probably knows everything, but anything we can find out on our own will help—particularly with the interpretations."

Helen stood watching the man and panda walk deeper into the Archives for a few moments, hands on her hips in thoughtful repose. Alexander came up and rubbed his nose along her knee. She reached down to scratch his ear.

"Let's see what we can find, Alexai," she murmured.

She pulled out a chair at the T'chell's table and let the cub hop onto her lap.

"Initiate search. Dr. Beh'ln Tchelakov. Research. Sartographic technology, theoretical advances, implementation. Subcategory: Nralda Keiretsu, fourth tier Director Carrelle Darstin, research and development, current projects. Primary focus: Tchelakov creatures, current whereabouts, speculation. Begin."

Helen leaned back in her chair and waited as the ghost drummed his fingers together in concentration.

❖ ❖ ❖

THE GHOST OF NORTON HEYWOOD STOOD BEAMING WARMLY atop the table at the end of the blue neo markers. Thankfully his table was built more or less to human proportions, as an expert on the Collistas' Dynasty should, Garrand supposed.

"Welcome Garrand Médeville, welcome," the ghost effused. "Dylan tells me that we have you to thank for this grand resurgence. We're all so pleased to be getting back up to speed. So much has happened in a mere 500 years! I'm almost back up to date, myself. A few more minutes now and I'll be able to tell you all you want to know."

Garrand pulled out a chair and sat. Sid walked once around the table before settling down next to the human.

"There now. What can I help you with?" the ghost asked. "Caste records, is it? And ship registries?"

"I'm looking for a member of the Gokazoku Kaigi, a woman. Captain of the Guard for a Vice Proctor in the Wyxian Proctorialship."

"Hmm. Hellius Barrett's neck of the woods, eh?"

"And a ship registered perhaps in her name, or in the caste's name. A small personal sloop, chrysalis-shaped." He tried to picture the slender vessel that he'd seen as *Destiny's Needle* had swung away from the Imperial frigate and the Gamborian Jave' o Wars. Uh, maybe Troat or Di'grietn design. I can give you more details if necessary."

"One moment please. Accessing."

"I'll need complete service records and most recent port of call. You may have to search every port authority core in the Wyxian volume to find it."

"That won't be a problem," Heywood said. "Ah, here we are. Gokazoku Kaigi records. Core assignments, no. Commendations, no. History and impact on Collistas affairs, hmm. Here we go: assignments to Carinaena's Shell. Okay, Wyxian Proctorialship, Captain of Lord Hellius Barrett's Imperial Guard..." The ghost glanced down at Garrand. "Current one?"

"Yes."

"Here she is. Vailetta Strom. Born 35,328 on Daulinbêres..." The information appeared on a holo display along with a small likeness.

Garrand studied the image—it was the fisher girl from Eemon Nores, the deadly looking warrior who'd had him dead-to-rights aboard the frigate. "That's her."

"Hmm. There's a few discrepancies here in her early files. I'm getting two listings under education—and several annotations." The ghost frowned. "I have so much to catch up on—I'm afraid I haven't had the chance to ferret out conflicting pieces of datum."

"It doesn't matter," Garrand said. "I am trying to locate here current whereabouts in real time. Her past is of no concern to me."

"Ahh... thus the ship registry. Very good, very good. You'd make a splendid archivist. Let's see. There is indeed a ship registered to one Vaietta Strom, Captain of the Imperial Guard. The *Lolovanti*, a Hurelein sloop—you were close on that one—and its last port of call was... ah, yes. Wyx itself. Underwent some major repairs. Thurston generator, inertial damper, and primary reactor coil all replaced—two and a half tonnes of armor plate removed..." the ghost tapped his chin as he scrolled down the list. "Saw some heavy damage recently. A battle perhaps?"

"Yes, that fits."

"Hmm. By this account, the repairs have not been completed." He looked at Garrand. "The ship is still on Wyx."

"What about the woman? Has she been reassigned?"

"Hmm. Captain Strom, Captain Strom..."

Garrand felt his fists tighten. His hands were cold.

"Ah, here we are. New entry. There's a ship departing Wyx with diplomatic status. Standard transport, blah, blah, blah. But under the passenger manifest there is a 'Vailetta Strom, special envoy to the ambassador.'"

Garrand edged forward. "What's the listed destination?"

"New Haivello."

Garrand looked at Sid triumphantly. *By Haven, they had it!*

"What's the estimated date of arrival?"

"Listed at four days hence."

Garrand tried to do some rough astrogation in his head. "We could make it," he thought aloud. "A little late, but we could make it." He looked at Sid. "Will she still be there? Are we on the Path if we head there now?"

The panda had a dreamy look in his eyes. "I believe so, Captain."

Garrand slapped the table and stood up quickly. "Go get Helen, see what she's found. Tell her we're lifting as soon as possible."

"Congratulations, Garrand. You've successfully interpreted a dream and applied that knowledge. You've found the Thief of Ships." Sid beamed proudly at his pupil. The *Griffin* had unraveled a fated event and explained it *before it happened*. It was what the tribe so desperately needed. A *Jhei Pōloc* to interpret the dreams and comment on the Path ahead of time.

"Yeah, now we just have to get to her in time."

Sid blinked sleepily: "In time?"

"She hangs by a slender thread, remember?"

"Of course. I will go tell Helen."

Garrand turned and looked up at the expectant ghost. "You have done me a great service, Heywood."

The ghost smiled back warmly. "We are pleased to be of service, sir. Thank you for convincing Senii Vilne to reactivate us."

"Well, don't let him turn you off for any 'reactor repair' this time."

The ghost chuckled. "Never you fear, citizen. The Great Senii Vilne Markks has some explaining to do. I think we'll be on for a long time now."

"Good," he turned to leave.

"I'll keep an eye out for information concerning you Garrand Médeville. We all will!"

Garrand stopped, a little shiver creeping up his spine. An entire planetary Archive keeping tabs on him…

"Come back and see us when you've found this Vailetta Strom. Come back so that we may have a real chat."

"As you will."

"Very good, then. Dragon's speed to you, sir!" the ghost effused, using the Collistas colloquialism.

Garrand considered this as he trotted back down the rows of desks. It must be lonely to be a ghost, and lonelier still being a ghost in a deserted city on a forgotten planet. He spoke into his comtab. "Bailey, get back to the ship. Get her prepped to lift. Make sure the pandas and Helen and Jean-Wa are aboard — you're in charge."

"We're leaving soon?"

"We're leaving *now*," Garrand said.

"You've found her?"

Garrand smiled. "That I have. Now go, and don't call me until you're ready to seal the primary lock."

"What course should I lay in?"

"Serpentine course out of this system — then best speed to New Haivello."

Helen stood up nervously as he approached. "What is it?"

"We're leaving," he said.

"Leaving? I was just starting to like it here."

"Well don't worry, you can visit again sometime. We've been invited back."

GRIFFIN TERMINOLOGY

Alexander: giant panda cub, third generation member or the Tchelakov Tribe.

Archiva: also known as Mardell's world. Location: unknown. After the destruction of twelve key data repositories during the War of the Three in 29,182 in which the entire ancestral records of deeds and fiefs for five thousand systems was lost, the network of information was deemed too important to lie 'scattered across the Shell like diamonds for the taking.' A central archival planet was deemed the solution, with a planet-wide system of data storage—a backup repository for the knowledge off an entire empire. The location was chosen in secret and the entire network was shunted through the planet's datacores where physical copies were recorded and stored in vast repositories. So vast was this archive that it became synonymous with the planet itself. The planet was discovered and later sacked (some say destroyed) in the time of Mardell III.

Armor Drip: versatile field armor developed by Pavelle Nest. Transported in liquid form and poured into a variety of molds on site, cerafiber bonds harden in under a minute after catalyst is added. Gives added mobility to light armor divisions.

Arnas, San Barrilito: battalion commander, 41st Imperial Marines; Shock Trooper.

Art Wars: a conflict that arose when the Sullust movement sought to curtail the rapid proliferation of Free Will artificials, specifically machines indistinguishable from humans. Fueled by fear and religious fervor, the push for curtailment quickly expanded into a genocidal Jihad that lasted from 35,110 until the Gelicus Art Convention in 35,307. Alternately known as the Gai'han Jihad, depending on one's point of view, the resulting conflagration plunged much of the galaxy into turmoil (see: Jihad, Gai'han, Free Will artificials, Sullust Movement)

Artificial: any of a wide class of mobile mechanical constructs possessing intelligence, self-awareness and the ability to learn through experience.

Bailey: Krellian Artificial, Varsis model VL1357-B8, incept date unrecorded. Master of Arms, Caius Minor, from 35,329 to 35,337. Assigned to Santos II as personal assistant to Captain of the Guard, Garrand Ai'Gonet Médeville in 35,337. Granted Free Will in 35,345. First mate on *Destiny's Needle*.

Barrelian Corvette: Highly-maneuverable armed escort ship, smaller than a frigate, ranging in length from 100-150 meter; often used in conjunction with a larger fleet of vessels. Barrelian designs have been manufactured for over 700 years.

Barrett, Hellius: An ambitious Vecklorn who inherited his father's seat in the Royal Regincira and was later appointed High Magistrate in the Emperor's Court, he was a trusted confidante who lost favor after rumors of an illicit affair with the Empress surfaced. "Banished" to the political chaos of Carinaena's Shell, where his charms could not impress Chyrella, he labored in relative obscurity for some time. The assassination of ruling Proctor Lekkson Nesbit elevated Barrett into control of the Shell's third largest Proctorialship. Commonly referred to as Lord Barrett (whether it be in reference to Vecklornian nobility, or claimed in ancient Caluras rite is unknown), his title is officially Vice Proctor of Wyx.

Bordëgian Academé: ancient school of preparation for service in the Imperial Navy.

Brotherhood of the Princes of Blood: Order within the Imperial Guard. Founded 34,512 on Daulinbêres (see also: Griffin).

Byrethylen Wraith: race of large (4 meter tall), amorphous, multi-tendriled vaporous energy manifestations. Wraiths prey on the neurological fears of their victims, manifesting themselves as the delusional images found in their victims' minds. Wraiths feed on all energy sources, but prefer the cerebrum's neural energy. Wraiths were once the scourge of the Byrethyl System, wiping out whole planets and rendering them barren and lifeless.

By the Barthsa: Dalis colloquialism; mild curse.

Carinaena's Shell: (Car-in-ae-na) the massive outer ring of stars that forms a donut-shaped shell around the central Core of the Gli-Dawun Galaxy. Named for the Lallalopsle ship Carinaena's Hope whose quantum drive failed at the edge of the galactic Core, and thus became the first "seeder" ship of colonists (see Dolke's Historical tome "Carinaena's Fate: the Colonization of Chance").

Carrack Class Cruiser: large, fast, heavily armored and gunned warship; Imperial classification of Battle Cruiser, top of the line capital ship.

Cerasteel: ceramic steel formed on site by combining polymer-bonded dryexcellon powder into molten steel. After cooling, the steel is superheated through conduction, bonding the dryexcellon and steel at a molecular level.

Cha'halen: rank in the military hierarchy of the Gambor; roughly equivalent to the Imperial rank of major.

Cheplus: Strahlinvek colloquialism; moderate curse.

Clipscanner: miniature (20 cm x 12 cm) personal datacore composed of digital reader, processing unit, fingertap board and display housed within a slim impact casing; noted for its versatility and interface capabilities.

Clipscan Visor: data relay that partially blinds user's real-time vision; primarily intended for use by artificials.

Coil: rechargeable storage field that uses magnetic coils to safely store massive amounts of charged ions. Capable of efficiently storing vast amounts of energy in a small physical space. Primary source of power for all energy dependent devices and engines.

Collistas Dynasty: (co-least-us) largest autonomous governing body in the Gli-Dawun Galaxy, ruled by a member of the Collistas family for 47 generations. The empire spawned from this stability now envelops much of the galaxy's core.

Core: (also: "Core worlds," "The Core") the densely populated center of the Gli-Dawun Galaxy; common designation for the vast volume of star systems currently under the domain of the Collistas Imperial Dynasty.

Coryl-Tuluyt Picket: escort warship of the fastest class; Imperial classification for its top of the line interdictors and blockade runners.

Crevlin, Jonathon: MSD, Imperial surgeon stationed on Wyx. Chief medical officer assigned to the Tchelakov 37 development team.

Cronix: a design line of datacores, a product of Si Bell Logiks, a proprietary arm of the Si Bell Keiretsu; Cronix datacores are commonly considered the industrial standard in Carinaena's Shell.

Dailyern Green: bitter, slightly caustic alcoholic concoction formed from the lesser of the two saps from the Yourb trees on Dailyern (the other, red sap, is a fatal poison) and Kakin malt. A drink favored by the vegrauts who conquered Dailyern six centuries ago, their strong constitutions and thick abdominal lining able to handle the toxins. The two ingredients are unstable when combined, thus the drink is served in two equal portions and it is left to the patron to mix them.

Dalintus Commission: formed by the Gelicus Art Convention in 35,312, charged with the judgment of Free Will artificials—the Dalintus seal signifying the highest possible conditioning against taking a human life. Dalintus qualified artificials permitted to design and create Free Will artificials without human intervention.

Danelle: lieutenant in the Imperial Guard, Gokazoku Kaigi; currently assigned to Wyx, Carinaena's Shell, linguist.

Darstin, Carrelle: Director of Research and Acquisitions, Nralda Keiretsu. Seat on the Nralda High Board, 4th Tier. Responsible for funding and perpetuation of Beh'ln Tchelakov's research concerning the next evolution of the sartographic chip (see: Tchelakov Tribe).

Dasko, Lee: lieutenant in the Imperial Guard, Gokazoku Kaigi; currently assigned to Wyx, Carinaena's Shell, decryption specialist, 1st grade.

Datacore: programmable electromagnetic device that can store, retrieve, and process data; the heart of all mechanical thinking mechanisms.

Datapad: any of a wide variety of specialized technical data readers; poor cousin of the clipscanner.

Daulinbêres: sixth planet in the Wopäs System, situated in a prime strategic location near the heart of the Gli-Dawun Galaxy; seat of the Imperial throne for 137 centuries.

Daurrian Shipyards: the vast Pragen spaceworks in high orbit off Bingham; the close proximity of the Hames asteroid belt for raw materials and the industrial processing complex on Bingham itself has made this yard one of the most efficient operations in the Shell, capable of turning out a full destroyer in under eight years.

Destroyer: very large, fast, heavily armored and gunned warship; a classification usually reserved for a fleet's largest and most advanced capital ships.

Destiny's Needle: modified medium cruiser designed by Garrand Ai'Gonet Médeville and built by Le'hadn Vercks in 35,347 for the express purpose of breaking the Talen quarantine on El Phobadia. Presented to Médeville by the Sandhalles Grip, Bestriyx Dagen, soon thereafter as a token of his esteem, in return for the rescue of his daughter. Subsequently played a principle role in the Tchelakov Revolt circa 35,355.

Drazon Vorge: refugee youth from Galipsus Minoirte; currently under the tutelage of Vice Proctor Barrett.

Dreadnaught: large, moderately armored and gunned warship; an older classification generally reserved for blockade interdictors and fleet escorts. Upgrades in quantum drive technologies have rendered many of the dreadnaught designs obsolete. Properly refit, dreadnaughts play an important role in many developing navies.

Dreighonäis: Tchelakov 37 colloquialism for dragons, which they refer to as "the serpents without a sea."

Dryexcellon: mineral ore principally mined in the Restepheron system and refined on planets throughout the Shell into highgrade fuels, powders and industrial byproducts (see: cerafiber, cerasteel).

E2: Eckreon 2; the Empire's top of the line massive datacore processor, integrating the latest sartographic series II technology with group "e" Cronix mainframes; used aboard all Carrack class vessels (see: sartograph).

Eckreon: a design line of Cronix datacores, the product of Si Bell Logiks, a proprietary arm of Si Bell Keiretsu; Cronix datacores are commonly considered the industrial standard in Carinaena's Shell.

Eemon Nores: icy seventh planet of the Niyl System, situated near the Krestyaninov Cluster.

El-Bouteran: only planet in the Pakken System, far removed from all major shipping routes in Carinaena's Shell.

Elytra: the anterior wings of Gamborian beetles that serve to protect the posterior pair of functional wings.

Exel: wild echrine of Maltus adapted for Se-faillus hunters on Letugia; sometimes kept as pets.

Fokathenais: deadly species of dragon; noted for their ferocity and intelligence. Adults can reach 20-25 meters in length.

Freetrader: colloquialism; broad term embracing what is in essence a wide variety of professions including (but not limited to) inter-system mercantile trading, freelance entrepreneurial merchandising, smuggling, and simple cargo hauling. Originally a term used to describe independent freelance entrepreneurs in early Colonial era, specifically the nine hundred year period that saw the Shell worlds successfully pioneered and settled (see: Great Diaspora). Working alone in single ships, Freetraders were an indispensable element of the colonization effort. The high risks and huge overhead involved in supplying hundreds of tiny colonies made it unprofitable to sustain and supply colonies on a corporate and/or commercial level. These entrepreneurs—private oneman operations flying single craft with low overhead—allowed colonies to flourish in their infant stages by bringing goods that could not be produced on fledgling worlds for decades. Private traders were colonists' lifeblood, shipping in needed commodities, spare parts, and resources in return for grains and foodstuffs for shipment offworld. Most Freetraders are thought of as colonial patriots of a sort. Without them, most colonies would have quickly failed and the Shell as we know it would not exist.

Free Will Artificial: a specialized class of mobile mechanical constructs possessing intelligence, self-awareness and the ability to learn through experience. Free Will arts are not designed with a specific underlying purpose. Without a rigorous code of conduct for higher functions, Free Will arts are left to choose their own course after inception. The Sullust movement sought to curtail the rapid proliferation of Free Will arts after the perfection of the indistinguishable-from-human designs. The resulting conflicts are alternately known as the Gai'han Jihad (see: The Purge) or the Art Wars (see: the Lashback). The 200-year upheaval plunged much of the galaxy into turmoil. Numerous commissions sprang up in the aftermath, attempting to regulate Free Will arts, and many prejudices still exist (see: Artificial).

Frigate: any of a broad variety of moderately armored and gunned warships, the classification of which differ widely from navy to navy. Historically: a moderate to large design; the workhorse of many a navy.

Gambor: race of large (3 meter tall) multi-limbed, smooth-shelled, winged beetles (sentient); home world of the Galzeki, tagged for garbage reclamation by Imperial Navy and site of 400-year-old civil war (see Po'tchantu's "Siege of Galzeki"). The Gambor have recently begun contracting their warrior services out to the Nralda Keiretsu in return for desperately needed munitions.

Gelicus Art Convention: contravened in 35,312, marking the official end of the Gai'han Jihad, its provisions forging an uneasy peace between the Gai'han Sullusts and the Free Will coalition lead by the Free Will artificial, Samuel. It's chief tenant: no machine was to be constructed indistinguishable from a human being. In compromise, the Sullusts lifted the death bounty placed on all Free Will artificials. Secondary precepts limited the creation of Free Will artificials: specifically, it was forbidden for artificials to create Free Will artificials (in essence procreate) without the Dalintus seal (see: Dalintus Commission).

Gokazoku Kaigi: Order within the Imperial Guard. Known as the "Brotherhood of the Silent Blade." Founded 34,819 on Daulinbêres.

Gravitic Repulsors: Fit beneath everything from cargo lighters to gunsleds to starships, Norgen generators project a harmonic field that negates the affects of gravity over a limited area focused in conical projections that dissipate over distance. The resulting gravitic null space creates buoyancy that is enhanced by standard field suspensors. The combined effect of the null space and the repulsor wave field is enough to allow most vessels, pallet, skimmers, and such to hover mid-air. In more elaborate configurations, they are enough to allow starships of massive tonnage to overcome the pull of planetary gravity wells and land and takeoff vertically.

Great Hall: Built 35,330 on Wyx; monument created to display the names of the fallen Imperial forces within the Wyxian Proctorialship.

Griffin: Collistas colloquialism; slang for Imperial Guardian, Griffin Order. Order within the Imperial Guard. Known as the "Brotherhood of the Princes of Blood." Founded 34,512 on Daulinbêres.

Gyropod: enclosed datastations typically found aboard military vessels, designed to insulate vital tech ensigns from the dangers of battle and aid their interface with the ship's datacore (see: Poddies).

Haven's End: Imperial colloquialism; mild curse derived from the infamous travails of Giin Bly Haven, officer in the Royal Regincira, whose life was ironically taken by the very men he risked everything to save.

Holocube: miniature holographic display unit roughly the size of an Imperial quantis. Projects a small static image of subject that can be viewed from all angles.

Holo Ghost: the emotional and neurological essence of a creature captured by electronic means and stored in a digital matrix much like a datacore. The mortal subject's neural activity and the brain's electro-chemical signature is transferred (either during the death throes, or soon after death) by electronic conductivity and hard wired into circuitry chips, much like the creation of an artificial. The imprint is stored in a Tarkanian containment field and is manifested as a hologram. The resultant "ghost" is cognizant and self-aware, many times with full memories and recollections intact, though the manifestation exists with a painful echo of former emotions. A common theological belief is that the souls of ghosts are suspended in K'ye, awaiting judgment.

Hurka-boy: Two-person, low altitude winged flying craft; used as versatile transportation in cities with a high degree of verticality, often used purchased in large numbers by taxi services.

Ident-link: mathematical symbol(s) or icon used to represent a person or artificial; any of a wide range of identifying markers imbedded or cosmetic; standard Imperial identification system.

Imperial Guard: For over 3 millennia, the Imperial Guard has protected the interests of the Imperial throne, specifically the well being of the Emperor and his highest Ambassadors (see: Proctors). The Guardian caste is one of the most ancient and revered schooling bodies in the Empire. The noble warriors within have sworn to honor the Emperor and uphold the sanctity of the realm. Each faction within the caste has its own Order, full of timeworn tradition and a legacy to uphold. New members of the guard are sworn into a particular order, whose tenets they must obey and traditions they most honor.

Jean-Wa: Do-lât Artificial, Preparation model D430, incept date unrecorded; six-armed master chef with detachable legs and wheels. Purchased by Garrand Ai'Gonet Médeville from the Baron Senn van Basel of Daruma.

Jhei Pōloc: Tchelakov 37 expression that translates into "the interpreter of dreams." The tribe believes they are fated to meet a human who will become their interpreter of dreams; this belief has become part of the tribe's Path of Fate.

Jihad: (ji-häd) a religious holy war; fanatical crusade for a principle or belief.

Jihad, Gai'han: (see also: Art Wars) the doomed crusade against Free Will artificials, humaniform mechanical sentients, sentient machines, and conscious datacores begun in 35,110 and concluded in 35,307. It's chief result: the disappearance of all indistinguishable-from-human artificials.

Ka'vaelus: Gambor warrior; Cha'halen first grade of the Vaelus burrow, Galzeki. Rumored to have personal ties with 4th tier Nralda Director of Acquisitions, Carrelle Darstin.

Keiltraoma: a state of conscious dreaming; the keiltraoma requires a mastery of the body's physiological and physical states, allowing the conscious awareness of the brain's unbidden neurological activity, specifically, the subconscious creativity know as dreams.

Kess: fourth planet in the Dell Transim system; site of Gort's Agro Supply.

K'iik Vla: idiomatic expression from the Lalen dialect; roughly: "The ability to survive at any cost." Often referred to as the third rule in Griffin Order doctrine.

Keiretsu: corporate entities that have bonded together in Carinaena's Shell for protection and profit—combining trade routes and resources to form interplanetary cartels complete with defense fleets. Some keiretsu control whole systems, having subjugated the populace through economic monopolies and trade embargoes. While avoiding outright war with the Collistas Dynasty, many keiretsu are involved in an escalating cold war with the Imperial Proctorialships in the Shell.

Krass: Fleet Sergeant, 41st Imperial Marines, 1st platoon; third squad leader, Shock Trooper, weapons specialist (2nd class), armorer's assist.

K'ye: the mythical "battleground of the gods," where the souls of the dead are said to be judged; purgatory.

Larkson Shield Generator: produces powerful resonating magnetic field capable of bending light around its focusing body. Used in conjunction with deflector arrays and an adequate system of null-dampers, the Larkson creates a viable protective field. Buffer coils store power bled from other ship systems and then feed pulses of energy to the shields' magnetic deflector fields. Energy that is not refracted or deflected is absorbed by null- dampers.

Leusta: giant panda, first generation member of the Tchelakov Tribe; Elder in the Tchelakov Tribe.

Lewg: lieutenant in the Imperial Guard, Gokazoku Kaigi; currently assigned to Wyx, Carinaena's Shell; master bladesman.

Lifter: huge obtuse transport shuttles, heavily shielded and fit with gigantic sublight reactors, but possessing no faster-than-light capability. Designed to safely and efficiently ferry cargo and men between planet surfaces and orbiting ships (see: Mules).

Lighter: mechanical construct of varying size fit with gravitic repulsors and possessing limited intelligence, designed to ferry cargo between vessels in docking bays.

Little Bit: Turkle Sphere II, model 339-74C, incept date 35,329; technical assist (modified) purchased by Garrand Ai'Gonet Médeville at the Syhan Fabrication Works on Tikus.

Lolovanti: light cruiser from the Daurrian Shipyards; Captain Vailetta Strom's personal vessel.

Lor Stanta Destroyer: warship of the largest and most heavily armed and armored class; Imperial classification of the largest capital ship currently in active service (700 meter).

Lyceum: large pavilion or open-aired amphitheater.

Magester, Urqual: Born 35,256; renowned stonecutter within the Wyxian Imperial Proctorialship; carves in the Great Hall.

Matrix: something within which something else originates or develops; material in which something is enclosed or embedded.

Médeville, Garrand Ai'Gonet: Freetrader, former Captain of the Imperial Guard, Griffin Order; purported leader of the Tchelakov Revolt.

Mules: Collistas colloquialism; slang for lifters.

Nesbit, Lekkson: Provost of Wyx and reigning Proctor of the Callus, Niramdi, and del'Trin system fiefs until his assassination in 35,347. Respected for his ability to create economic bridges between vastly different cultures. With the help of his ambitious vice proctor, Hellius Barrett, nurtured the Wyxian Proctorialship into one of the largest and richest Imperial fiefs in Carinaena's Shell.

New Haivello: 4th planet in the Skarsgård System; part of the Wyxian Imperial Proctorialship.

Niramdi System: minor star system in the Outer Reaches (II Gallen Wei); hidden staging area for Free Will resistance during the Gai'han Jihad (see: Thrassin, battle of).

Nralda: Keiretsu; one of the largest and most powerful operating in the Shell.

Offloader: mechanical construct of limited intelligence designed to remove cargo from vessels quickly and efficiently.

Orae'teleute: "Until the end is near"; Imperial battle cry.

Path of Fate: an expression unique to the Tchelakov Tribe; a series of events that are destined to transpire. The Path of Fate is a map of something that does not yet exist, but will inevitably come to pass (see: seitparen). To the Tchelakov Tribe, the future is fluid and ever-changing, with some paths more likely to occur than others, and some events almost impossible to avoid. The Path of Fate is the culmination of all dreams and all variables, the part of time that will come to be known as 'the past.' Seeing the Path before it becomes the past is the tribe's legacy, a blessing so coveted that it threatens to destroy them.

Phase Emitter: general diagnostic tool for setting correct power configurations on coil-based reactors and generators. Uses pulses of energy to calibrate null dampers.

Picket Cutter: small-to-medium sized, extremely fast and lightly armored warship; primarily used as lead escort ships, blockade runners, and strike interdictors.

Plascrete: a lightweight, strong building material formed by mixing industrial grade polymer plastic aggregates with cementing agents and catalysts that cause the plastics to set and bind the entire mass. Can be poured on-site making it useful in fortifications and mobile battle situations.

Poddies: Collistas colloquialism; derogatory reference to pod-tech ensigns.

Pod-tech: Collistas colloquialism; tech ensigns who spend much of their time suspended in gyropods.

Praetor: Imperial magistrate, adjucatal overlord, ranking below a consul.

Proctor: the chief magistrate of an Imperial fiefdom.

Proctorialship: the principle sphere of influence or domain of specific Imperial fiefs created during the Great Shell Diaspora. Proctorialships are doled out to lords and barons within the Imperial Court as the Emperor sees fit. The relative domain of the fief may be expanded in the Emperor's name at the ruling proctor's discretion.

Provost: Imperial planetary governor.

Quantis: circular trebian alloy coin. Five Imperial credits. Accepted coin of the realm in most systems along with local currency. Although credit chits are more widely used, some small denomination coins are more efficient for limited purchases, such as food and beverage.

Quantum Drive: crucial middle element of all interstellar ships' three-tiered drive system; sub-light engines propel ships up to the brink of light speed (speeds and acceleration dependent upon design, size, efficiency, etc.), the quantum drive breaches the light barrier, lifting the ship into quantum space, and the light engines propel the ship through quantum space itself.

Reactor Core: chamber that powers all sub-light and quantum drives. The chamber is filled with cryxthlen gas at extremely high pressure. This gas, through which a series of directed neutron sparks pass, contains charged particles accelerated by the power field of the coils that wrap around the reactor core. As the field oscillates, it accelerates the charges back and forth, making them collide energetically with the cryxthlen atoms. Many of the gas atoms are actually torn apart by the collisions, yielding even more charged particles to collide with cryxthlen atoms, creating an exponentially expanding energy source. The cryxthlen acts as the fuel source that is slowly depleted as some atoms are not spilt by the collisions in the core, and thus are converted directly to energy without yielding any new charged particles.

Roto'mo: Single-person, low altitude flying craft, featuring a turbine-based rotor mounted overhead.

Sartograph: highly specialized mathematical construct utilizing Dr. Sartok's revolutionary chip and representing a quantum breakthrough in 4th dimension physics decay. Used to create time-based models which accurately forecast the relative probability of any given circumstance; the visual output of such a projection.

Sartok: probability chip capable of assessing statistical future outcomes through rigorous analysis of past and present conditions (see: Sartograph); named after its creator, Naius Packden Sartok, theoretical mathematician and founder of the Seilhenn School of Advanced Logistics.

Scupper: non-sentient tech art designed by Mardell the 4th; noted for unique spider design.

Seitparen: an expression unique to the Tchelakov Tribe; an event or series of events that are unavoidable; something that is destined to happen. The seitparen are a series of events seen ahead of time that will eventually become known as 'the past.' In terms of prophetic visions, it is the currently accurate map of the actual future as opposed to the myriad and chaotic possible futures that could occur. Determining and shaping events that will become part of the seitparen or "Path of Fate" are twin goals of the Tchelakov Elders, and part of the genetic legacy bestowed upon them by Dr. Beh'ln Tchelakov (see: Path of Fate, sartograph, tromaveint, Tchelakov Tribe).

Senii Vilne Markks: Universally renowned chef (dead, suspended). Originally from Dexbit; lived 34,671- 34,742. (see: Holo Ghost).

Servo Limb: mechanical construct: any augmented lifting or reaching device.

Shecut: brigadier general (retired) of the Imperial Marines, 6th Army, special envoy to Carinaena's Shell.

Shields: (also: Larkson Shield Generator) shield combat was in vogue for almost 300 years until advances in optical targeting made the generators more hazardous than helpful. Still, some usefulness can be found, particularly in close arms combat (see Tolmer's "Optical Advances and other Technological Foibles" & Ku'bii's "Offensive Retreat—the Rise of the Projectile").

Shiva: Carrak class cruiser; flagship of the Imperial Third Fleet; currently assigned to the Wyxian Proctorialship.

Shock Troops: Imperial commandos, generally bred for cunning, viciousness, and absolute loyalty. Raised from birth as soldiers, completely immersed in the caste D'ai Mital, the cult of the warrior. The caste training emphasizes ruthlessness, survival and instills a near fanatical devotion to unit commanders; historically known as "the Emperor's elite."

Sid: giant panda, second generation member of the Tchelakov Tribe; youngest Elder in the Tchelakov Tribe, in charge of information retrieval.

Stanzer: Imperial picket crippled during the Battle of Sardis (35,345) by Ditraln Secessionists; sinking after atmospheric re-entry, the superstructure still rests in 2 kilometers of water off the shore of Callen High. Captain of the Imperial Guard, Garrand Ai'Gonet Médeville, rescued the *Stanzer*'s crew and passengers against direct orders and sacrificed an Imperial battle frigate in the process. That ship, the Deil-Karo, became the first command frigate lost at sea in 10,000 years.

Strahlinvek: language spoken by most of the trading cultures in Carinaena's Shell; a simple trade language, its root forms easily derived from thousands of other dialects. Some variation of the language is spoken by almost every race that has spacefaring ties, facilitating exploration and colonization.

Strom, Vailetta: Captain of the Imperial Guard, Gokazoku Kaigi; currently assigned to Wyx, Carinaena's Shell. Illegitimate (and some say favored) daughter of Emperor Collistas. Nicknamed Myshka, or "Firebird," by the Emperor, the young Vailetta spurned courtly life and set out to make a name for herself independent of her royal lineage (and some argue, her father's stifling protective care) taking the name Strom as cover to her true identity and entering the Bordëgian Academé as an anonymous student. The Gokazoku Kaigi culled her from the top of her graduating class. She quickly rose to the prestigious position of Captain within the sect and accepted a post commanding Vice Proctor Hellius Barrett's Imperial Guard.

Su'lairn: Gambor warrior; Tginsahi of the Lairn burrow, Galzeki. Honor Guard to Cha'halen first grade, Ka'vaelus.

Sullust Movement: Religious order; Gai'han Sullusts believe in the genetic superiority of the Gai'han bloodline carefully cultivated for over seven millennia. After the capitulation of Gallen Wei in the War of the Three in 35,242, the Niramdi system became the focus of the Gai'han practice of 'holy sterilization.' This process of indiscriminate extermination of non-Sullust humans and artificials forced the Collistas Dynasty to re-evaluate their position of support for the movement. Some believed the Sullusts were becoming powerful enough to threaten the Emperor himself. After skirmishes along the edges of Carinaena's Shell, the Thrassin Campaign marked the Collistas Dynasty's first foray into the Gai'han Jihad in support of Free Will artificials.

TacOps: idiomatic for tactical operations; the neural nexus of Imperial battle command that analyses and processes all information, provides a link between human experience in the field and raw datacore projections, and coordinates the various arms of Imperial power. An integral part of the command structure of all Imperial warships.

Tai-wren: "the shadow of the maker"; anyone who has pledged their life to protecting another.

Takens Root: native Chellian beverage, fermented for at least thirty years, usually served chilled with a garnish of fresh root.

Tarkanian Containment Shell: Hardened cerafibrous shell that houses a strong electromagnetic field; capable of safely storing incorporeal lifeforms and manifestations.

Tchelakov 37: colloquial expression referring to the original giant pandas engineered by Dr. Beh'ln Tchelakov (see: Tchelakov Tribe).

Tchelakov, Beh'ln: visionary genetic engineer whose highly guarded research into the next evolution of sartographic technology resulted in the creation of a new species (see: Tchelakov Tribe). His fusion of sartographic technology with a sentient-level intuition resulted in a quantum leap forward in 4th dimension physics decay and the science of future probabilities.

Tchelakov, Helen: courier/agent of the Nralda Keiretsu; daughter of Beh'ln Tchelakov.

Tchelakov Revolt: A blossoming conflict in the Wyxian Proctorialship the origins of which center around the pursuit, capture, and escape of the Tchelakov 37, circa 35,355.

Tchelakov Tribe: the giant pandas elevated to sentience and successfully fused with Dr. Naius Sartok's probability chips. The pandas' resulting mental matrix became viable probability engines, capable of using intuitive processes to make deductive leaps and accurately predict the future. Early iterations of the technology were only viable during dream state.

Tech Art: any of a wide class of mobile mechanical constructs designed to perform a broad range of technical tasks. Non-sentient, imbued with one (or several) highly technical skills, but possessing little overall intelligence due to high degree of specialization and desire for cost efficiency.

Tginsahi: rank of "Honor Guard" in the Gambor warrior caste.

Thiretsen Reed: any of a genus of tall, erect herbs of the nightshade family with little foliage and tubular flowers, cultivated for its stalks; the stems of cultivated thiretsen prepared for use in smoking.

Thola: Tchelakov 37 colloquialism for artificials, who they refer to as "noble sentinels of steel."

Thrassin, Battle of: The Thrassin Campaign marked the Empire's first foray into the Gai'han Jihad in support of the Free Will artificials. Though technically a stalemate (the Gai'han drive was halted, but the Sullusts were not driven out of the system until 37 years later), most historians view the battle as a clear victory for the Free Will Coalition.

Thurston Shields: proprietary design of defensive shield known for its massive buffers, ample null-dampers and wide field modulation. Generally considered the best.

Torg: class 1 master assassin, assigned to Vice Proctor Hellius Barrett, Wyxian Proctorialship. Much speculation exists concerning this soldier's original identity (see Vo Kamp's "The Emperor's Butcher"); it is said that Master Torg was charged as Vailetta Strom's personal Tai-wren by the Emperor himself.

Tortian: portable field assault cannon, tripod mounted.

Torvel Class Frigate: war vessel intermediate between a corvette and a ship of the line; Imperial classification of an escort defense ship between a corvette and destroyer in size.

Trioxin: short for Trioxin Battle Plate; armored drop suits vastly enhancing a soldier's strength, speed, sensory input, and firepower. In a fully operational Trioxin suit, it is said that just one Imperial Shock Trooper can easily outfight a dozen heavily-armed men. Unsuitable for some theaters of operation.

Trogand: race of large (2.7 meter tall) reptilian beasts with thick-plated hides, large dual-horned heads, and broad mouths full of 5 cm long teeth. The Trogands' gregarious disposition and meticulous attention to detail make them well suited for bureaucratic service.

Tromaveint: Tchelakov 37 colloquialism for the waking dream; a vision.

Turkle Sphere: Syhan artificial design. All drive components and core matrixes housed within one-meter diameter sphere. Rugged and highly versatile. Primarily used as tech arts though some instances of sentient models can be found.

Tvultàk Skullers: small, highly-maneuverable cruiser used as inter-dictors and strike craft; aging but rugged and adaptable design favored by mercenaries and smugglers. A particularly dangerous configuration is the Gamborian Jave 'O War.

Varsis: Krellian artificial design, manufactured without interruption for nearly 160 years between 34,687 and 34,846. The inherent simplicity of the design along with the Varsis' unparalleled learning curve made the design one of the Krell's most successful to date.

Vegraut: race of large (2 meter tall) graceful quadrupeds that ruled most of the Outer Reaches for over a millennium. Their sympathies toward the Free Will artificials during the Gai'han Jihad nearly lead to their extinction as the Sullusts made no distinction between arti-ficials and those who protected them. Today, their empire lies in ruin, and their numbers are estimated at less than 200 million.

Vell'lairn: Gambor warrior; Tginsahi of the Lairn burrow, Galzeki. Honor Guard to Cha'halen first grade, Ka'vaelus.

Wyx: 4th planet in the Bline system, seat of the Wyxian Imperial Proctorialship, one of the largest fiefdoms in Carinaena's Shell.

Yarvek-EZ: Virtruna caste, cybernetics specialist, 9th class, currently assigned to Imperial Battle Cruiser *Shiva* as pod ensign; bred in the Imperial Vats on Wyx for mathematical genius.

Yuzbek Sharlott School: medical research facility specializing in transgenics; radical medical sect destroyed in 35,324.

Yuzbekistin: 5th planet in the Core system of Wilkens Folly, site of the Biomaterial Implant Facility and Sharlott Research grounds; a level 8 quarantine is currently in place on the entire system, reason unknown.

TIME LINE

33,811 Last recorded contact with the seeder ship *Carinaena's Hope*.

34,290 Beginning of the Great Shell Diaspora. Major colonization efforts will continue for over a millennia.

35,110 Beginning of Gai'han Jihad.

35,307 Final battle of Gai'han Jihad. Gelicus Art Convention holds first open hearings.

35,312 Ratification of the Gelicus Art Proviso signals formal end of the Art Wars. Compromise includes ban on all indistinguishable-from-human artificials. Dalintus Commission formed to judge and regulate Free Will artificials.

35,337 Garrand Ai'Gonet Médeville graduates from Bordëgian Academé, receives commission in Imperial Navy. Selected for membership in the Brotherhood of the Princes of Blood, Griffin Order of the Imperial Guard. Varsis artificial Bailey VL1357-B8 is assigned as his personal combat assist.

35,341 Médeville is made Captain of the Imperial Guard.

35,342 Médeville accepts post on Santos II as Captain of Proctor Birmaldon's Imperial Guard.

35,343 At Battle of Sardis, Médeville distinguishes himself by rescuing Proctor Birmaldon from Ditraln Secessionists. In the course of battle, the Imperial picket *Stanzer* is disabled and left in a decaying orbit around Sardis. Médeville disobeys a direct order and commandeers a battle frigate to rescue seven of his men left aboard the *Stanzer*. Both ships are lost, but the Guardsmen are saved. Médeville is court-martialed and discharged from Imperial service.

35,345 Artificial Bailey is granted Free Will on lunar colony Fortrivance.

35,346 Proctor Lekkson Nesbit assassinated. Vice Proctor Hellius Barrett takes control of the Wyxian Proctorialship.

35,347 Médeville contracts with the Sandhalles Grip, Bestriyx Dagen, for the rescue of his daughter. Designs modified light cruiser for express purpose of breaking Talen quarantine on El Phobadia to reach the young Miss Dagen. Ship built by Lehadn Vercks in Lo Kamer-Daun Shipworks; christened *Destiny's Needle*. After completion of mission, Bestriyx Dagen presents Médeville with *Destiny's Needle* as a grateful token of his esteem.

35,355 Médeville contracts with Helen Tchelakov for transport of 37 "exotic bios."

About the Author

PHILIP WILLIAMS IS an author, artist and sculptor. A graduate of the University of North Carolina, Chapel Hill with a BFA in Studio Art, he has enjoyed a successful career creating powerful, gas-welded steel sculptures as well as designing and building unique furniture. Philip is a dedicated father of three and an avid soccer player.

Visit him online at *www.thegriffinseries.com*.

THE GRIFFIN SERIES

Ashes of Honor
The Dreams of Men and Pandas
The Dragon's Price
A Path of Majesty

Garrand Ai'Gonet Médeville's adventure
continues in Book 4, *A Path of Majesty*

THE GRIFFIN SERIES

THE GRIFFIN
ASHES OF HONOR
PHILIP WILLIAMS
CAT WILLIAMS

THE GRIFFIN
THE DREAMS OF MEN
AND PANDAS
PHILIP WILLIAMS
CAT WILLIAMS

THE GRIFFIN
THE DRAGON'S PRICE
PHILIP WILLIAMS
CAT WILLIAMS

THE GRIFFIN
A PATH OF MAJESTY
PHILIP WILLIAMS
CAT WILLIAMS